THE MYSTERIOUS JOHN SOLOMON
AND JOHN SOLOMON'S BIGGEST
GAME: THE ADVENTURES OF
JOHN SOLOMON, VOLUME II

H. BEDFORD-JONES

THE MYSTERIOUS JOHN SOLOMON

AND

JOHN SOLOMON'S BIGGEST GAME

THE ADVENTURES OF JOHN SOLOMON, VOLUME 11

H. BEDFORD-JONES

COVER BY
PAUL STAHR

ILLUSTRATIONS BY
ROGER B. MORRISON

STEEGER BOOKS • 2023

THE MYSTERIOUS JOHN SOLOMON

EDITOR'S NOTE: It is ten years since John Solomon, one of the most popular of fiction characters, has made his appearance in any magazine. We have urged Mr. Bedford-Jones to give us more of John, but he was unable to do so, being out of touch with the famous little cockney—not knowing, indeed, whether Solomon were still alive or not.

While in Rome last year, Mr. Bedford-Jones was one day leaving the Chigi Palace when, under the deep arch to the left of the entrance, he sighted the unmistakable figure of the cockney. Next moment Solomon had disappeared. He could not be located; every one denied all knowledge of him, and Mr. Bedford-Jones was forced to leave Italy without finding his man. A month later, while *en route* to Africa, he was approached by a stranger and handed a note in the neat calligraphy of John Solomon. A meeting followed, and from this chance we are enabled to introduce our readers to what Mr. Bedford-Jones terms the strangest and most remarkable of all the adventures of that strange man, John Solomon.

CHAPTER I

PARISIAN PLOTTERS

UPON A bright April day in Paris a young man came down the steps opposite the Rue de Castiglione and entered the Tuileries gardens. It was a warm and sunny morning. Children played in the gardens, people were everywhere enjoying the flowers and fresh air. The young man strolled along until he found a bench occupied by only one other person, and sat down.

One might look twice at him. As he took off his hat and lighted a cigarette his face was striking—bronzed from the eyes down, but white of forehead, sure mark of weeks under a torrid sun and a sun-helmet lately worn. His features were rather harsh, forbidding, almost bitter, as though life had used him most unkindly. His eyes were remarkable. When Dick North looked at any one—as he looked at the other man on the bench—his cold gray eyes were half asleep, they held no animation, they seemed queerly devoid of life. When he smiled, this changed all at once—but there it was. The look of a stricken man.

"Werry fine day, sir, ain't it? Werry fine," said the other occupant of the bench.

In some surprise North surveyed the speaker. He saw a pudgy little man whittling tobacco from a plug into an old clay pipe; a rather small man, none too well dressed, wearing a Basque beret over one ear, with wisps of gray hair escaping from about the edge. Wide blue eyes turned upon North with no more expression than the eyes of a china doll.

"Fine day for fine folks," said North, with a curt laugh. "You're an Englishman?"

"No, sir; American," said the other apologetically. "Naturalized citizen, sir. By the way, I'd take it werry kindly if so be as you'd tell me why you give up a building of that 'ere reclamation project down in Libya."

"Eh? What's that?" North's eyes came wide awake. He was startled. "You know me?"

The blue eyes twinkled at him in a most astonishingly friendly fashion.

"Well, sir, them as asks questions get less 'n they asks, says I," came the reply. "But questions is all werry good in their place, as the old gent said when the 'ousemaid asks if 'e was minded to marry 'er. About that 'ere reclamation project, Mr. North—"

"Who are you?" demanded North. "I never met you in my life!"

THE PUDGY little man chuckled, held a match to his clay pipe, and chuckled again.

"More questions, dang it!" he observed mildly to the world at large. "I gives 'im a 'int, and 'e goes and does it again! Why, Mr. North, it might be I could put you in the way o' making a couple o' thousand pounds, so to speak. Maybe more."

North's gaze swept the speaker. "You don't look it," he said. "Whoever you are, I don't know you. As for ten thousand dollars—huh! Can't be done in Paris without a thousand or two to start with. And I haven't a thousand francs to my name."

"This 'ere is an age of miracles, sir," said the other humbly. "Yes, sir, just like that! And Paris is a mortal queer place, Mr. North."

"How d'you know my name?" North regarded the smaller man curiously. "How do you know so confounded much about me? Suppose you tell me that for a starter."

The other chuckled wheezily. "I've been inwestigatin' of you, as the old gent said when 'e went and 'ired the pretty 'ousekeeper.

Now, then, about that 'ere reclamation project and you leaving of it 'alf done—?"

"I didn't leave it; I was fired," said North, and laughed shortly. "Since you know so much about me, you ought to know that. An investigating committee from Rome found graft everywhere; the cement was actually crumbling in the foundations of the dam. They wired Mussolini. I was kicked out of Africa inside two days, and lucky at that. If I hadn't been an American, they'd have jailed me."

"Werry likely, too," said the other, and his blue eyes were as deep and expressionless as the sky above. "And who might be the grafting parties, sir, in your own mind?"

"Probably one of my Italian assistants," said North, and shrugged. "How could I tell? They didn't give me a chance to look into it."

"Well, sir," said the other wheezily, "if I was you I'd go to 13 *bis*, Rue Montorgeuil, about eight o'clock tonight, and ask for Mr. Solomon. If so be as I ain't mistook, 'e can tell you about that 'ere two thousand quid, and also about your reputation."

"My reputation?" North flushed. "I haven't any. I'm wrecked, ruined, done for as an engineer! My reputation is buried in Libya. They wouldn't even grant me a trial!"

The innocent, childlike blue eyes of the other man dwelt upon him briefly, then the pudgy little stranger rose.

"This 'ere Solomon might be able to 'elp you, sir," he said deferentially. "You go to that 'ere address to-night, just like that! About eight."

With a nod the speaker started away. North checked him.

"This does not concern us. The man
intended to murder you. Come."

"Here, hold on! You haven't said who the devil you were, or—"

The other turned. "All in good time, sir. If I was you, I'd be werry slow about that 'ere deal with them American promoters. A man is mortal apt to be deceived in 'is fellows, as the old gent said when 'e found the butler a kissing of the 'ousemaid."

The little old man, walking rather stiffly, moved away, leaving North absolutely petrified with amazement.

He had been startled enough when this queer little man spoke his name, asked about his disgrace; but how on earth could the

fellow know about this new deal? It was a dead secret. Harden
and Billings had sworn him to silence—had not told even North
the details. They had merely discussed a prospective job; and here
this man knew all about it! The thing was astounding.

Impulsively North started to follow the man, then found him
gone, lost in the passing throngs. He sank back on his seat and
groped for a fresh cigarette as he tried to get a grip on himself.
Dingy little rascal with the blue eyes—some tout, some hang-
er-on of hotels?

A grimace swept North's face—a grimace of hopelessness,
of rebellion against futility. A month previously he had been
working on a huge reclamation project in Libya, engaged by the
Italian government, his future brilliant.

Overnight he was utterly wrecked. A committee from Rome
had uncovered graft, undeniable graft. He had been clapped
under arrest, and promptly deported from Italian territory, a
ruined man. His appeals, his demands for trial, for further investigation, were vain. He came to Paris disgraced, penniless, his
career ended.

He started suddenly. What had the man said—Solomon
might help him? Nonsense. Who was that man, to effect
anything with the dictator of Italy? A bitter laugh twisted
North's lips.

"The fellow was drunk. Yet he certainly knew me.... Well, I
don't know what to think. I'm up against it. Why did he warn
me against Harden and Billings?"

Bewildered, he left the bench, ascended to the Rue de Rivoli,
and hailed a taxicab. He went directly to the American consulate
and sent in his card to the official who was handling his case in
Rome. He was ushered in at once.

"MY DEAR Mr. North," said the consular officer, "I've no
news, and, frankly, I expect to have none. Our embassy at Rome,
under the circumstances, is helpless to obtain any fair hearing
for you. You know, the Fascisti believe in ruthless efficiency—"

"Oh, I know," said North. "By the way, do you people happen

to know anything about a man named Solomon, in the Rue Montorgeuil?"

To his surprise, the official stared at him hard for a moment.

"Sorry," came the slow reply. "I cannot give you any information about him."

"So you know him, eh?" North shrugged. "What's the answer? Is he crooked or not?"

The other smiled slightly.

"Let me ask whether you know him, Mr. North?"

"Well," said North, "I have an appointment with him for this evening."

He received a swift, almost startled look.

"Then let me congratulate you," came the reply. "Rumor says he is one of the most powerful men in Europe. I can give you no information about him, except to say that he is thoroughly reliable."

North departed, feeling rather dazed. The most powerful man in Europe? That was putting it too strong. Rumor said the most powerful man in Europe was a Greek financier, Sir Basil Condax, whose money was unlimited and whose finger was in every diplomatic pie. This man Solomon probably had a pull somewhere, that was all.

North walked to the Hotel Continental, having an appointment there for luncheon with Billings. Last night, he had looked on the tentative offer from Harden and Billings as a providential helping hand; now, oddly enough, he was inclined to be critical.

Dick North was not effeminate, and he was not sentimental. He had worked his way up in a rough school; he had been on engineering jobs in Bolivia, in Canada, in the Mojave and, last of all, on his own hook in Libya. His first independent job had wrecked his life, but it had not wrecked him by a long shot. He was ready to fight, and to go the limit—if only he were not up against a stone wall!

North came to the Continental, turned in beneath the arch, and made his way direct to the suite occupied by Harden and

Billings. He found Billings dictating in fluent French to a stenographer, and the promoter shook hands cordially.

"Harden will be in presently," said Billings. "Sit down—I'll have this letter cleaned up before he comes."

Billings was a stocky, powerful man of forty-odd, with gray-ish-red mustache, tight lips, a coldly keen eye. He had come to France on some wartime commission and had remained ever since, as an attorney and man of affairs, preferring it to petty politics at home. Harden had not been here so long, but was of New Orleans French descent, and so found France agreeable.

The door of the adjoining room opened, and Harden ushered out two men. North was somewhat surprised to find them Italians and, from their dress and manners, evidently men of position. Then Harden was warmly shaking his hand, having bowed out the swarthy pair.

"Be right with you. I'm leaving Paris to-night and a bit rushed. Ready, Billings?"

Harden was a lean, bronzed, outdoor man with an air of extreme optimism and aggressive self-confidence; he always spoke very positively. He had a large nose, thin-slitted dark eyes, and the cut of his jaw might be described at will as either strong and manly, or very brutal. North knew that until lately Harden had been selling agricultural machinery among the huge farms of Algeria and Morocco.

The three went out together, finding a quiet, old-time Gallic restaurant behind the Louvre department store. Not until they were settled at a comfortable corner table, with the *plat du jour* and a good wine ordered, was business touched upon. Then Harden rubbed his sinewy brown hand and smiled across the table, at North.

"Well, old man, prepared to close with us to-day?"

"No," said North, who was usually given to blunt speech.

"Eh?" For an instant the eyes of Harden narrowed and flashed. "How come?"

"I can't give you a definite answer before to-morrow," said

North. "I'd like to know more about your project. Also, I must see a friend of mine to-night in regard to my own business in Rome. I want to get some action there if possible."

HARDEN NODDED a little angrily. Billings, the usual spokesman for the pair, intervened with his urbane manner.

"North, I'll tell you confidentially that our project is close to Tunis."

"Tunis? In Africa?" said North.

"No, in France." Billings chuckled. "Algiers, remember, is a definite part of France and not a colony. However, we can't tell you more until we have your answer. If you want references as to our responsibility, that's natural enough. But as to telling you any details—"

"Nonsense!" plunged in Harden aggressively. "We can trust North—in confidence."

"Entirely," said the surprised North, as the other glanced at him inquiringly.

"Good." Harden nodded. "We're acting for certain Italian gentlemen who are securing a concession from the French government for a large irrigation project on the Tunis-Algiers border. There you are, in brief. I suggest that, if you like to look us up, you might see Signor Dominetti. So think it over."

North nodded. Dominetti was an Italian exile, a nobleman who moved in high social circles in Paris. And this bit of information gave a little light on the situation.

France was feverishly worried, in true Gallic fashion, about the large Italian population of Tunis, having the idea that she would lose her Tunisian colony overnight whenever Mussolini issued a call to arms—an absurd idea, but deeply rooted. France did not love the glorious united strength of the new Italy. And Tunis, being more Italian than French, worried her vastly.

The waiter arrived. When he had departed, Billings tasted his wine and caressed his red-gray mustache.

"Don't mind saying," he observed, "that we've interested

Dominetti in your case, North. Shouldn't be a bit surprised if we effected something at Rome for you. This is on the q.t."

"Mighty good of you," murmured North dutifully. And from this instant, he began to suspect.

He had asked no help from Harden or Billings. If they were tied up with the Royalist group of Italians, they certainly had no influence in Rome. North was far too well versed in the varied phases of the situation to swallow any such chaff.

The luncheon proceeded to an amiable conclusion. It was agreed that North would give his definite answer on the morrow, and the two partners professed themselves content; but North doubted that. He caught occasional glances between them, hinting at some hidden meaning. He was puzzled by their eagerness, their warm friendliness, their confidence that he would take the job. Neither of them was a philanthropist, but their talk was entirely of his own welfare.

"Well, good luck all around!" said Harden, shaking hands at parting. "Not going our way? All right—I'm confident of your decision. And if you need any salary advance, just tip us the word. *Au revoir!*"

They departed by taxi. North walked over to the river and strolled along the Seine, thinking hard and getting nowhere. Something about it all worried him, puzzled him, warned him in a subconscious way, though he could lay his finger on nothing definite.

"And who was it knocked me out, down in Libya?" he pondered, not for the first time. "One of those Italian engineers, that's sure! At a venture, I'd say it was that assistant of mine, Caporni—he's a scoundrel if there ever was one! Yet I haven't a particle of evidence. On the face of it, Dick North was guilty as hell. While I don't blame Mussolini for kicking me out, I do blame him for not giving me a decent chance to clear myself."

At eight that night, North came to the address given him by the pudgy little man, in the ancient street almost overshadowed by Notre Dame—the old, mysterious, ghost-ridden section of

Paris now about to be demolished and rebuilt in "city beautiful" fashion.

The house before which his taxi dropped him was a solid stone building, without a light showing anywhere. The ancient and massive bronze gates were ten feet high, but in one of them was set a small door, which was standing ajar, giving entrance to the usual courtyard of these old-time Paris dwellings.

North stepped inside.

CHAPTER II

THE MYSTERY OF THE WALL

A S N O R T H stepped into the entrance, a shadowy figure in the street behind him also slid through the opening; but he was unaware of it. North saw an entresol light to the right, and opened the door. A typically Parisian *concierge,* a heavy-jawed lady occupied with her knitting, looked up inquiringly.

"Does M. Solomon live here?" queried North, rather confusedly.

"But certainly, *m'sieur,*" came the response. "Straight ahead, across the court."

Thanking the good dame, North closed the door, passed through the entrance arch, and bore straight across the court-yard. It was unlighted, but windows around emitted thin gleams of light. Ahead of him loomed a white object like a statue, midway of the courtyard. Abruptly, without the slightest warn-ing, this statue moved, and spoke in English.

"Good evening, Mr. North. Did you come alone?"

"Yes," said North, halting in surprise.

"Come with me, if you please."

The statue revealed itself as a man in snowy white robes, prob-ably an Arab. North followed him toward the dark walls ahead, where a dark doorway loomed. At this instant, a sudden shrill, gasping cry wailed up and was checked; there was the crash of a body falling.

North swung around. A splutter, and the whole courtyard was illumined by a ghastly greenish radiance. A dozen feet behind,

North saw the body of a man outstretched on the cobblestones, a long curved Basque knife in his hand. No one else was near.

"Good Lord!" exclaimed North. "This is—"

"Come!" His guide, a lean dark man, touched his arm. "This does not concern us. The man intended to murder you. Come."

With an effort, North forced himself to obey. It was all unreal. The doorway ahead swung open, and Dick North passed from shock into further unreality—into a dream of the Arabian Nights brought to life.

An Arab in snowy white salaamed profoundly, took his hat and stick, and ushered him into a huge room. His guide had disappeared. North had a confused impression of a strange radiance like sunlight coming from crystal panes in the walls—a light wherein the natural colors of everything were transmuted into strange hues. He vaguely noted gorgeous jeweled lanterns and chandeliers, rich rugs and hangings, brocaded walls. Then another Arab appeared and held open a curtain for him.

"Solomon Effendi awaits you, Mr. North," he said in English.

Dumb, North passed into a smaller, plainer room—a room absolutely bare except for a large desk and several chairs, and one magnificent Shiraz rug upon the floor. From a large crystal pane in the ceiling came the same strange light, making red lips purple and white skins a ghastly yellow—yet a pleasant light withal.

Two men here. One the same little pudgy man whom North had met in the park, puffing at the same old clay pipe; the other a dark, handsome, highly dressed gentleman who looked rather startled at the intrusion. The cockney looked up and nodded at North.

"Werry glad to see you, Mr. North, and I 'opes you won't mind excusing me a moment or two. This 'ere ain't no private conwersation, as the old gent said when 'e met the pretty 'ousemaid a strolling in the park. Now, Your 'Ighness, we needn't 'ave no secrets from me old friend Mr. North, so go right ahead, sir, if you please!"

North dropped into a chair, bewildered, perplexed. Then, as the dark man spoke, his bewilderment passed into a sharp, vivid interest.

"Very well, Mr. Solomon," and the speaker's voice rose in sharp anger. "You are an absolute liar. You make charges that have no foundation. You say I was connected with the murder of those men—it is false! I had nothing to do with it."

"Your 'Ighness," and the old man at the desk spoke apologetically, "I says as 'ow I don't want to 'ave no dealings wi' bloody murderers—"

"But it's a lie!" cried out the "Highness" angrily.

The pudgy little man removed the clay pipe from his mouth, leaned back in his swivel chair, cocked one foot on an open desk drawer, and waved his pipe at the blank wall before him.

"Werry good, Your 'Ighness," he said, and his left hand touched a button in the top of the desk. "S'pose as 'ow we admits a bit o' proof, sir—just like that!"

THE DARK gentleman looked at the wall. North looked at it—and to his amazement saw a picture there, and the picture moved, focused! North glanced around. The opposite wall was blank also. There was no machinery in the room. He could find no logical explanation.

Two men in gorgeous uniforms showed in the picture. One was this dark man at the desk, the other an officer who saluted him stiffly, turned, and walked out of the picture. The dark man sitting at the desk gasped, clutched at his armchair—saw himself stride along that blank wall, enter a motor car and be driven away.

The pictured car whirled through streets, halted. The dark man in uniform got out and entered a building. Then he was standing at a window, smoking a cigarette, looking down into a courtyard where six men stood in line, blindfolded. A file of soldiers drew up, presented arms, aimed, fired; the six men toppled grotesquely over. The dark man at the window laughed and flung a remark over his shoulder. The officer who had first appeared, came into the picture, saluted. The dark man laughed, gave him a cigarette; and suddenly all the picture was gone.

The handsome dark gentleman at the desk had collapsed. He was staring at the pudgy little old man with frightened, haunted eyes—eyes that burned against a withered face.

"Well?" he said, nervously wetting his lips. "I—I don't understand."

"There you be, sir, just like that," said the cockney, his wide blue eyes betraying no emotion whatever. "And if I ain't mistook, there's summat more a comin' on that 'ere wall."

The dark man jerked about. Words came on the wall; luminous, shining words in an alphabet North did not know, but took to be Russian. The dark man cried out terribly.

"What do you want?" rang his voice, tortured. "Name it, name it!"

The man at the desk pushed toward him a document and a fountain pen. The dark man collected himself to read the paper; then he lifted frightful eyes.

"You unspeakable devil!" he exclaimed, and reached for the pen. He dashed down a word. "Take it, damn you!"

"And a werry good thing, Your 'Ighness," said the cockney solemnly. "If you 'adn't signed this 'ere paper, you'd ha' been a dead man to-morrow morning. And there ain't no good in bein' dead, as the old gent said when 'e kissed the 'ousemaid—"

But the dark man had left the room, staggering. The cockney swung his chair about, sucked at his pipe, and looked at North.

"That 'ere prince," he observed, "is a mortal bad lot, 'e is; made 'is blessed family a lot o' trouble, sir. Now 'e's took care of. And 'ow are you, Mr. North?"

"Out of my depth," said North, and smiled a little. "Are you Solomon?"

"Yes, sir, and werry much at your service," said the other, with a wheezy chuckle. In the wide blue eyes was a twinkling comprehension of North's amazement. "You're fair bursting to be asking of some questions, sir?"

"Of course. This moving picture business—the man with the knife outside—you don't know about him, I suppose?"

Solomon touched the button on his desk. North looked up, saw a picture come again on the wall: the courtyard with the man lying there, dead, knife in hand. Solomon pulled an extension telephone from the side of the desk. He was speaking in Arabic, as North realized. Then he gestured again to the wall, and North looked up. An exclamation broke from him. He saw a bloodless dead face—and recognized it. The picture faded.

"You know 'im, sir?" asked Solomon.

"My Lord, yes!" exclaimed North. "Caporni—my late assistant in Libya!"

Solomon sighed wheezily. "And werry likely 'e was a going to do you in, and one o' me own men got 'im. It's a werry bad 'abit, but it does get done, as the old gent said when 'e kissed the 'ousekeeper. If so be as you'd like to smoke, sir, go ahead."

NORTH LIGHTED a cigarette, and tried to marshal his wits.

"Hocus-pocus or plain magic?" he inquired, waving his match toward the wall. Solomon knocked out his pipe on the floor, produced a plug of villainous black tobacco and a knife, and leisurely began to whittle a fresh load.

"I ain't as young as I was, Mr. North, for a fact," he observed reminiscently. "I've 'ad me good days and me bad uns; I've 'ad me share in life, and a werry good time I've 'ad, too, if I do say it as shouldn't. And now 'ere I be in Paris—a doing what? Well, sir, I'm 'elping of me friends, just like that. And I ain't doing it by magic, but by science—me not being as spry as I was in me younger days. Science, Mr. North, is a wonderful thing."

Solomon paused, teased out the tobacco, stuffed his pipe. North sat fascinated. Here was a queer old man, insignificant, shabby, uneducated; yet holding something terrible in those placid blue eyes. A maniac? Certainly not. What, then? As though to his thought, came the answer.

"I must be telling you as 'ow I 'ave more money than I care for,

Mr. North," said Solomon. "Spending money is a mortal 'appy occupation, but a werry ticklish one, as the old gent said when 'e 'ired the pretty 'ousemaid. You'd be surprised, Mr. North, if I was to tell you how many chemists and scientists are a-working things out for me in laboratories! These 'ere pictures, now," and Solomon waved his pipe at the wall, "are all werry fine in their place; but their place ain't nowheres but here in this room. It's the same wi' me. As long as I'm setting 'ere with these 'ere violet ray lights to keep me from getting old. I'm all werry good; but I'm needing a younger man to do me odd jobs, so to speak."

A buzzer sounded beneath the desk. North was wondering whether he were in a dream or listening to the ravings of a maniac; then he was abruptly shifted to acute realization that he dealt with hard and sober fact. Solomon took up the telephone, listened, and spoke.

"Werry good. Put 'im on the amplifier and leave this 'ere connection," and he laid down the receiver, and went back to stuffing his pipe. A voice leaped out of the air.

"Stinson speaking, Mr. Solomon. Just reached the Marseilles office—didn't dare send word before getting here. Dominetti's agent in Alexandria died on Thursday. I have his papers. They include a remarkable scheme for mining and wrecking the Suez Canal just west of the lakes. Every detail is perfect. The proof of its having been planned by Fascist elements is elaborate and perfect. That's all of moment."

Solomon picked up the receiver. "Werry good, Mr. Stinson," he said. "Don't come on to Paris, but catch the night boat out o' Marseilles. It ain't safe for you in France, sir. You go by sea to London and 'and over them there papers to Lord Northing with me compliments. You ain't 'ad no report from Jerusalem?"

"You know Johnson was killed on Wednesday?" said the voice.

"Yes, but I ain't 'ad no report," said Solomon wheezily.

"I have a report sent me Wednesday. The Franco-British boundary agreement with Angora was arranged and was to be signed Wednesday night. Evidently Johnson was murdered

before the meeting and the documents were lost. I ordered
Meacham there at once from Bagdad, by air. You'll probably
hear from him in the morning. Any further orders?"

"That's all, sir," said Solomon.

He resumed his methodical filling of the villainous old clay
pipe. North sat silent. He knew this was no hocus-pocus; his
mind was already grappling with the situation. Those pictures
on the wall had some explanation, as had this conversation;
television and radio, of course, carried to their logical extremes.

"This 'ere light"—and North found the mild blue eyes rest-
ing upon him reflectively—"is one o' me own inwentions, sir.
Quartz rays developed for service in the 'ome, so to speak. Werry
beneficial I find it, and it's 'elping to an old man like me. Well,
sir, I 'opes as 'ow you didn't take on that 'ere project for them 'ere
gents this noon?"

North swallowed hard at this shot, but was past showing
surprise.

"I deferred a decision until to-morrow," he said.

"And a werry good thing, too. That 'ere Harden is by way o'
being a scoundrel, sir. If I may make so bold, 'e told you as 'ow
Dominetti is behind 'im?"

"He told me certain things in confidence," returned North.

"And s'pose you took 'is job, but was to be workin' for me all
the while, sir?"

"If you'd propose such a thing," said North calmly, "I'd not
care to be associated with you. I don't work for any man and
betray him."

Solomon chuckled wheezily, lighted his pipe, and touched the
button on his desk. North's eyes leaped to the wall.

He saw a map outlined there; it was the country about La
Calle and Tunis, with the Algerian border. A star suddenly
glowed red at a certain spot.

"There you are, sir," said Solomon, "this 'ere irrigation project.
The scheme is for you to be buildin' of it with Italian workmen

from Tunis. All of a sudden they puts on black shirts, just like that, and we 'ave a Fascist march on Tunis."

"WHAT?" NORTH stiffened as he sensed the possibilities of such a thing. "You don't mean it seriously? Why, if Italy did such a thing it'd mean war!"

"Italy wouldn't be a doing of it, sir; wouldn't know a blessed thing about it. But France would never believe that for a minute. Before it got ironed out, Italy would 'ave a mortal black eye, and somebody would clean up millions in stocks, just like that!"

"Oh!" said North, slowly. "A Royalist frame-up?"

"No, sir; a Dominetti frame-up," and Solomon's wheezy chuckle leaped out. "This 'ere Dominetti is a werry clever man, sir, and a werry big man in 'is way, and 'e 'as an organization of the smartest crooks in the world, just like that. That 'ere gent will never 'ave a thing pinned on 'im, so to speak. Harden is one of 'is big men."

North thought fast. "If what you say is true," he rejoined slowly, lighting a cigarette, feeling for words, "then—then this irrigation job would have been pinned on me. My record would be aired. Hm! Did this crowd have anything to do with my getting kicked out of Libya?"

Solomon chuckled and sucked at his pipe. "You're a getting on, Mr. North! I've been inwestigatin' things a bit, sir, and I wouldn't be surprised if we'd uncover something yet. That 'ere Caporni, your assistant—'im that got killed outside—'e was one of the gang. I expect 'e was on your trail, ready to knife you if so be as you was a coming to see me. Dominetti, 'e knows I'm after 'im. Human life ain't nothing to that man, sir."

"Nor to you, apparently," said North dryly, remembering how Caporni had died.

"It's werry cheap, as the old gent said when 'e caught the butler a kissing of 'is wife. I've 'ad me eye on you, sir. I've 'ad to pick me men careful like, and I've picked you."

"Thank you," said North half ironically. "Salary and duties?"

"Ten thousand dollars a year and expenses, sir. Expenses may run to 'alf a million. Two months' trial. If so be as you likes me and I likes you, money ain't no object. Your job right now is to fight this 'ere Harden."

"He's going to Algeria," said North, recovering from this staggering proposal.

"Not much 'e ain't!" and Solomon chuckled. "Not 'im! 'Is job is to kill the Duke o' York, who's a coming to Paris day after to-morrow on the quiet, so to speak. Your job is to stop 'im."

"Eh?" North stared hard at the pudgy little man, met those blank blue eyes, and doubted his own senses. "Are you trying to string me?"

"Dang it!" exclaimed Solomon, with a trace of irritation. "If so be as the duke was shot by a Fascist, where would Italy be? Ain't you got sense enough—"

"Dang it yourself," said North, cutting in. "Use your magic pictures! Use your organization! If this fantastic thing is true, then send out warnings, have Harden arrested—"

Solomon sighed wheezily. "Dang it, Mr. North, where's your 'ead, sir? Tricks—that's what them pictures are. And I ain't doing of no arresting or warning. If so be as you find a snake coiled in your bed, sir, what d'you do? Kill 'im, just like that. In me younger days, when I was a bit spryer, I could 'andle these 'ere jobs me own self, but I ain't what I used to be, as the old gent said when 'e fired the 'ousekeeper. You and me together, sir, we'll 'andle this 'ere gent. Two of me best men was killed last month, and we've got to look spry, Mr. North. Most of me men 'ere are Arabs, and this ain't no job for an Arab."

North puffed at his cigarette. Inwardly, excitement stirred him. He had begun to grasp what sort of man this was sitting here before him—or at least, he thought be did. The possibility gripped him. It might be all a fantastic dream, of course, but if by any chance it were true—and the consulate had certainly known Solomon—

"And now, sir," said Solomon abruptly, "is it yes or no?"

North blinked. "Yes."

Solomon opened a desk drawer. "Werry good, sir. You'll move to the 'Otel Imperial to-morrow morning; a suite's ready for you there. I'll 'ave your man bring around your car at ten, sir. And now, if you'll be so good as to turn up your right sleeve, and put on this 'ere glove?"

North asked no questions. He took the long right-hand gauntlet that was handed him, rolled up his sleeve, and donned the leather. He perceived that an aperture of peculiar shape was cut in the back, so that it came just at his wrist. Solomon turned a wall-switch, and another light behind his desk was turned on—a light set into the wall behind a crystal or quartz pane, stronger than that overhead. North could see the running mercury fusing and bubbling behind the glass.

"While it's a gettin' 'ot, sir," said Solomon wheezily, "I might say as 'ow I'm a going to mark your 'and a bit. We'll keep a doing this from time to time, as the old gent said when 'e kissed the 'ousemaid. You'll 'ave me own mark on your wrist, like all me men, and then there can't be no mistakes. Sunburn, it is."

He produced a watch, held up the back of North's hand to the crystal pane, and counted the minutes carefully. North perceived that the diagram cut in the leather was being reproduced by the violet rays in a sunburned pattern on his wrist. And of a sudden he realized what this diagram was—two interlaced triangles, forming a six-pointed star, known to all the Eastern world as the Seal of Solomon.

"Werry good, sir." Solomon switched off the light, put up his watch, and resumed his pipe. "And now the car's a waiting for you, Mr. North."

"Eh?" North, laying down the glove, gave Solomon a sharp look. "And what am I to do?"

"Don't trust nobody, sir, unless 'e 'as me mark on 'is wrist, just like that. You'll 'ear from me to-morrow, sir. Good night, and a werry good job all around, I calls it!"

Dazedly, North took his departure. He was in a whirl, mentally. The whole adventure was fantastic, incredible. This pudgy little man with cockney accent, his new employer? This dealing with titled gentry and international politics—was it real or fake? When he came out into the courtyard he found it brilliantly lighted. A liveried chauffeur and a powerful Hispano were awaiting him, and to his amazement North saw his own initials on the car door in a large silver monogram.

"Hotel Vignon, *m'sieur?*" asked the chauffeur, an Arab.

"Yes," murmured North. So they knew where he lived, then, knew his little hotel behind the Madeleine! He felt helpless, bewildered. He had scarce collected himself when the car swung out of the Boulevard Haussmann and a moment later was standing at his hotel entrance. The chauffeur opened the door and saluted, white teeth gleaming.

"I am Yusuf, *m'sieur,*" he said. "I will be here at ten in the morning."

North nodded and entered the hotel.

In the key-box he found a note awaiting him. It requested him to call at the consulate at eleven in the morning, as there was a most important communication for him from someone which would give him extreme gratification.

Dick North went to bed, hoping he would wake up sane on the morrow.

CHAPTER III

IN THE NET

NEXT MORNING North was wakened by the arrival of his coffee and rolls. When the maid had departed, he sat up suddenly in bed, spurred by remembrance. A dream or reality? Then he looked at his right wrist. There, faintly yet distinctly outlined in the vivid red of sunburned skin, was the symbol formed by two interlaced triangles.

"That much is true, anyhow!" thought North, and reached for his tray. "But what about the rest of it? I think somebody has been pulling a game. We'll see at ten o'clock."

That visit of the previous night seemed more like halluci-nation than reality; he still felt there must have been a trick somewhere. The letter from the consulate, however—no joke about that! Something had happened in Libya or Rome, beyond question.

At ten o'clock, Yusuf appeared for his luggage. He was a merry-eyed Arab, with the salute of a soldier. North had picked up a little Arabic in Libya, and tried it out on Yusuf with laugh-ing results.

He found the car adorned with his own monogram awaiting him in the street.

From this point Dick North yielded to the fate which had enmeshed him; a very pleasant fate, it seemed. He was carried to the Hotel Imperial, one of those imitation-palatial structures which the French call tourist-traps; here he was received with deference and led to a suite on the second floor—in Paris the

third floor. The suite was the acme of luxury: a bedroom, a large
tiled bathroom, with a sitting and reception room, all very large,
their brocade-curtained windows looking out upon a vista of
the Champs Elysees. A valet appeared and offered his services,
which North refused; and Yusuf presently arrived with the last
of his bags.

"Orders, *m'sieur?*" said the Arab. "Shall I unpack your things?"

"I'll do it." North inspected the man curiously. "I must go to
the consulate at eleven. Are you wholly at my service, or have
you other duties?"

"None but your orders, *m'sieur.*"

"Do you speak English?"

Yusuf grinned. "No, *m'sieur.*"

"How long have you been with Mr. Solomon?"

"Ten years, *m'sieur.* And my father before me served Solomon
Effendi many years."

"Eh?" North's brows lifted. "How old is Solomon?"

Yusuf shrugged. "Solomon Effendi has no age, *m'sieur.*"

Seeing that he would learn nothing, North dismissed the
Arab and set about unpacking.

He had not half finished when his telephone rang, and the
desk clerk announced that a M. Dupont had called to see him.
North ordered him sent up, and went on with his work. Presently a knock came, and the door opened to admit a typical
Frenchman of the small banker type—broad in the chest, with
an enormous, carefully brushed beard, an impressive manner,
and a red ribbon at his lapel.

"Good morning, M. North," he said, and with a bow extended
a card. "I was sent to ask that you come to this address at noon
or before, to meet my friend M. Solomon."

North was relieved, for he had been wondering when he
would see Solomon again, and whence his instructions would
come. A glance at the card showed him that the address was a
villa in Auteuil. After his visit to the consulate, then.

"At noon, M. Dupont?" he inquired.

The other bowed.

"If that is convenient. May I have the privilege of picking you up, M. North?"

"Thanks; I have my own car, and I shall probably be running around town all morning," returned North. "I'll be there at twelve, or a little before."

M. Dupont bowed and withdrew impressively. North chuckled at memory of those luxuriant whiskers; the lower class Frenchman's idea of fierce mustaches and wild hairs as a sort of protective coloration always amused him.

He went on with his unpacking, and then for the first time opened his morning paper and searched for any news of Caporni. As he had expected, the paper contained nothing about the dead man in Solomon's courtyard. News is not a matter of catching the next edition, anywhere east of the Gulf Stream. Perhaps the matter had been hushed up.

How far was Solomon a charlatan, a hot-air artist? How much of last night's business had been staged for effect? How much of that melodramatic crook-talk was pure bosh? North thought about this, then suddenly wakened to the fact that he had no choice. He must either accept the pudgy little man at full face value, or reject him utterly as a fraud. No halfway measure would do. Yet, there was no reason for fraud.

"And I'm not worth setting such a stage for," thought North soberly. "If that man is genuine, I've dropped into something big. If he's a fraud—well, he's no worse than Harden *et al.!* I must pass by and let those birds know that I'm not playing with them, too."

So he descended, got into his car, and went to the Continental. Neither Harden nor Billings was there, somewhat to his relief. He left word with their secretary that he could not consider their offer, scribbled a brief note to the same effect, and departed.

AT ELEVEN sharp he walked into the consulate, to be
met with staggering news. Rome had wired that his case was
reopened. The Libyan operations were developing into a gigantic
scandal in which North appeared entirely guiltless; one official
of the company had committed suicide, two were under arrest,
and Caporni, the chief assistant, had disappeared. North was
asked not only to resume his post, but was invited to come to
Rome immediately.

"Which means only one thing," said the smiling consular
official. "They'll do the right thing by you. Congratulations, Mr.
North! I suppose you still feel bitter against the Duce?"

North shrugged. "No; he's all right. Well, I don't know just
what to say to this; you see, I've accepted another position in
the meantime."

The other gave him a sharp look. "Not with—"

"The Mr. Solomon whom I mentioned yesterday."

"Oh! Then, if I were you," and the official smiled slightly, "I'd
talk it over with Mr. Solomon; perhaps he can straighten things
out very simply."

North departed in sober mood. He felt no exultation over
his probable justification; he was, instead, lost in wonder. Had
Solomon known of these things beforehand? How far was his
system of agents real, how far was it bluff? And how could Solomon straighten things out? The official's knowing smile, coupled
with what Solomon himself had said the previous night, threw
a sudden sharp ray of light on North's problem.

"Can Solomon be a sort of agent for Mussolini, then?" he
asked himself. "Perhaps. Blast it, I have to accept the man at
face value. There's no alternative! This Arabian Nights dream
is solid fact!"

He gave Yusuf the Auteuil address of M. Dupont and settled
back on the cushions, and dismissed his ponderings. Heading
across the Place de la Concorde, the Hispano swept out for the
Crenelle bridge with a tremendous burst of speed and power;
the luxury of it was incredible. Turning into Rue La Fontaine,

Yusuf swung into a side street of steep cobbles that climbed the hills of Passy, and presently halted before a villa surrounded by gardens and a high wall.

"You needn't wait," said North, when Yusuf had rung the bell at the gate and held open the car door for him. "I'll probably leave with M. Solomon, or take a taxi when we've finished. Take the afternoon off and enjoy life."

Yusuf looked a little surprised, but saluted, grinned, and obeyed. North turned to the gate, which was opened by an old woman in a lace cap.

"M. North?" she said. "You are expected. Enter, if you please."

North walked up a trim garden path of gravel to the house beyond, set well back from the street in spacious grounds. As he approached, the door was opened by a man all in black, who ushered him into a room on the right of a long corridor.

"If *m'sieur* will have the kindness to be seated, I will advise M. Dupont."

North found himself in an oppressive reception salon which looked as though it had not changed in the least detail for at least fifty years. The satin walls, the heavy window-drapes, the ornate crystal chandeliers, the bad paintings and excellent portraits, were all in the approved taste of a past generation. North even fancied there was a musty smell in the air, as though the place had been long shut up.

Dupont came into the room, whiskers and all, and greeted North with a warm handshake.

"Ah, my dear *monsieur,* I am charmed to have you beneath my humble roof!" he exclaimed. "M. Solomon has just telephoned; he is delayed and will not be here for twenty minutes. It is a little luncheon, you comprehend; the three of us. We shall discuss certain affairs, settle certain matters. M. Solomon tells me that you are about to take over some business matters for him—you have joined his following, eh?"

"Yes," said North, accepting the chair offered. "You have known him long, *monsieur?*"

Dupont waved a hand in the air.

"Oh, not long—a matter of fifteen years or so. You recall, he was established in Port Said at one time? His little shop was a famous place in those days. I was attached to the Bureau des Postes there, at the time. A wonderful man, M. Solomon—his influence with the Arabs—ah!"

And M. Dupont eloquently blew a kiss to the chandelier. North was interested.

"Influence with the Arabs? I didn't know that," he returned. "Of course, I really know little about him."

Dupont laid one finger along his nose, glanced around, and leaned forward with an expressive wink.

"But, my dear *monsieur*, you know about the business in hand, *n'est-ce pas!*"

North remembered abruptly—the Duke of York in Paris! And there had been an item in the morning paper about the arrival of the royal guest.

"Oh, of course, of course," he rejoined, leaning back. Dupont beamed, then looked around and came to his feet.

"Ah, the little Madeleine. My dear, this is M. North."

NORTH ROSE. A young woman, slim and dark, with masses of black hair braided and coiled about her head, was entering the room. She extended her hand, and North awkwardly bowed over it with the conventional phrase. Her eyes were fastened upon him with a certain intensity, and as he met her gaze, he thought to himself that he had seldom met a more unattractive young lady. She was beautiful enough, yet a peculiar feline savagery was written in her face.

"My niece," said Dupont in his grandiose way, "who manages this little house for me. Madeleine, my dear, M. North will join me in a glass of my birth-year Vouvray—the famous *crû* of '82! Every drop of it is in my own cellar, *monsieur*, it has an aroma, this wine, of the real nectar and ambrosia of the Elysian Fields—or was it Olympus? I am a little vague as to the classical allusion, to tell the truth. However, you shall judge of the vintage for yourself."

The black-clad servant entered with a silver tray. North glanced again at the girl, as she took the bottle when it was opened, and poured the wine into long slender glasses. Her features were peculiar, strange in their odd expression—some effect of her brilliant eyes and dark, heavy brows, that was hard to define. Then she was handing him a glass, and the smile upon her lips changed all his impression of her, gave him a quick warmth.

"Success!" exclaimed Dupont, lifting his own glass reverently, looking at the honey-colored wine, sniffing it with the air of a connoisseur. "Success to us all—to you and to me, *monsieur*, to our little Madeleine, success!"

North tasted his wine. The first drop on his tongue sent a pleasant fire through his veins. It was not a wine, but a heavenly ichor, unlike anything he had ever tasted before. Or was it the glowing eyes of the girl that thus affected him? He laughed suddenly, and raised his glass.

"Aye, success to us all!" he said, and drank.

He heard Dupont's laugh, a rich and hearty laugh that drew his eyes to the man. Then he saw something, as Dupont held glass to light. The man's right wrist, thick-haired, bore no sunburned emblem. What was it Solomon had said? "Don't trust nobody, sir, unless 'e 'as me mark on 'is wrist."

North put down his glass. "I'd like to use your telephone a moment, if I may," he said.

"But certainly, *monsieur!*" exclaimed Dupont, cordially. "Come, it is in the little salon."

North went with him to the door. Then something queer happened. The doorway vanished. Dupont's whiskered visage became all blurred. The walls wavered and fell away, and the hard bleak boards of the floor beyond the carpet-edge seemed very close and distinct. North caught himself, sagged down—and his memory failed.

Dupont turned, looked down at the inert figure, and then flung a laugh at Madeleine.

"Good! Make all arrangements here, my dear. We shall be ready in five minutes. Emile!"

The black-clad servant entered. There was no confusion, no haste; everything was ready and was done with admirable precision. Dupont and Emile lifted North and carried him out of the room, through the house to the rear, and across the garden path to the old stable, whose doors were standing open. A large closed car was standing there.

North's inert form was placed inside the car. The black-clad Emile darted into the stables and presently emerged with chauffeur's cap, and white coat. M. Dupont walked around the house to the front gates, where he engaged the old lady in lace cap in conversation, and yellow bank notes glinted in the noonday sun as she counted them over.

The car came down the drive to the gates, and halted. In the rear sat Madeleine, two suitcases at her feet; a robe was flung over the form of North, hiding it from sight. Emile opened the high gates and got in; Dupont got in beside him; a moment later the car was rolling out into the narrow cobbled street. The old *concierge* closed the gates again, as the car swiftly turned left and went leaping downhill toward the Seine.

The street was quite empty except for one of the omnipresent Algerine peddlers who infest Paris. A huge bale of imitation rugs made in Lyons was slung over one shoulder, imitation pearls glittered about his neck, a dirty fez was cocked over one ear; he was leaning against a wall, dozing lazily in the warm sunlight.

As the car turned down the street, however, this peddler wakened from his doze and took a sharp step out to the edge of the sidewalk. There he held up one arm high, shaking a cascade of pearls in the air; then he crossed the street to where the old *concierge* was closing the gates.

"Nice pearls, *ma'm'selle*," he said. "Fine pearls! Rugs from Constantinople!"

"Get out, you dirty one," spat the old dame, and slammed the gates fast.

The Algerine grinned, shrugged, called Allah to witness his shame, and went slouching away down the street.

CHAPTER IV

HALF A SHOE

IT WAS dark when North came vaguely to his senses; vaguely, for his tongue was thick and his head was dizzy, and his brain was slow to comprehend and translate anything that went on. After a time he found soft hands on his face, was dimly aware that he was being helped to sit up; a woman kissed him and laughed, softly but terribly, so that he was swept by a swift, keen fear. Then he was drinking a cold draft.

For one instant he came full to himself, saw the girl Madeleine sitting beside him, and met her eyes as she watched him and held an empty silver cup. Then, even as he started to speak, fog came upon his brain again and he could not remember anything further.

North sat there on the bed, his eyes wide open, and after a moment Madeleine turned and set down the cup. From the doorway advanced Dupont.

"Good!" said the girl, calmly. "Now he is ready. Tell M. Harden that I am bringing him."

"But there is delay," said Dupont, spreading out his hands. "If you—"

"Fool!" said Madeleine, looking at him. "Don't you know better than to voice objections? When you talk to me, hairy ape, watch your tongue!"

She took a step toward him, her face very white, her eyes dark and large. Dupont's jaw fell, and as he turned and hurried out of the room he crossed himself hurriedly.

Madeleine went back to the bed, took North by the hand, told him to get up. He obeyed, and stood there docile. He was fully dressed. Madeleine smoothed his clothes a little, pulled at his necktie, then stood looking him in the face for a moment, curiously. Those singular features of hers were cold, predatory, not nice to look upon.

"You are handsome, my fine fellow," she said, and leaning forward, kissed him on the lips. "Perhaps I shall save you for myself—why not? There are worse men in the world. Well, come along now, tell what you know, and to-morrow we'll talk things over, you and I. Walk after me, and speak when you're spoken to, like a good chap."

No expression came into North's face. He stood there like a wooden man, looked at her, through her, as though not seeing her. Obviously one part of his brain was awake, for he obeyed her command at once, and walked after her to the doorway. His eyes, wide and unwinking, no longer sleepy and careful, looked unnatural, but otherwise he appeared quite himself.

Madeline left the room, and this automaton, who had been Dick North, walked after her, along a passage. Windows gave glimpses of gardens, a high stone wall inclosing them; the house itself, like the other in Auteuil, gave every indication of having been a luxurious abode of the past generation. Stained glass windows, delicate painted ceilings, brocaded walls, heavy panel-ing, and everything kept in the pink of condition. A maid in trim apron and Breton lace cap appeared, saluted Madeleine and passed on.

Now they were in a room—the grand salon of the house, with windows on the garden and at the far end a glass conser-vatory filled with rare plants. A large table of Buhl work, deep rugs, cabinets of the little *objets d'art* so loved by French minds, gorgeous walls of yellow brocade; and men. At the table sat Harden, with two men sitting at his right. His bronzed face with its big nose and thin-slitted eyes lifted, and he shot a glance at Madeleine and the automaton behind her.

"Good work, girl," he said in French. "Let him wait. Reports coming in—something's gone wrong. Don't know what."

The telephone buzzed. Harden took up the desk receiver and lifted it. For an instant a blaze leaped in his eyes.

"Gone, you say?" His voice fairly crackled. "And no word from him? He was to have been there to meet Piacenza at six thirty—All right."

He laid down the receiver and crooked his finger at one of the two men, obviously an Italian. The man stood up quickly.

"Billings has disappeared," said Harden. "He didn't meet Piacenza at six thirty, and hasn't been to the Continental. Go find him. Need money?"

The Italian shook his head and departed without a word. Madeleine spoke with an assured air which told clearly enough her position. She was no hireling.

"What could have happened, then?"

Harden leaned back and gazed at her sardonically. "My dear girl, how do I know? Wait and see. You haven't met Le Crotal? He's innocent of French—speak English. Here, Rattler, this is the prize skirt," and Harden turned to the other man and spoke in English. "Get me?"

"Yeah. Pleased to meet ya," and Le Crotal, or the Rattler, stood up, jerked at his hat, and shook hands with Madeleine. He was an Italian-American, weazened, sharp-eyed, with a merry and thin-lipped smile that warmed his cold face.

"I am please' to meet you, Meestair Crotal," said the girl, laughing a little.

"SIT DOWN, Madeleine," said Harden indifferently. "The Rattler's an imported Chicago gunman, and he'll do the work. Fiave and Ciro are ready for the martyr role—they'll parade their black shirts and so forth, and their guns will show they fired the shots. All's clear."

The telephone buzzed. Harden spat a word into the receiver, listened, laid it down.

"To-morrow at three, then," he said, meeting the eyes of the girl, and bit at a cigar. "The Duke of York leaves Etretat in the morning. He gets in at two. There'll be the usual didoes at the station, with committees and so forth. He'll get to his hotel at three. We'll have everything set for then. Suit you, Rattler?"

"Yeah." The Rattler stood up. "Now we're all set, I'll blow. I got a date with a dame for to-night."

Harden looked up sidewise at him, and under this look the Rattler recoiled slightly.

"Let me tell you something," said Harden in a low voice. "Go on and keep your date, but you show up here at nine in the morning, get me? If you don't, there'll be somebody right close on your tail to see that you do. Don't think for a minute that you'll be alone to-night."

The Rattler grinned. "All right, big boy," he said, and reached under his arm. "Here's my rod, see? I ain't lettin' these here cops pull no Sullivan law on me."

Harden took the pistol and put it in a drawer, laughing. "Go on, Rattler; go on!" he said. "Be a good boy and forget the cops. If you get pinched, sing low, and you'll be sprung in ten minutes. This is my town, see? Have a good time. There's a taxi waiting for you."

The Rattler nodded to Madeleine and sauntered out.

Left alone, Harden looked at the girl, met her eyes, tensed a little.

"Trouble," he said, meeting her unspoken question without evasion. "We did well to get this North. That devil Solomon is going to raise Cain with us, somehow. I can't place him or his men.

"We can't discover a thing about him, what he's doing, how to reach him. Billings had a lead—and has disappeared. Jack and Florio are on the job; Florio telephoned this afternoon that they had struck something and would have news to-night. Nothing's come—"

The telephone buzzed. Harden picked it up, and his voice leaped shrill.

"What—he is? All right. You can send him in. But give him a drink first."

Excitement blazed in the girl's eyes, flamed in her cheeks, as she leaned forward.

"Who?"

"Jack." Harden tried hard to control himself, but failed. "He's outside. Came in a taxi, in bad shape. Can hardly walk. Something's cracked, I tell you!"

"Bah!" Madeleine shrugged, took a cigarette from an open box, lighted it, and shot a glance at the immobile, wooden figure of North to one side. "Cracks can be mended, my dear boy! You and I are not fools. There is only one mistake you make—when you tell Le Crotal that this is your town. Paris is nobody's town."

"Unless somebody has brains," and Harden smiled thinly. "Let Jack in, will you?"

She nodded, rose, walked out of the room to the outer door, that opened on a *porte-cochère* in the garden.

A door opened, slammed. Into the room, ahead of Madeleine, burst a shambling, terrible figure. A man, disheveled, unhurt in the body, yet his face so paralyzed by unutterable and fearful horror that the impassive Harden came to his feet at first sight of him, and stood staring. The fellow almost collided with North, evaded him, came to a halt before the table and dropped both hands on it. He leaned there, panting, two great eyes fastened upon Harden. His features were twisted, contorted, as though some spasm were upon him.

"Good God!" cried Harden abruptly. "Jack, Jack, what's the matter?"

"I don't know," said the other, and then slid himself into one of the two chairs, buried his face in his hands, remained motionless. Harden made a sign of caution to Madeleine, who had returned and was looking at the newcomer with a frown that was largely contempt.

"Take your time, Jack," said Harden. "It's all right now. Where's Florio?"

JACK'S BODY moved in a convulsive shudder, and he lifted a more controlled face.

"He—he *isn't*," he returned in a shaky voice. "That's all there is to it—he *was*, and now he *isn't*. There isn't any Florio. Listen, Harden! It's got me. I don't know what it is. Something in the air. It hit him square. I—I know it's got me—I got to tell you. Look here, you know Rue Jasmine, down Avenue Mozart? In Auteuil?"

"Yes. The little short street," said Harden.

"Uh-huh. New house been built there, couple o'blocks off the avenue," went on Jack. His voice was controlled, but weaker. "We got a line on it to-day. Low house, two stories, not any windows on the ground floor; and a door that's solid brass. Solid stone house, see? Tracked a man there from Solomon's place—he was the chemist Pearson, the Englishman. We hung around all afternoon. There's a garden in back. We got in there from next door, after dark. Lights all in the back. Car entrance from the side; the house is on a corner. See? Boxes inside. Cases. Chemicals."

"Good!" cried out Harden, and his fist slammed on the table. "Hear that, Madeleine? We've got Solomon's damned laboratory or whatever it is! By heavens, we've got it—"

A fearful groan from Jack interrupted him, silenced him.

"Listen, listen!" cried out the man, almost desperately. "You fool, listen! I've got to tell you. It's—got me! We were there, Florio and I, at the window—on a tree, see? Inside, there was machinery. Pearson was there, and another man. Don't know him. They were working at the machine. Can't describe it. Pearson looked up, saw Florio's face there—the window had no blind or shutters. Then there was a flash. That was all."

Jack shivered again, threw out both hands, then clapped them over his face.

"That was all," he said faintly. "I climbed down. Florio was gone. Gone, you understand? There was nothing left, just one of his shoes. It was on the ground there, by me. Nothing in it. No blood. No foot. Nothing. A shoe—half of it. And I knew something had hit me. I got away—had a taxi waiting—had to tell you. The light was green—green—"

"Buck up," exclaimed Harden, whose bronzed face had gone white. "You're off your nut about Florio. I expect he'll be along almost any time now."

The man in the chair laughed, his face still in his hands. It was a horrible thing to hear, this laugh; even Madeleine straightened up at sound of it; stood with hands clenched. Then the laugh died, and the man slumped down.

Harden gasped, and slipped around the corner of the table and put his hand on the man's shoulder. "Here—no! No use."

Jack slid forward and tumbled out of the chair, and lay sprawled on the floor. He was dead. Harden straightened up and met the gaze of Madeleine. She had gone deathly white, but now she shrugged a little, disdainfully.

"Well, what does it matter?" she said, and showed her white teeth in a smile. "Learning always commands its price."

"You she-devil!" said Harden, and then he, too, laughed and pulled himself together. "Good girl. You're right. I'll have him taken care of—then we'll see what else we can learn, eh?"

The impassive figure of North stood there, eyes wide open, a thing of wood.

CHAPTER V

THE UNWITTING INFORMER

THE LATE unfortunate Jack removed, Harden lighted a fresh cigar, pushed the cigarettes toward Madeleine, and watched her light one.

"I admire your nerve, girl," he said quietly. "You're the best I ever met. What do you make of Jack's story?"

"True enough," said Madeleine. "It proved itself. He didn't have a mark on him. Well, you remember this English chemist Pearson? He's the man mixed up in that so-called death ray affair a year or two ago. It did not work."

"It works now," said Harden wryly. "At the same time—ah! Dominetti will know all about it. Take the telephone in my study, will you, and report this business to him? Meantime, I'll be questioning our young friend here."

Madeleine nodded. "Just a moment, though," she observed reflectively. "I like this M. North of yours, and I should be very sorry to have anything happen to him."

Harden smiled grimly. "Oh! So that's it, eh? My dear girl, haven't you smashed enough men in your time? Believe me, North would far rather die and be done with it than remain a prisoner to you—and waken from the dream wrecked and broken!"

She shrugged lazily. "Never mind him; think about me, my dear," and she arose. "Remember, I am rather emphatic about it!"

Harden waved a mocking hand. "Very well; we shall not disagree upon so small a point, I promise you. If you want this

poor devil, you shall have him. You gave him the usual amount
of the dose?"

"Quite; it hit him at once." Madeleine glanced indifferently
at North. "He'll remember a little, not very much, afterward;
he'll take it all for a dream. You can ask what you like, and he'll
answer truthfully enough."

"Yes, we've had pretty steady luck with your subjects so far,"
and Harden chuckled. "Well, get that report to Dominetti.
We've got to know at once just what sort of a thing we're up
against. We can't risk any failure to-morrow. And tell him about
Billings; I'll report as soon as we learn anything definite."

Madeleine nodded and passed out of the room.

Harden, puffing reflectively, swung his chair around and
looked at North, frowning a little, as though finding it hard to
realize that the flesh-and-blood man here before him was no
more than an automaton, a creature whose brain was half dead.

"Well, North, ready to talk?" he asked crisply.

"Of course," said North, without change of expression.

"That's fine, fine! Sorry you didn't throw in with me and
Billings?"

"No."

"Why not?"

"Because you're crooked, of course."

"Oh!" Harden grinned at this. "And who told you this?"

"Solomon."

"Remarkable man! Tell me all about his house in Rue Montorgeuil, how you got into it, who was there, and all about it."

North obeyed. He described his visit to Solomon's house in
detail, while Harden sat in a queer amazement, half incredulous,
half exultant. When his own name came up, Harden started.
Madeleine was entering the room, but Harden paid her no heed.

"What's that again?" he cried out. "He said that I was going
to kill the duke?"

"Yes," said North. "And that I was to prevent you."

"You look as if you'd do it." Harden drew a deep breath, and looked at Madeleine. "You hear that, girl? Listen, North! What details did he go into about the killing?"

"None. I was to hear from him later."

Madeleine took a hand in the probe, emptying North's brain as though it were a measure holding apples. They got out of him all that he knew about Solomon, which was none too much, yet it raised them both to a keen pitch of eager excitement. When it came to the mark on his wrist, North explained this, showing the token and telling how it had been done.

"Well, that's about all—and it's enough for this time," said Harden, leaning back. "Any news from Dominetti?"

Madeleine nodded. "Enough, and I don't like it," she returned. "He says it is not what we think; it is no death ray, but something else. An atomic disturbance, he called it. I do not understand at all."

"H-m!" Harden's eyes narrowed to slits. "Nor I. Did he say we'd have any trouble?"

"He said that we would have no trouble whatever tomorrow," returned the girl, "provided instructions were followed exactly. The duke goes to his usual hotel in Rue St. Honoré. We are to be in the second floor apartment at two thirty, and to be ready from that time on. Your man from America will use the machine rifle that you and he have prepared, and the two blackshirts will do their part."

Harden made an impatient gesture. "And Billings?"

"Has not been found. Dominetti is leaving by the night express for London, and trusts everything to us."

"Yes." Harden sneered. "He's going to be out of it, and to-morrow afternoon he'll be selling empire stocks short as hell—what a clean-up! Well, girl, we get a good fat percentage. You've arranged everything at the apartment?"

She nodded composedly. "Of course."

HARDEN PUFFED for a moment. "Only one thing I'm afraid of," he said slowly. "Billings knows everything. If by any chance they've got him, he's likely to talk under torture."

"Then we must discover whether they've got him or not," said Madeleine. "If they have, we must change all our arrangements. If a mere accident has happened, as may very well be the case—"

The telephone buzzed.

Harden lifted the receiver, listened for a moment. "Yes," he said in French. "Yes, *monsieur*, this is M. Harden. I did not catch the place—oh! The *gendarmerie*—at Caen, you say? Yes, all right."

He listened again, and his eyes darted to Madeleine. Then he smiled suddenly, and broke into voluble thanks.

"You will do everything, if you please," he replied. "Tell him that I will arrive to-morrow evening. Yes, and a thousand thanks once more."

He laid down the receiver, leaned back, and broke into a laugh—a hard, arrogant laugh.

"Billings," he said. "He was with a lady in a car; his lady friend from Grenoble, you comprehend? That was from police head-quarters at Caen. There was a smash-up on the road today. The lady was a bit hurt, nothing much; Billings was cut a bit by glass, no great damage—mostly shock."

Madeleine leaped into activity. She came to the desk, seized the telephone, and spoke in rapid French—even Harden could scarcely follow it. Then, after a moment, she laid down the receiver and turned.

"In this game, *mon ami*," she said coolly, "one does not take chances. Any one might put in such a message. I have called back the police station."

A buzz. With a nod of comprehension, Harden responded to the call.

"Yes, it is M. Harden again. Will you have the great kind-ness to see that the lady is supplied with flowers? Thank you, *monsieur*. I shall, of course, arrange with you to-morrow."

"Good head, Madeleine," he said approvingly, when he had hung up. "Hadn't occurred to me, but it's best to take no chances. Well, that clears things up in fine shape. Will you attend to this North?" He glanced at the American, half frowning. "I tell you, young lady, the best thing is to finish him at once. Let Emile 'take him for a ride'!"

The girl shrugged. "Leave him to me. He'll wake up some time to-morrow, and Emile can look after him until we have attended to the business. We come back here, I believe?"

"Of course. Emile will be waiting with the car to run us here. We pick up our bags, put this man in the car if you want him, and become American tourists bound for the Belgian border. Nothing could be more simple."

"Agreed." Madeleine turned to North and touched his arm. "Come."

They passed out of the room, followed by the cynical gaze of Harden. When they had gone, Harden took a fresh cigar, laughed shortly, and called Dominetti's number, making report that Billings was located and not hurt to mention. Then he lighted his cigar and sent a thin wave of smoke toward the painted ceiling.

"Odd fish, this girl!" he muttered. "I'm thankful she never fell for me. She's a devil in disguise! I could almost feel sorry for—"

A buzz. Harden picked up the telephone, listened. His face changed, became bitter, cold and hard.

"Bring him in," he said, and then, from the table drawer, produced an automatic fitted with a silencer.

Presently three men came into the room. The man in the center, shoved forward by the two others, was an Algerine peddler. He bore no rugs baled over his shoulder, but dark throat and arms were slung with imitation pearl strings. He looked at Harden with frightened eyes and babbled incoherently.

"He has been hanging about in the street, *monsieur*," said Emile, one of the two captors.

"In the name of Allah, the Compassionate!" broke out the

Algerine, falling on his knees and extending his clasped hands toward Harden. He was a sharp-faced man, very dark. "I meant no harm, *m'sieur!* I have sold nothing all day—I am weak and faint—I have not even five sous to buy a crust of bread, and it is a long walk back to Boulogne."

Harden took up the automatic, and his eyes were like ice.

"What is that mark on your right wrist?" he said, and pointed. The Algerine looked at his wrist, upon which was faintly outlined, against the whiter skin of the forearm, the Seal of Solomon.

"That, *m'sieur?*" said the man in surprise. "That is the mark of my tribe. Preservation against the Evil Eye—"

Harden laughed. "And against bullets also?" he said.

He fired twice; deliberate, unhurried shots. The noise was very slight. The Algerine, knocked sidewise by the impact of two bullets in his brain, fell over in a sprawl of dirty robes and imitation pearls. Harden laid down his weapon and looked at Emile.

"Emile, you know the house in Rue Montorgeuil?" he said. "Good. About dawn, take this carrion and lay it beside the door, and drive off quickly. Before you go, take white paint and make this design upon his forehead."

With a pencil he swiftly drew the two interlaced triangles forming the Seal of Solomon, and Emile took the paper. Harden watched while the limp clay was carried out of the room, then he resumed his cigar, and smiled thinly.

"So you want war, Mr. Solomon?" he murmured. "Good. You shall have it, up to the hilt!"

TOWARD NOON of the following day, North wakened.

As previously, his wakening was fogged and unreal. This time he presently realized that he lay in bed, amid very sumptuous surroundings; the room was ornate, in the extreme of French delicacy. North rather got the idea that it must be a woman's room. The heavy silk draperies of the bed, the gay and beautiful things all around, the satin curtains, the thousand and one little things bespeaking a lady's boudoir, startled him into wider wakefulness.

A voice came abruptly to him and pierced like a knife through his vague cloud—it was the voice of Madeleine, from an adjoining room. He remembered little of what had passed since Dupont had drugged him; confused words, an inchoate floating jumble of phrases and things. Danger lay in this girl's voice, however, and he instantly relaxed again, closed his eyes, lay quiet. She must have come close to him, for he caught a bitter-sweet perfume, then she spoke again.

"Luncheon is served, Emile? Very well. Come back in half an hour and bring a tray—he should waken soon. And be careful. We leave directly after luncheon."

Emile? The black-clad man at Dupont's house! Was he in the same house? North could not tell. When he opened his eyes again, he was alone in the room. He looked about, lifted himself, sat up. He felt no pain, but every motion was mental torture;

the drug had affected the controls between brain and muscles. Drugged, no doubt of it! How could he clear his head? In half an hour Emile would be back; what then?

North staggered about the room. The windows were closed by the ever-present volets—thin steel shutters closed with bar and padlock, locked. The door was locked. There was no help in sight; nothing! Sinking upon a chair, North clasped his reeling head in both hands and fought for self-mastery, desperately, vainly. For a moment or two his brain would be clear as crystal, then fog would descend in a swirl.

He fumbled in his pockets, found cigarettes and lighted one. It sickened him after a half dozen puffs. He dropped it, set his foot on it. He went around the room again like a man half blind. A door; a closet, filled with dresses; a niche that held a dressing-table—and another door, curtained. To his amazement, it opened to his thrust.

A room almost exactly similar—Madeleine's room, then? Closed shutters, locked door; he had the run of these two rooms, no more. Again he sank down, and after a minute realized that he was seated before a dressing table.

Perfume, toilet water—bottles of it! His hand shaking, he reached out, seized the first bottle in reach, gulped down a thin swallow. It burned him like fire, but it reacted on his brain like driving wind on fog. For a space, everything came clear.

Daylight of the next day—and where was he? Strength came back to him. He tried doors, in vain. He tried the shutters, in vain. He remembered Emile was coming back—how much time had passed? No telling. Sudden hope flooded upon him. There was a fireplace, and by it an iron-and-brass poker, no child's toy. He seized it, hurried back into his own room, saw his clothes on a chair beside the bed, and feverishly climbed into them. He was nearly dressed when, without warning, a swirl of cloud descended on his brain; the brief stimulus of the alcohol had worn off— Like a man stricken, he toppled over, fell on the bed, mechanically pulled up the covers. Then darkness was upon him.

A man's voice broke the swirling waves. "He'll not wake up for a bit. I must go with the car. Remain here, in this room, you comprehend? Watch him, he may be dangerous. If he makes any trouble, shoot him."

Emile, now wearing chauffeur's cap and coat, departed. The door closed. Another man brought a tray to a table: a short thick-set man of peasant type. North closed his eyes, after that one glance, and lay quiet. Again his brain was swept clear. He had the poker in his hand, beneath the coverlet. He remembered now; they were going away.

With sudden decision, North swung his feet clear, sat up on the edge of the bed. The short man turned, saw him, caught up the tray and brought it to the bed. "If *monsieur* will eat a bite—"

The man did not perceive his danger in time, and then he perceived nothing else at all, for North came up like a flash, and the heavy poker smashed his skull, so that he and the tray together fell forward across the bed with a subdued crash. The man had a gun; good! North leaned over, reached for it—

The fog came down upon him. He battled against it desperately, but in vain. Success in his very grasp, under his hand—and lost! He came to his knees, caught at the bed, slowly went down and lay, this time, very quiet.

WHILE THESE things were going on in the house of Harden, events in all the rest of Paris were moving toward their appointed destiny.

The Gare St. Lazare was bustling, its dingy old train-sheds and corridors filled with every one who had a uniform to wear, while National Guards, *gendarmes* and agents thronged the passages. Passing potentates and kings were nothing in the life of Paris, but the smiling duke from across the channel was dear to all hearts—easily the most popular, after his royal brother, of all the titled visitors who found France a playground.

In the Rue St. Honoré, a pudgy little man walked stiffly along, between his teeth an old clay pipe; curious glances were directed at him in passing, for his mild blue eyes seemed fixed on vacancy,

and the Basque beret over one ear gave him a grotesque appearance.

As Solomon passed the entry of the National City Bank, a
man came down the steps, halted him, shook hands, passed the
time of day, and went his way. Solomon went on to the corner
of the Rue de Castiglione and was held up by a traffic block. He
opened his hand and glanced at a crumpled piece of paper. It
was a cable from London, not addressed to him, and unsigned:

> Heavy selling all Empire stocks since noon.

Solomon tore up the paper and crossed as the traffic surged
over.

On the other side of the street, a man in chauffeur's uniform,
a dark man idling in front of a shop-window, asked a light for
his cigarette. Solomon produced a box of matches.

"Merci, effendi," replied the man, saluting, as he returned the
box. With it was a key. "The place is empty so far."

"They come in ten minutes," said Solomon in Arabic, and
went on.

Half a block away was a large hotel, much frequented by
English people of rank who came to Paris; it fronted on the
Rue de Rivoli, but its carriage entrance was here in the Rue St.
Honoré. Opposite this entrance was gathered a little throng of
loafers, about the front of a tiny bar with the oblique tobacco
sign flaming over its doorway. Just as Solomon got here, two
agents and half a dozen operatives of the Sûreté, the detective
headquarters of Paris, suddenly appeared with an officer.

"Hold that man," said the officer, pointing to Solomon. "The
rest of you, on your way!"

Two operatives took charge of Solomon, who regarded them
placidly and sucked at his pipe. The others sent the idlers on
their way, after the manner of French police—not a pleasant
manner as a rule. The officer came to Solomon.

"M'sieur, your *carte d'identité?"*

Solomon chuckled wheezily and produced an identification

card from his pocket. "Two men with workmen's smocks or overcoats over Fascist uniforms," said Solomon. "They'll probably be waiting about here."

The officer returned the card with a bow, made no comment, and vanished with his men. Solomon turned into a doorway, whose stairs gave entry to the offices and apartments above.

Two minutes later he was sitting at the window of a second floor apartment, whose door the key had fitted. Directly opposite and beneath, was the hotel carriage entrance. Solomon produced plug and knife, and began whittling off fresh tobacco and teasing it in his palm. The apartment was fairly well furnished, but unoccupied; it was probably one of those apartments used by the clients of divorce lawyers who desire to establish a "residence" in Paris, where bailiffs may serve papers.

"Dang it!" observed Solomon mildly. "This 'ere apartment must 'ave a back way, but I can't find it. I expect as 'ow it lets out on the Place Vendôme. That there Billings didn't know a thing about it, neither."

He looked down at the street, sighed, tapped down his pipe, and withdrew to another room.

Presently feet were heard in the outer hall, and the door was opened. Harden entered; behind him were Madeleine and the Rattler. Harden closed the door, then swung around as a sharp cry broke from the Rattler:

"It's gone—it's gone! Looky there! We left the gun waitin' by the window—"

Harden's jaw dropped in consternation. There was no machine rifle in the room. Yet he and the Rattler together had arranged everything.

"Lemme out!" Like a flash, a pistol appeared in the Rattler's hand; snarling, smitten with panic, he shoved Harden aside and leaped at the door.

Taking alarm and to flight like a wild beast, he was gone at a bound, and the door slammed behind him. The other two stood there paralyzed, staring at each other. Madeleine's lip curled disdainfully.

"S O !" S H E said, gazing at Harden in contempt. "This is the end of your fine scheme—oh, you Americans! Bah! You make me sick!"

A wheezy chuckle caused them both to turn.

"Good afternoon, sir and miss," said Solomon, standing in the entrance to the next room. "A werry fine day it is, and werry 'appy I am to see you both. If so be as you'd care to go over me accounts with you, Mr. Harden—"

An incredulous oath burst from Harden. The eyes of Madeleine were wide, startled, amazed

"Solomon! John Solomon—you devil!"

Solomon chuckled and held a match to his pipe. His blue eyes were wide and blank.

"Now, Mr. Harden, don't you go being all upset, as the old gent said when the 'ousemaid broke 'im the bad news. I 'opes as 'ow you and me will be having a werry polite talk. If I was you, miss, I wouldn't leave—it ain't 'ealthy. That 'ere Rattler was in a terrible 'urry, and if I ain't mistook, it ain't give 'im no luck."

Pointing his words, there was a commotion in the street below; cries, whistles, the sharp bursting sound of a shot. Madeleine darted to the window, then swung about.

"They've got him!" she said, her voice shrill. "This is a trap!"

Harden woke up. A pistol showed in his hand, and he wrenched open the door with an imperative gesture. His face was hard, cold, merciless, his eyes blazed with triumph.

"The get-away, girl!" he cried. "Give me a whistle if it's clear. We've got big game enough right in our hands. Quick! You, Solomon, keep those hands up—"

Madeleine darted past him. Harden was transformed. In his eyes gleamed desperation, exultation, the harsh menace of death.

"You damned little rat!" he said, low-voiced, and advanced to Solomon, shoving the pistol against his body, reaching out with the other hand, searching him. "No gun, eh? Well, we'd sooner have you than any one else. How'd you learn about this? Speak up, damn you!"

Solomon chuckled. "Mr. Billings told us a mortal lot, sir," he rejoined apologetically. "And 'e ain't in no 'ospital at all. No, sir, Mr. Billings is a laying in me own 'ouse this werry minute."

Harden exploded in a vitriolic curse. "So that's it? Well, you've slipped up! One thing he didn't know was the getaway; and we'll fix you, mister!" From the hall came a quick, thin whistle. The pistol jerked. "Step out ahead of me. March, or I swear I'll blow hell out of you. March!"

Solomon, helpless, obeyed the menace. They stepped out into the hall. Harden gripped him by the nape of the neck and hurled him into the opposite doorway. Madeleine was holding the door open. She swiftly closed it, shot a bolt.

"Got him!" cried Harden. "Quick, girl, go ahead! One yell out of you, Solomon, and you get drilled. March!"

The three passed into the next room and were gone.

CHAPTER VII

SETTLING ACCOUNTS

THE PLACE Vendôme was its usual bustling self, and nobody observed three people who emerged from one of the old, courtyard entrances between shops, and entered a waiting car. The lady got in first; the two men, arm in arm, were not remarked; the door closed and the car darted away and was lost in the traffic stream.

It swept around, circled the Place de l'Opéra, shot out the Boulevard Haussmann to the Étoile, and presently swooped down the sharp hill past the Trocadéro to the Seine. Then, at the Pont de Grenelle, it slid off through Auteuil and two minutes later was passing the high iron gates of the Villa Montmorenci—that cluster of houses in private grounds which forms one of the most secluded spots in all Paris. The car slowed down before a crumbling old house in a corner of the grounds, passed a lodge at whose door a man stood at attention, and halted.

This was the house in which Dick North lay helpless.

Harden escorted his prisoner into the house. Madeleine paused and turned to the chauffeur.

"We will be in the salon, Emile. Go and get M. North and bring him. If necessary, use handcuffs; that man may have to be tamed."

Emile saluted and the car circled the house. Madeleine went in, and joined Harden and John Solomon in the salon.

"Sit down," snapped Harden. "Madeleine, watch him." He picked up his desk telephone and gave a number. "Who's in charge there to-day?" he inquired when the response came. "Well, you can wire Dominetti that I've got Solomon right here under my gun. Any orders out regarding him? Oh! All right. Then change the wire to read that he's dead; he will be in five minutes. All right."

Solomon listened to all this without any expression showing in his face. His placid blue eyes were unwinking. He fished for his knife and plug, and began to shred tobacco into his palm. Harden opened his desk and produced his silenced automatic from the drawer.

"Well, big boy," Harden said jocosely, "you've run a grand little bluff on Dominetti, huh? But your string's played out. What's all this bunk about you and Pearson having some sort of a death ray—eh?"

"Beggin' your pardon, sir," said Solomon, "it ain't bunk. That there is a werry scientific fact, as the old gent said when 'e kissed the 'ousemaid."

"You're nuts," said Harden in contempt. "If you had such a thing, you'd pull all kinds of tricks with it. I know all about you. You're a fat little fool with more money than brains, and you have sense enough to hire brains. Well, you're finished."

"Yes, sir?" said Solomon, tamping his pipe. Madeleine stood at one side, holding a small pistol. "Beggin' your pardon, sir and miss, I'd be werry glad to 'ave a settlin' of me accounts, if so be as you don't mind. That 'ere Arab you went and killed last night—'e was a werry good man, Mr. Harden, and sorry I was to see 'im murdered."

Harden laughed harshly, his eyes fastened on Solomon.

"Know about it, huh? What's all this bosh about accounts?"

"Me accounts, sir and miss—'ere they be, all shipshape and Bristol fashion," said Solomon. His hand went to his pocket, regardless of the silenced revolver that darted up at him. He produced a small red notebook, and, with an apologetic air, laid it on the desk. "If you'll 'ave the kindness, sir and miss. Prowidence is a werry mysterious thing, Mr. Harden, and I'm mortal sorry for you and this 'ere poor misguided female—"

"Shut your trap," snapped Harden. "Madeleine, look at that book. Watch out for tricks."

Harden kept his eyes and weapon steadily on Solomon. Madeleine, putting her pistol on the desk, picked up the notebook, a disdainful smile on her lips. She opened it, turned a page or two.

Her smile became frozen. Her eyes dilated, and across her face stole a mortal pallor. Whatever this woman was, whatever her past had been, in this moment one could feel only a pity not untinged with horror. Her face contracted, and suddenly she dropped the notebook and clutched at the desk, and stared at Solomon with terrible eyes.

"You damned fool!" said Harden in amazement. He put out one hand and took the notebook. "One move from you, Solomon, and you're done for."

"Yes, sir," said Solomon placidly, and held a match to his pipe. "Only it's you as is done for, Mr. Harden—just like that."

HARDEN LAUGHED. He opened the little red book, glanced at it, and a change came into his face. Upon his lips burst an oath of rage. He flung down the book and swept up the silenced automatic, aiming at Solomon. His eyes were narrow, vindictive, terrible in their determination.

"You rat!" he said slowly. "Take it, then—"

A voice broke in upon him from the doorway.

"Up with 'em, Harden! Up!"

North was standing there. In one hand he held a frightful object—a poker of iron and brass, from which slow drops of red fell to the carpet. Emile had come upon him as he wakened again from that deathly sleep. In the other hand North held an automatic pistol.

"Drop that gun—drop it!" rang out his voice. Harden's hand laid down his automatic and drew back along the desk. He stared at the newcomer as though petrified. A low sobbing groan broke from Madeleine. "Up," commanded North, and took a step forward.

With the rapidity of light Madeleine snatched her own pistol from the desk, fired twice. Harden's hand leaped to his weapon; the silenced *chug-chug-chug* of its viperous shots sounded queerly amid the crashes of blasting reports. Then Harden sagged forward a little and a rush of blood broke from his lips.

Madeleine screamed horribly—the scream of a mad beast, instinct with rage, with fury, with a mortal hurt. She made a leap toward North; as she did so, Harden's finger, convulsive in death, pressed the trigger of his weapon twice. The woman spun around—both bullets had smashed into her body. As she collapsed, Harden's head fell forward on the desk.

John Solomon put one finger in his pipe and tamped it calmly. He had not moved.

North's hand let his weapon fall. Very white, he caught the curtain at the doorway, gripped it to him, held himself erect. Behind him was a rush of feet, a shrill medley of voices. He half turned, swayed, then slowly his hand slipped on the curtain folds and he sank down.

"Solomon Effendi!"

Dark men, half a dozen of them, burst into the room.

JOHN SOLOMON, pudgy, placid as ever, sat beside North's bed and carefully cut off tobacco from a very new, black and shiny plug of T & B, and loaded his clay pipe.

"You're a werry lucky young man, sir, that's all I got to say," he observed calmly. "That 'ere drug is about wore off, but bullets don't wear off so good!"

"Listen to me a minute," said North, coming to one elbow. "I don't understand a lot of things—you couldn't have known that I'd show up at the right moment! If you got hold of Billings and made him talk, and then spoiled their whole game, then why did you let yourself get trapped?"

"I couldn't rightly 'elp it," and Solomon's eyes twinkled.

"Besides which, I 've a mortal lot o' trust in Prowidence, sir; and I 've me own ways of reaching me own ends. So when I knowed as 'ow that 'ere Dupont 'ad caught you, I went and caught that 'ere Billings, and I wasn't mistook in trusting of Prowidence. Now, sir, this 'ere is a sleeping draft the doctor left for you."

"Hold on," said North. "See here—how did you get hold of me in the first place? Remember when we met in the Tuileries Gardens? Was that an accident or not?"

"Them as asks questions, sir, gets less 'n they asks, says I," and Solomon chuckled. "Accidents 'ave a werry queer way of 'appening to me, sir, they 'ave that! As a matter o' fact, I'd been on your trail ever since 'earing o' that there matter down in Libya. When I likes a man, I likes 'im werry much indeed, as the 'ousemaid said when the old gent up and kissed 'er. You and me can 'ave a trip to Rome, Mr. North, and you can go back to Libya—"

"I stick with you, if you want me," said North, and smiled.

John Solomon put out a hand and gave North a surprisingly firm grip.

"Werry 'appy I am to 'ear you say so." Solomon put down his pipe. "Now you take this 'ere drink, sir."

North swallowed the potion—and this, so far as he was concerned, ended the story.

> *But—the story is not ended!*
> *What was this mysterious "Death Ray?" What were those re-markable pictures on a blank wall? Who was Dominetti? These queries and a dozen more will be answered in the longest and best John Solomon story ever written—"John Solomon's Biggest Game"—a book-length novel soon to appear in the Argosy. You will see John pitted against all the forces of destruction, with the fate of half the civilized world hanging in the balance; and the lit-tle blue-eyed cockney coming face to face with defeat—the glorious defeat that has made the sagas and hero-stories of the world an inspiration to following generations.*

JOHN SOLOMON'S BIGGEST GAME

CHAPTER I

DECK CHAIR INTRIGUES

WITH THE Statue of Liberty three days behind her the *De Grasse* had settled down into the usual routine of her east-bound trips. Deck chairs were adjusted to the liking of the passengers, the smoking room crowd had come down to steady bridge hours and the serious business of drinking, acquaintances were being rapidly cemented. Passengers were beginning to recognize their own stewards by sight, and had discovered that their French was less comprehensible than their English. Surest sign of all, the radio was working steadily.

On the fourth morning, a steward delivered a Marconigram just received from Paris, to a Mr. Frank Halsey, who had an outside B deck cabin all to himself.

Halsey was a tall, slender man of distinguished appearance, his dark hair tipped with gray, his aristocratic features unusually handsome in their strength and regularity, his dark eyes very piercing from beneath heavy lids. His attire displayed quiet luxury and good taste, and without a ripple he had fallen into a group which devoted the afternoons to contract at rather high stakes.

Opening the envelope, Halsey spread out a long message in French—and in code, at that. He sat down at his writing table, took a folded sheet from a notebook, and with pencil and paper set about deciphering the message. This task occupied him for a good half hour. Then, a gleam in his dark eyes, he lighted a cigarette and scrutinized the result of his labor. This result was, to say the least, astonishing—the more so that it was unsigned. Obviously, the signature "Gelli et Cie," appended to the code message meant nothing. The translated communication read:

> Courier believed Miss Tully Cabin B 67. Ascertain every-thing possible. Imperative you attempt nothing, but inform Boris at Le Havre of discoveries. Remain with Lee as per original orders, advising immediately results.

Halsey read this over, then tore the transcribed sheet into tiny fragments. Busy again with pencil, he scribbled out a message addressed to Signor Dominetti in care of a Paris bank. The message was laconic:

> Unable bribe Lee. Taking other measures. Already know Tully.

This he translated carefully into code, destroying the origi-nal. Dressing with his usual precision, he went on deck, sought out the radio cabin on the upper deck, left his message, and descended again.

A B A F T T H E smoking room, where a few deck chairs occu-pied a favored spot, two people were seated, talking. The man was short, rotund, saffron, a Chinaman whose oblique eyes were merry and sparkling. His English, like his clothes, bespoke an Occidental university. He looked up and rose as Halsey came toward them.

"I have your chair, Mr. Halsey—"

"Keep it, keep it, Dr. Lee," and Halsey drew up an unoccupied chair. "Good morning, Miss Tully! May I join your little circle? In time for morning broth, I hope."

"So do I—I'm hungry already!" and the girl laughed. "Dr. Lee and I have discovered mutual friends; he was at John Hopkins for two years, and delved into the mysteries of physics under my own Professor Loomis."

"Indeed?" Halsey smiled at the two, but his eyes lingered a moment on the girl's face. June Tully must be close to twen-

He searched the unconscious Chinaman's luggage.

ty-five, he thought; and dangerous. She was dark, lithe, expressed a keen vivacity in every word and motion. Halsey added: "I've heard of Loomis—he's made a lot of discoveries, hasn't he? I didn't know you had a proprietary interest in him."

"I have, though," and the girl's eyes were serious. "I was his secretary until lately, and he's a wonderful man! In fact, he got me the position I'm taking up in Paris. You've lived there a long time, Mr. Halsey—how many years?"

"Several," returned Halsey and negligently proffered cigarettes. "Long enough to build up an importing business back home. Unfortunately my brain doesn't run to science, like that of your professor, or to politics, like that of Dr. Lee here."

The yellow man laughed softly.

"Politics, with me, is an aftermath of science," he observed. "Besides, I do not have much to do with politics. In China, those of us who know the Occident have been drafted into service, that's all."

Halsey said nothing. He knew very well that Erh Lim Lee was a highly important man in China, was even said to control its foreign policies; and might conceivably at the present moment be on his way to Geneva to lay certain matters before the League of Nations; but this was not supposed to be known, so why mention it? Then June Tully broke in, eagerly.

"Did you ever meet a man in Paris, Mr. Halsey, by the name of Solomon?"

"Never heard of him," said Halsey. "A friend of yours?"

"Of my father's, yes—I never met him. I thought you might know of him."

"Not, by any chance," and Dr. Lee leaned forward, "one John Solomon?"

"Yes!" The girl turned toward him. "You don't mean to I say that you know him?"

Dr. Lee made a deprecating gesture. "Oh, not at all. I have heard the name, that's all. I can't even remember where I heard it, but—ah, here's the broth! Now we can pass to more serious matters!"

The stewards appeared with trays, serving broth and biscuits. The steward with the broth presented his tray to Halsey; a look, a swift lightning glance, passed between them. Halsey handed a cup to the girl, another to Dr. Lee, took one himself.

The three sipped their broth, chatted, nibbled at biscuits. Presently Dr. Lee rose, refusing another cigarette. His cherubic face looked slightly pale, and on the plea of having letters to write, he departed.

MISS TULLY glanced after him with interest.

"He's a singular man, Mr. Halsey. A wonderful scientist, they say, and now one of the big political men in the new China! I'm glad to have met him, for I've heard a lot about him."

"Nice chap," agreed Halsey. "So you're going to Paris for the first time? If you'll permit me, Miss Tully, I'd be glad to be of service to you in any way. But perhaps you have friends there?"

"I have letters, but no friends," and she nodded eagerly. "Yes, I'd be only too glad, indeed! I speak French pretty well, but it's all strange and new country to me over on the other side. If I—"

There was a dull sound. Stifling an exclamation, the girl

leaned over swiftly, even before Halsey could stoop. Her hand-bag, a very handsome one of carved leather, had fallen to the deck. She recovered it, and broke into a laugh.

"Silly of me, to carry a perfume vial when I'm bound for Paris! And even more silly to be afraid it had broken! Feminine inconsistency for you."

"And, as always, entirely charming," said Halsey, smiling. His smile was warm and could he very winning. He came to his feet. "Well, if you'll excuse me, I'd better follow Lee's example and get a duty letter off my mind before luncheon."

"And I'll promenade to work up more appetite. Until later, then!" answered the girl.

Halsey bowed and departed. Once around the corner of the deck house, his careless gait quickened. He strode forward rapidly, and made his way below—not to his own deck, but down to the lower level. With quick glances at the cabin numbers, he passed without hesitation to 134. No one was in sight as he turned into the alley containing this number. He paused at the door, listened, tried the handle.

"No, a sick man doesn't lock doors!" he murmured, and entered the cabin.

Upon the lower berth was outstretched the figure of Dr. Lee, who occupied the cabin alone. Sick, perhaps; very certainly asleep. Halsey gave him one attentive look, then locked the door.

In the cabin were two suitcases and a small trunk, from whose lock dangled a bunch of keys. Halsey went through all three pieces of luggage, very systematically. With scrupulous care he disarranged nothing, replaced everything, appearing to know exactly what he was seeking. His treasure-trove came to light midway through the trunk, in the shape of a heavy manila enve-lope on which were brushed three Chinese ideograms. It was unsealed.

Halsey sat down, lit a cigarette, drew a sheaf of papers from the envelope, and a glitter of satisfaction lightened his dark eyes as he glanced through the papers. Separating certain sheets from the rest, he drew out pencil and notebook and rapidly jotted down a long list of notes. This occupied him a good fifteen minutes. When he had finished, he put the papers together again and was slipping them into the large envelope when, inside, he discerned something he had overlooked. This was a small sealed envelope. He drew it forth, and a long, soft whistle came from his lips.

It was addressed to John Solomon, Rue Montorgeuil, Paris.

HALSEY TURNED it over and over, sharp excitement in his features.

The paper was thin; without steam and patience, it was impossible to open the envelope and escape detection. He glanced at the sleeping man, then came to abrupt decision.

"It's worth the gamble!" he muttered, and tore open the envelope. There was disclosed a single sheet of paper, bearing only a string of Chinese ideograms. Halsey cursed softly, but pocketed this and the envelope.

In five minutes everything was exactly as he had found it. He left the cabin and had regained his own cabin just as the first luncheon call was sounding. Sitting down, he wrote out two messages, then worked getting them into code. The first, addressed to Dominetti, was brief:

> Mailing full text aboard ship, also at Plymouth. Have got letter Lee carried addressed to Solomon.

The second message was longer, and was addressed to one Boris Glazunoff at the Hôtel de la Marine, Le Havre:

> Suggest you meet ship Plymouth, making plans action on reaching Le Havre. Lady extremely dangerous, probably forewarned. Impossible obtain results without using force. Believe she suspects me.

Reading over this last message, Halsey nodded, eyes shrewdly reflective.

"She's a deep one, all right," he murmured, as he finished

transcribing the message in code. "Either she's going openly
to Solomon and knows nothing, or else she suspects every one
and uses his name as a bait for suckers. I incline to think she
knows exactly what she's about. Also, I incline to think she and
I might get on well together. If so, the good Boris will find his
way made smooth."

He laughed a little, and was rising when there came a tap at
his door. To his call, it opened. The deck steward, he who had
carried the broth, stepped furtively in and closed the door.

"Right," said Halsey, reaching for his pocketbook. He drew
forth a sheaf of lavender thousand-franc notes and counted off
five. "Here you are, my friend. You're certain there will be no ill
effects?"

The steward bowed greasily. "None, *m'sieur*," he rejoined, "save
perhaps a headache. I trust *m'sieur* is satisfied with my services?"

"Quite," said Halsey dryly, visualizing the unconscious form
of Dr. Lee.

When the steward had departed, Halsey lighted a cigarette
and adjusted his cravat. He scrutinized his reflection in the
mirror, and appeared to be quite satisfied with himself no less
than with the services of the steward.

"If Dominetti were not a fool," he murmured, "I might have
worked the same little trick with the girl. But no! He was so
cursed afraid that I couldn't handle the two jobs, eh? Well, just
for that I'll see what can be done in another manner! I've met
deep ones before this—and never liked them half so well as I
do her!"

With which cryptic utterance he went forth to send his
messages and make himself thoroughly agreeable to June Tully;
and in this not unpleasant, if faintly ominous, fashion ended the
prologue to the savage and merciless drama whose scenes were
laid among the rain-wet streets of Paris.

CHAPTER II

A MAN'S ARM

O N T H E day before the *De Grasse* docked at Le Havre, the consulate of the United States at the same uninviting city severed relations with its assistant consul. More properly, James Warden severed relations with his diplomatic career, and yielded up his office; not from any necessity, but from choice, for private reasons.

So far as the Department of State was concerned, his reasons for such action were rather obscure. He was twenty-eight, and was a very promising "career man" in the foreign service. Besides, he had recently come into an inheritance which assured him the financial case needful for rising high in diplomatic circles. However, he had resigned, and there was an end of it—so far as the consulate was concerned.

The *De Grasse* was due to dock at ten. A little before nine, Warden secured a place in the boat train to Paris, checked on his trunks, and retired to the café of the vast roofed-in wharf. Here he settled down at a table, ordered a Rossi with water, and prepared to pass the time agreeably, while all around thronged porters, customs men and women, and commissionaires of all sorts, with a swiftly increasing throng of folks come to meet the arriving boat.

Jimmy Warden appeared to view his immediate future with cheerful equanimity; he was, in fact, a distinctly cheerful sort of person. Slightly over six feet, of wide and powerful build, he was a man to attract attention. His gray tweeds spoke eloquently of the Boulevard Haussman and the finest tailoring, his crisp blond hair and fresh complexion carried out the athletic promise of his build; but it was his face, and the personality it expressed, which drew the eye. A wide, strong face it was, with level and well-balanced eyes, holding that indefinable air of assurance and command which comes to a man who has the ability and means to be entirely independent. Jimmy Warden not only said and did exactly what he liked, but he got away with it.

While he sipped the scarlet drink before him, he ran over the phrases of a letter he had received two weeks previously. The writing was angular, fairly large, very even and feminine; the letter was from a girl whom he had not seen for a year, but whom he was very far from forgetting. His eye dwelt upon the significant phrases:

—have given up my position and am sailing on the *De Grasse,* so if you're not too busy with state affairs to run down and say hello, you'll have the chance. I've been offered a fine position in Paris, by an old friend of my father's; but I'll tell you more about it when I see you—if I do. Probably you'll be too occupied with tennis matches or government business or something to pay any attention to half-forgotten friends from home. In which case I'll depend on somebody else to get me through the customs, and I'll go on to Paris, and you can have Havre all to your comfortable self.

Anyway, Jimmy, you'd better be on the dock when I get in, or you'll be sorry.

Sincerely,

JUNE

Mr. Warden folded up the letter and pocketed it, a smile playing about his eyes. He was not the type of man who smiles readily, despite his very cheerful air, but now he was eagerly amused and expectant.

"Nobody'd call that a love letter," he confided to the sparkling Rossi, "but if I choose to regard it as such, that's my business! And won't June get the surprise of her life when she hears I'm out of the consulate, eh? Wonder what sort of a job she's taken

in Paris. Hm! We'll look into that, young lady. I have absolutely nothing to do in life except to show you a good time and
persuade you to become Mrs. James Warden—and gosh, how I
wish it wouldn't take persuasion!"

HE GLANCED up, still half smiling, and met the glance
of a passing American—a bronzed and vigorous man of about
his own age, whose firm and rather severe features touched some
chord of recognition. The other turned and came to his table,
hand outstretched.

"Warden, isn't it? Met you in the consulate here last month.
North's my name."

"Of course! Sit down and join me," said Warden heartily.
"You were down from Paris to arrange about clearing some
scientific instruments, weren't you? I'm out of the service now,
and staying over to meet a friend on this boat. You're here on
the same errand?"

North nodded, sat down, and accepted a cigarette. A man
in chauffeur's cap and dust-robe approached him and saluted—a dark-looking man, possibly an Arab, as Warden noted
in surprise.

"The car is just outside, *m'sieur.*"

"Good. Watch for a reply to that radio I sent the boat, Yusuf;
it would probably be at the office upstairs."

Yusuf saluted and departed. Warden observed his companion approvingly.

"Not a bad notion that! I'll have to get me an Arab and a car,
too! I like the idea. And an apartment out Auteuil way. Here's
happy days—the nights are always happy! I'm out of a job, and
thanks to the estate of a beneficent uncle, I'm going to step out
and enjoy life."

North chuckled as he sipped his drink.

"Yes, you look as if you were on a lazy man's holiday," he
retorted. "I can see you playing the Paris lounge-lizard—not!
Out of the service, eh? You and I might have a talk one of these
days, Warden. I know of something that would appeal to you."

Warden studied the other man for a sharp instant. He knew practically nothing about North, but he was a good appraiser of men, and behind North's words, behind the direct, piercing eyes, he could read unsaid things.

"So long as it's not serious, I'm agreeable," Warden returned lightly. "Aren't you in the engineering line or something? Seems to me I recall reading something about you—reclamation project down in Libya, wasn't it?"

North nodded a bit wryly. "Yes. But I'm in Paris now, in a very different line. Of course, your place in the diplomatic service vouches for you, Warden, so I've no hesitation about speaking frankly to you. Seriously, you're exactly the sort of man I'd like to get in touch with. By the way, did you ever hear of a chap in Paris by the name of John Solomon?"

"Lord. Yes!" Warden chuckled. "Little pudgy cockney with gray hair and wide-open blue eyes? He was down here raising hell about three months ago. I was acting consul then. This bird came down to meet somebody who had no passport and wanted me to fix things up. I couldn't do it, of course, and hanged if he didn't telephone the ambassador! About an hour later he had wires from Paris that made him cock of the walk, too. Never could understand how he did it. What about him?"

"Nothing much," and North smiled little. "Tell you later, maybe. I motored down to meet a lady for him—a secretary he's brought over. Family friends and all that. By the way, what d'you know about a couple of murders in Paris yesterday; hear anything on the inside?"

WARDEN FROWNED. "You mean Ferguson and Huntley—those two chaps whose car was halted in the Bois, and both of them shot? No, I don't know any inside stuff about it. Just robbery and murder. Why? Know them?"

"Yes," said North, his voice touched with acid. Then he dismissed the subject. "Warden, I've got a hunch that you and I can do business, and I'm playing it. Shall we talk?"

Warden threw back his head in a quick, hearty laugh.

"Not a chance, North, not a chance—at any rate, not for the immediate present! I'm a gilded butterfly of leisure. Here, I'll give you the lowdown: I'm here to meet a girl from home, who's going to Paris. Have met her several times, off and on, and she's the sort to remember. I'm going to Paris, savvy? And I'm going to show her the old town, and I'm going to give the best imitation of the rush act that you ever laid eyes on."

"So that's it!" North's eyes twinkled cordially, and he lifted his glass. "Well, old chap, here's all the luck in the world!—How's our time going? Half an hour yet—time to bounce another Rossi off your tonsils, so let's have it."

The order was given. A moment later, the trim figure of Yusuf appeared, holding an envelope. He came to the table and handed the message to North, who tore at it and drew forth a sheet of paper. One glance, and his face changed.

"The devil!" he said, in evident consternation.

"Nothing wrong, I hope?" asked Warden.

"Everything." North read the message again, with a puzzled frown. "It can't be—something wrong here! She'd have no reason to do that!"

"Women don't need reason; they function without it," said Jimmy Warden.

Disregarding him, North held out the message to Yusuf, who read it. "Telephone Solomon Effendi," North ordered, and the Arab departed with a smart salute. North laid the message on the table, and stared blankly at it.

Warden studied him in silence, attention caught by this further mention of Solomon. What had that fat little old man to do with this energetic and highly capable American? In North's manner was a hint of recklessness that Jimmy Warden liked—a hint of capability in any emergency, a hint of thorough readiness to cope with anything at any time. Yet here the man was struck blank and in evident dismay by the receipt of a radiogram.

"There, read it!" and North, looking up, shoved the message across the table. "Why the devil would she do that, now?"

Warden picked up the paper. Then his jaw dropped. The message, from the purser of the *De Grasse*, stated that Mlle. Tully had left the boat at Plymouth, but her luggage was coming on to Le Havre.

"Good Lord!" exclaimed Warden. "Why, I'm here to meet June Tully myself! She can't be the one? I've got her letter in my pocket—said to meet her here!"

"What?" North was suddenly alert, his voice crisp, his eyes glinting sharply. "Is that so, Warden? Something wrong for sure, then! She had absolutely no reason to leave the boat at Plymouth. She was bringing vitally important messages, dispatches. D'you see what it means? She's in London now, instead of being here. That is, she'd have reached London by last night."

The two men sat staring at each other for a moment. It was Warden who broke the silence—broke it aggressively, resolutely, a steely flash in his gray-blue eyes as he leaned forward and addressed North.

"See here, now. I don't understand much about this, but I mean to. I don't know you at all well, but I rather think you're straight. June Tully means a whole lot to me, and I'm going into this thing hard. This isn't like her at all. It's no fool woman's whim. North, come across now or never. Cards on the table, or not?"

NORTH NODDED quietly. "Yes, so far as is possible," he said.

"All right. Her letter said she was taking a position with an old friend of her father's. Is that your beggar Solomon?"

"Yes," said North. The incoming steamer had been sighted near the mole, and all around was a surge and throng of people, but the two men sat regardless and heedless.

"From your hints," pursued Warden, "there's more to Solomon and your business relations than meets the eye. Suppose you cough up what you know about June Tully; either we go into the thing separately or together—and I don't propose to act blind."

"Right," said North crisply. "Just a minute, there's Yusuf coming back."

Warden glanced at the approaching Arab, then scrutinized North anew. He had the feeling that North was absolutely straight, that he was a man to be liked and to be depended on; but at the same time Jimmy Warden knew too much about France and Americans in France to take anything for granted.

Yusuf came up, hesitated, and at a curt order from North, delivered his message.

"Solomon Effendi said you were to find her," he stated. "If necessary, see or communicate with Wright in London. That was all."

"Good. Have the car ready," said North, and squared around toward Jimmy Warden.

"We're in it together, then," he said quietly. "At the moment, I'm not able to speak freely about Solomon. Let's stick to June Tully. Her father and Solomon were friends years ago, I understand. She's been a sort of secretary and assistant to Professor Loomis at the Johns Hopkins University for a couple of years. Solomon and one or two gentlemen associated with him have been in touch with Loomis, and Miss Tully was engaged to come over here and act as secretary for Solomon—more with a view to helping her financially, I think, than for any other reason. She was bringing some very important papers from Loomis, embodying the result of his latest experiments and discoveries. He's the chap who has revolutionized physics in the past few years, you know. That's all."

"Maybe," said Jimmy Warden, who did not look at all cheerful or humorous now. "Maybe. Not enough for me. Anybody interested in getting those papers?"

"Yes," returned North. "Nobody knows she has them, so far as we're aware, but I came down to meet her, just to be on the safe side. Do you, by any chance, know of an Italian prince, an exile in Paris, who's named Dominetti?"

Warden made an impatient gesture.

"I've heard something about him; can't recall just what. Signor Dominetti, prince of something-or-other—one of the royal rotters who fill France, eh?"

"No, not a rotter at all," said North. "A wealthy, unscrupulous, and extremely able man. We'll discuss him later. To put it briefly, he's got the finest gang of crooks you ever ran up against—brainy men, not mere criminals. He plays for huge stakes, and usually wins. Those two chaps we mentioned, Ferguson and Huntley, were murdered by his agents; they're two of Solomon's best men, or were."

"See here," interrupted Warden, his eyes wide. "What kind of dope do you use, anyhow? This sort of stuff you're talking—"

"Is hard fact," broke in North. "Swallow it. You can digest it later. We've no time to jabber now; we've got to act, and act quick. Are you satisfied? Do we go in this together?"

"I must, for June's sake. You're on, North!"

"Good. Got your passport?"

"In my pocket," Warden said.

"I'll get busy and charter a plane. There are a couple of Goliaths at the aviation field here. We'll get over to London at once. If you have any luggage, Yusuf will take care of it for you. I'll be back in ten minutes and we'll meet at the upstairs office. We'd better get right out and board the *De Grasse*—she'll be a good half hour docking, as she has to be turned around in the basin. That'll save time for us. You can get a copy of the passenger list, and have them get a tug ready to take us out. If you can't swing it as a diplomat, I'll turn the trick. Upstairs, in ten minutes."

Almost before Warden realized it, North was gone, striding rapidly away.

JIMMY WARDEN paid for the drinks and made his way to the company offices on the upper platform. He was slightly dazed by the astonishing information he had just collected, but the vigorous, forthright words and manner of North, the man's swiftness to grapple with emergency, were heartening and confidence-inspiring.

That there was some pressing danger to June Tully was more than plain, however much else might remain unexplained. And this, with Warden, swept away all thought of other things. Except for North, he might have accepted her non-appearance as being some whim or as the result of a meeting with friends; in the circumstances, however, this did not appear very logical.

Being, naturally, quite well known to the local officials of the French Line, Warden had no hesitation in proffering a request that he be sent aboard the incoming boat at once. He met with ready assent—in fact, other small craft were going out to her as she came up the basin; and North appeared just as he was being supplied with a guide and the written warrant. A tug was brought in, and before the three men reached the wharf level it was waiting for them.

"All set," said North. "Got that passenger list?"

Warden turned it over. Their guide received his tip, and the tug set out on the instant, heading for the slowly moving bulk of the liner. North scanned the passenger list without comment.

"First job is to see the purser," he observed. "No easy matter, in the landing rush, but we'll do it. There's a fast plane ready for us; we should make Croydon in two hours. Keep your eyes open, Warden, in case you spot any one aboard who might be a crook. It's a long chance, though."

The tug circled, came in under the side of the crawling liner, and presently Jimmy Warden found himself climbing the ladder to the luggage gangway opening. North was at his heels, and a moment later they were being led to the exalted presence of the purser—the busiest man aboard at this moment. Warden's card was sent in, and word came back that the gentleman must wait. North touched the steward's arm.

"Go back," he said curtly. "Tell him that he sees us without a moment's delay, or that my friend M. de Retz, the general manager of the company, will put a new purser aboard this boat to-morrow. Go!"

They were passed immediately into the purser's cabin, where

the bearded and bemedaled officer received them most politely, if unwillingly.

"*Monsieur,*" said Warden, "one of your passengers, a Miss Tully, left the ship at Plymouth. It is essential that we obtain, without delay, all possible details of her departure, and if you will kindly assist us—"

The purser flung up his hands. "But, *messieurs!* We are about to dock! There are a thousand details which demand my attention—"

"Pardon me," intervened North. "This, *m'sieur,* is a detail which will demand the attention of the Foreign Office, and comes ahead of private matters. Let me advise you to coöperate with us; an efficient man of ability, like yourself, can see the advantage in so doing."

Warden started slightly. The Foreign Office of France—was this, then, something of international import? North would not have dared intimate such a thing unless it were so. The purser, too, was instantly impressed by the hint. He sent for a certain steward, and then faced his two callers.

"So far as I know, *messieurs,* the lady decided suddenly to land at Plymouth," he said. "Her luggage is being taken on to Paris. More than this, I cannot say."

"Her friends aboard ship?" demanded Warden.

The purser shrugged, then turned as the door opened and a cabin steward came into the office. He interrogated the man sharply.

"But yes," returned the steward. "Mlle. Tully decided very suddenly to land, and took only her hand luggage. She was with a M. Halsey. Another gentleman came aboard at Plymouth, and she went ashore with him. M. Halsey is still aboard."

"Good," said North. "You will have the kindness to point him out to us. That is all, gentlemen."

THEY DEPARTED with the steward, leaving the purser astonished at the abrupt end of their talk. Five minutes later the steward pointed Halsey out to them.

"Know him?" asked North. Warden shook his head. "Come along, then."

"You don't want to question him?" asked Warden.

"Hell, no!" snapped North, a frown corrugating his brow, his eyes alight. "Don't you get it? Somebody met her, pretending to be from Solomon. She fell for it."

"Have you any idea where to find her?"

"Not a ghost."

They were descending again into the small boat. So swiftly had all this passed, that the liner was still swinging in her slow curve for the dock. North lighted a cigarette, and said sharply:

"I'll get off a wire to our man in London. You get the morning papers—the Paris journals will be in by this time—then grab Yusuf and take him to the gangway. Point out Halsey. We'll have that bird trailed; he's mixed in the game somewhere. I'll meet you at the car. Must put my wire in code, which takes a bit of time. Give Yusuf your luggage checks. See you later."

They drew in at the landing steps. North was away with his swift, nervous stride. Warden tipped the boatmen and set forth to find Yusuf, outside the train shed. He located the Arab standing beside a powerful Hispano, and beckoned.

Back again at the wharf edge, Warden stood eying the slow-moving hulk of the approaching liner. Presently he located the figure of Halsey at the rail, and indicated the man to Yusuf.

"You have him spotted? Good. M. North will give you orders concerning him. Now, the Paris papers, and back to the car."

A sheaf of morning papers under his arm, Jimmy Warden had not long to wait before North came striding up. A brief colloquy with Yusuf, and the three got into the car. North seized on the papers, spread them out, gave Warden a sharp glance.

"Notice the name of a Dr. Lee on the passenger list? He's a big man in China. I'll bet he's mixed up in this business— Oh, the devil! Would you look at this!"

He indicated a front-page story, and Warden leaned over to read. It was a ghastly story, treated with grim humor; on the previous evening a man's arm, from hand to elbow, had been found lying in a side street just off the Avenue Mozart, the main thoroughfare of Auteuil. The arm was still clothed in shirt sleeve and coat sleeve; arm and garments were badly charred at the elbow.

"What's it mean?" Jimmy Warden frowned. "Some sort of hoax?"

"Not a bit of it," said North grimly, and tapped the paper. "It means just what this story says. Listen! 'It is conceivable that the arm of a man could be burned from his body, but how is one to imagine that the body could be burned from the arm? Gentlemen of Paris, I propose to you a mystery such as the great Poe never imagined!' And there you are, Warden. A man's body vanished, burned, destroyed utterly—and the arm left lying in the street!"

"Eh?" Jimmy Warden eyed his companion suspiciously. "Look here, North!"

"Oh, forget it!" said North wearily and leaned back. "There's a war on, that's what it means. The chap who owned that arm was probably one of the gang who murdered Ferguson and Huntley. I don't know the details, probably will never know them. I can tell you this much: John Solomon has his back against the wall, and he's fighting. There's going to be a hell of a muss before we're done!"

Warden shook himself slightly, and looked out at the bridges and narrow streets of the harbor district flashing past.

"I don't get it," he said slowly. "A war? With what sort of weapons?"

"The devil's own," said North. "If you must know more, ask Solomon, when we get back to Paris. We'll maybe get the night mail plane back. Wright will meet us at Croydon and should have news."

Half an hour later Jimmy Warden was in the air, the throbbing motors of their Goliath pointed for England.

CHAPTER III

MURDER WAR

THAT TWO-HOUR plunge through the air over the
Channel left Jimmy Warden in a somewhat bewildered
frame of mind. He was, indeed, sorely tempted to think that
North was violently insane. This, however, was no more than a
temptation to escape from horror. In his heart he knew North
to be as well-balanced as himself.

His puzzled questions produced little result, for North simply
would not talk about the mysterious John Solomon. It was clear
that North was laboring under a strain, and finally he said as
much to Warden.

"Let things slide until we get to London, old chap. Something big has broken loose, and I don't know what it is. I must
see Wright, see what's happened, find out about June Tully, and
then the three of us will talk things over."

And with this Jimmy Warden had to content himself.

However, from the welter had evolved certain glimpses which
fired the ex-diplomat's imagination. His slight acquaintance
with Solomon had showed him a curious little man of whom
he had not thought twice. Clearly enough, this notion must be
revised most thoroughly.

North was far too practical a man and Warden knew too
much about European affairs, for the question of intrigue to be
dismissed as unparalleled. Jimmy Warden could put his finger on
a well-known American living on the Riviera, who was actually
a go-between for dope and hashish smugglers; he knew of an

artist in Deauville who was the brains of a widespread black-mailing outfit; he knew too many inside stories about Americans in Paris, to deny outright the possibility of anything he heard. He did not deem it at all unlikely that this Dominetti could have a far-flung organization of crooks, who might even be dabbling in international politics—for such things, in Europe, are apt to have a well-defined if unhealthy connection.

That Solomon might be connected with a counter-organization of some sort was much less credible to Warden. As a practical man, he was inclined to scoff at such a thing. It simply was not done, except in fiction. The difficulties were too many and obvious. At the outset, the Paris detectives, the *Sûreté*, would never permit of such a thing. Financially, it was most impractical; what had any one to gain, considering the vast expense? And yet—and yet, how else explain North? How explain June Tully's disappearance?

These facts were patent enough and admitted of no argument. She had vanished; North was in search of her, and he, Jimmy Warden was flying to England on the same errand. This much could be accepted.

The background remained hazy. That story about the double murder, that newspaper yarn of a man's arm found in the street—what could it all mean? Warden was too sensible a man not to know that for the most fantastic of appearances there must always be some cold and clear explanation; intricate details can always be resolved into simplicity.

" 'Swallow it now, digest it later'—remarkably good advice at that," he reflected, while the motors roared outside the airplane cabin, and the blue Channel merged ahead into the green of the English fields. "Only, why the devil should June Tully be tangled up in this mess? I don't like it a bit."

North shoved one of the newspapers at him, indicating a paragraph. This concerned the session of the League of Nations convening within a few days at Geneva. It read:

The immediate interest of both Paris and London will center upon the address of the Chinese envoy, Dr. Lee. It is known that he will present certain demands upon the opening of the session; and it is greatly to be feared that these demands will aim at the abolishment of the French and English spheres of influence and trade in China.

Warden gave his companion an inquiring glance, but North merely shrugged and made no comment. A puzzling affair; Warden could not conceive what this, or the presence of Dr. Lee aboard the liner *De Grasse,* had to do with either Solomon or June Tully.

As to the expected Chinese blow-off at Geneva, he knew well enough that both London and Paris were most uneasy. The new Chinese government was capable of anything, and if backed up by Japan, their agitation might well cause the collapse of both British and French trade in the Far East. Diplomatic circles had been buzzing with this topic for the past month.

JIMMY WARDEN laid aside the paper. Apparently this involved situation had three angles: the international, with which he was little concerned, the scientific and murderous, in which he did not entirely believe; and the very personal angle of June Tully, which was all that mattered. He resolved to confine himself to the main issue, and let the others go hang until they could be viewed in a clearer light.

Croydon at last—the town which had grown up out of a hangar and an airplane. The Goliath circled, swooped down, and presently came rushing to earth, taxiing across the sward to the cement landing-place. North was scanning the groups of men eagerly, and now turned to Warden as the latter rose to open the door.

"No sign of Wright! I told you things were happening!" he exclaimed. "Come on."

They descended, and as they had no luggage, went direct to the passport bureau, where Warden's diplomatic passport speedily removed all red tape. They passed on through the customs shed without examination, and came into the open air. As they did so, a Mercedes car came roaring up the drive, and North uttered an exclamation.

"Great Scott! There's Wright's car, with Fisher driving! Didn't know Fisher was in England. Hello there! Didn't expect us so soon, eh? Fisher, shake hands with Warden; he's O.K., so shoot ahead. Where's Wright?"

Fisher was a slender, red-haired man, very freckled. He gave Warden a quick hand-grip, then glanced at the porters and others in the offing.

"Hop in," he said, motioning to the car. "You chaps haven't lunched? We'll get a bite here, then."

They got into the car and Fisher backed out, turning into the narrow lane that ran to the stores. As he swung about for the restaurant, he flung back a few words.

"Wright's dying. Happened on the way here. Smashed up my car. Had to go back and get this big brute. Damned near got me, too. Pile out—I want a drink before we talk. Need it."

"Good Lord!" said North softly, but made no other comment.

The three men entered the restaurant, secured a corner table, and as the closing hours were not in force, speedily had a drink before them and their order given. Warden caught a swift scrutiny from Fisher, then the latter gave North his attention.

"Truck crashed into us halfway here," he said. "Deliberate, of course; barged us up against a wall, crushed us, and went on. Poor Wright was badly smashed up. I had to drop everything and hop back for this car, in order to meet you. Bruised me up a bit, but no great damage done. Fortunately, I got here two days ago to assist Wright—there was nothing much happening in Brussels—and I have things pretty well in shape to carry on."

"Wright, killed!" said North, low-voiced. "And no warning?"

"Not a smidgeon. Didn't suspect anything going on. What's it all about?"

"Later. First," and North lighted a cigarette, with an effort at ease, "what about Miss Tully? Discover anything?"

"Haven't had time," said Fisher. "I put the whole force on it, or rather Wright did, and we'll have reports when we get into the office. Won't be hard to trace her and the man who took her ashore at Plymouth; the landing slips and passport cards will take care of that. We got a wire off to Plymouth before leaving town, so we'll find an answer awaiting us."

"Right," said North. "You got in touch with Paris, about Wright?"

"Sent off a wire before I got this car and rushed off to meet you. Well, here's the grub, so save your breath. But I want to know what's busted loose."

THEY ATTACKED the food set before them, and while eating North talked by snatches, to give Fisher an idea of things. Jimmy Warden, meantime, kept very quiet and listened with both ears. He was both startled and bewildered by what he had just heard, but was settling down to the grim realization that he had been drawn into something which seemed to cut down, sharply, the usual life insurance expectancies.

"So far as I know," said North, between bites, "all hell's broke loose, Fisher, just when least expected. You know about Ferguson and Huntley being killed in the Bois? I left Paris early this morning, so haven't the latest news, but we had word from Alexandria last night of something wrong. Simmons was sick, it seemed."

"Died this morning," cut in Fisher. "Poison... Item: Our Madrid office was bombed before daybreak. Nobody hurt, but everything destroyed. Just before we left the office, got word from Berlin that Swenson was badly hurt in some sort of accident, not explained. Is it war?"

"Looks that way, with all the casualties on our side." North turned to Warden, who was conscious also of the sharp regard of Fisher. "Well, Warden, you see what you're getting into. It's bad, and there's no quarter. I can't offer you any explanation; Solomon will have to do that. However, if you want to back out, do it—and small blame to you."

"Thanks, I don't use reverse gears," said Jimmy Warden quietly. "I don't give a hang about Solomon or your outfit, but—"

"June Tully's in our outfit," said North. "You may as well know it."

"Then count me in to the limit," was Warden's laconic response.

"Good." Fisher grinned and lifted his glass. "Wait until we begin to hit back! I'd love to be in Paris for the next week. Here's luck, Warden. By the way, North, Dominetti's in London."

"You're sure?" North's eyes were keen. "When!"

"Last night, by plane."

"Let's get out of here."

The meat hastily finished, all three men got into the Hispano, crowding into the front seat. Fisher headed the car for London. All of a sudden. Warden placed this red-headed man, and the realization fairly shocked him.

"Not Irvington Fisher?" he murmured in North's ear, and the latter nodded slightly.

Two years previously Irvington Fisher, attaché to the United States embassy in London, had been something like a lion to all the cubs in the service. They had all heard of his brilliant work in Russia. Independently wealthy, of the highest attainments, Fisher had been boomed as the great coming diplomat; then, abruptly, for no known reason, he had dropped out of the service. And now Warden realized why. Fisher had gone into this mysterious work with Solomon!

"Listen, old chap." North turned to Warden, speaking quietly, steadily. "A few things you must know; can't tell what may happen. We have reports on all plane service, but so has Dominetti, you know; he's probably aware by this time that we're here, and why, and so forth. Solomon's headquarters is in Rue Montorgeuil, Paris—13 *bis*. I've sent in word about you already. Remember the address, in case you need it.

"Now, we don't know exactly what we're up against. Dominetti is, of course, pretty well known himself, but so far as his gang is concerned he stays completely under cover. We can't get a thing on him. We know his activity, but can't prove anything. We haven't even located his headquarters of operation; and that means a very good deal. It'd prove more to you about Dominetti if you knew our crowd better; we're not exactly fools."

"OBVIOUSLY NOT," agreed Warden. "But Solomon—"

"Never mind him now; you would not believe what I told you, so let it wait," and North lit a cigarette. "Stick to Dominetti. He operates on a huge scale in the market. He is dead against the new Italy, he's enormously wealthy, and he aims at power through wealth. Last year England tried to make France deport him, and failed; since then he's hated England viciously. They say he has a big hand in Wall Street affairs. You can see for yourself that, with a little advance information on international matters, a man could clean up heavily. Well, our crowd is out to block him, that's all."

"Why?" demanded Jimmy Warden dryly. "As a matter of philanthropy?"

"Ask Solomon, not me," returned North. "That's his business. Now, things look pretty serious; from all indications, Dominetti or his agents have set out to smash the various units of our organization. He and Solomon both keep in touch with affairs over half the world, and I expect he's got two men to our one. Probably he has some big coup in hand, and is afraid of interference. So there's the layout, in a general way."

"I'd like to know more about Solomon," said Jimmy Warden.

North laughed a little.

"Yes? The old chap has knocked about the Arab countries most of his life, I gather—speaks the language like a native. And money is no object to him. More than this, you'll have to learn for yourself."

Warden was forced to accept the definite tone of this statement. He made up his mind to believe all or little of this fantastic nonsense according to later events; yet in his heart he had a feeling that it was by no means fantastic. Still, he fought against too easy credulity, and resolved to say little but to listen much.

"Chancery Lane office?" demanded North, and Fisher nodded.

Now came the big curving sweep past Trafalgar Square, and into the Strand, dodging huge busses and crawling taxies, reaching out for the narrow bustle of Fleet Street. Fisher swung off into Chancery Lane, and halfway to Holborn swerved the car into the curb. A man stepped out, saluted, and took the wheel.

"Not blown up yet, apparently," said North, looking at the dingy office building into which Fisher led the way.

Jimmy Warden followed up two flights of dark stairs, and Fisher swung open a door. At once the dingy office world of London vanished. Here was a long room beneath a huge skylight, with half a dozen men working at desks, and every office appliance of the western hemisphere in sight, from electric typewriter to stock ticker. At the rear of his room was an inclosed office, for which Fisher headed.

"What news from Wright, Bob?" he demanded of a man, halting as they passed the desk. The other looked up and made a gesture which needed no interpretation. The three went on.

Fisher's office—in reality that of the ill-fated Wright—contained a large desk, a shelf of books, and several chairs. Fisher went to the desk, where a stack of papers awaited him.

A knock at the door, and a dapper Englishman entered and waited.

"ALL RIGHT, Maravin," said Fisher. "This is Mr. North, from headquarters, and Mr. Warden. What luck?"

"Sorry, sir, very little," said Maravin. "Miss Tully disembarked at Plymouth with a chap named Boris Glazunoff, a Russian. Came up to London, and we haven't been able to trace them here at all. I may have word any minute."

Warden started. "Glazunoff!" he exclaimed. "That's the chap who's been hanging around Havre and Deauville for the past

month. A heavy gambler. He got into some mess over at Deauville last week. What's the answer?"

Fisher shrugged. "No telling. All right, Maravin, keep at it.
Minutes may count. Here, North! If we— By George, what's
this? Maravin, how did this get here?"

He held up a paper. Maravin glanced at it. "It came by
messenger ten minutes ago, sir."

North took the paper, whistled, passed it to Warden. It
displayed very fine copper-plate writing, every line and stroke
beautifully formed:

> Send Mr. Warden to the Savoy at once. To the lounge.

Warden found the others regarding him quizzically, half
smiling.

"What's it mean?" he demanded.

"That's Solomon's writing," returned North, a hint of excitement behind his smile. "It means, that Solomon is in London—
why or how, I can't say! Perhaps he has picked up Miss Tully's
trail himself. Probably he remembers you."

Warden rose. "Right. I'll walk over to the Savoy, then. Shall I
come back here if nothing happens? Or will you keep in touch
with me there?"

"I'll keep in touch with you," said North, and shook hands.
"Good luck, old chap! As soon as we have news, you'll hear
from me."

Jimmy Warden departed.

Behind him, North and Fisher settled down to clearing up
Wright's unfinished business. Various callers arrived, reports
were made out, letters written; for twenty minutes they were
kept busy. It was a warm day, and both men removed their coats.
One might have noted that each of them bore a peculiar mark
upon his right wrist; a mark, apparently sunburned there, in
the shape of two interlaced triangles, the symbol which from
time immemorial has been known in eastern lands as the Seal
of Solomon.

Maravin came into the room.

"Radio call from Paris, sir," he said to Fisher. "It's for Mr. North. The connection is through already."

North took up the telephone receiver at his elbow.

"Hello!" he said. "Hello! North speaking."

Fisher went into the outer office with some papers. North, alone in the room, suddenly stiffened in his chair and a look of incredulity swept into his face. A wheezy voice which he knew very well indeed had come to him.

"If I was you, Mr. North," it said, "I'd get back here to Paris, just like that."

"GREAT SCOTT!" exclaimed North. "Look here, John, where the devil are you? Thought you were in London?"

A chuckle responded. "There's some things, sir, as aren't humanly possible, as the old gent said when the 'ousemaid mentioned marriage. I'm werry busy right 'ere. That 'ere chap Halsey is a bad egg, Mr. North, a werry bad egg. You'll best leave Mr. Fisher to take care of Miss Tully, and Mr. Warden can give 'im a 'and—"

"Hold on," exclaimed North sharply. "What about this note from you, telling Warden to come over to the Savoy?"

Three minutes later North burst into the outer office. Every one there was gathered in a group about one of the front windows. North called out hurriedly.

"Fisher! Hey, Fisher, where are you? There's hell to pay! That note was a forgery. Drop everything else and—"

North checked himself. White faces turned to him. As he approached the group he saw the figure of Irvington Fisher in a chair, supported by two of the men.

"What's up?" he snapped.

Maravin gestured toward the window, which had been open, but was now closed.

"Mr. Fisher was passing the window and fell. A bullet through the body—looks bad."

Fisher struck down, openly! For an instant North stood silent, then collected himself.

"Right. Somebody get a doctor—Already summoned? Maravin, run over to the Savoy in a hurry. Get Warden out of there; that note was not written by Mr. Solomon. A forgery. Find Warden and bring him here."

The doctor, already summoned, could do Fisher no good; Fisher was dead before his wound could be dressed. A wild bullet, on the face of it; but this was very strange, happening in London.

North knew there was nothing strange about it. He knew that another, and one of the best, of Solomon's agents had fallen to the sinister and unseen forces of the enemy. Useless to call in the police. That bullet, probably fired out of some window across the street from a silenced weapon, would never be traced.

North was putting through a connection with Solomon when he received a telephone call from the Savoy.

"No sign of Warden here," reported Maravin. "The doorman noticed him enter, but he isn't here now!"

North hung up the receiver with a sinking sensation.

Fisher gone, Wright gone, all trace of June Tully lost—

"And now they've got Warden!" he muttered savagely. "Damn it! My turn next, I suppose."

CHAPTER IV

OUT OF THE TRAP

JAMES WARDEN walked into the Savoy with a feeling of no little satisfaction. He was about to come face to face with the pudgy little cockney who had suddenly assumed so mysterious an air of importance in the world—and he rather thought he would set his own doubts at rest in short order.

Besides, as he told himself, not for the first time, this man Solomon had something to answer for. Any one who dragged Julie Tully into a maze of murder would certainly answer for it, if Jimmy Warden knew anything about the matter.

His own apprehension regarding June was keen enough—had, in fact, increased to a very lively fear. This walk through the Strand had rather cleared his head, had tended to reduce him to a normal viewpoint. Warden was now prepared to face Solomon and, if necessary, throw all this fantastic intrigue overboard. He would probably be able to help June more by going direct to the embassy and getting Scotland Yard to work on the trail, than by parleying with agents of mystery and possible crime.

With this in mind, he strolled through the lounge, seeking some trace of the short, pudgy figure he remembered quite clearly. It was really ridiculous to think of a man like that occupying any such position as North ascribed to him—an illiterate little old fellow with gray hair and wide blue eyes. More likely, he considered, Solomon was some sort of crank; heaven knew there were enough cranks loose in the world, capable of anything!

"Mr. Warden, sir?"

Turning, Warden saw at his elbow a darkly handsome man attired in the most correct morning costume. A foreigner, he thought at once.

"Yes," he rejoined.

The other bowed.

"I believe you expect to meet a gentleman here? I was asked to request you to go to Suite Eighteen—on the third floor."

With another bow, the speaker turned and sauntered out of the hotel, leaving Warden in no little astonishment. He might have been accosted as a casual acquaintance, instead of by a man whom he had never seen before.

A half scornful laugh broke on his lips. Evidently, Solomon liked to do things in a most roundabout and mysterious fashion! Well, such child's play must come to an end, and at once. With this resolve, Warden made his way to an elevator.

Naturally enough, the thought of possible danger never for an instant crossed his mind. Such a thought, in the midst of this huge American-model hotel, was absurd. When he reached the third floor, Warden found number eighteen and knocked. A voice bade him enter, and he opened the door.

To his surprise, he found himself not in a hotel room, but in one of a suite of rooms, apparently offices. Here against a window a man sat at a desk, regarding him with polite inquiry. The American spoke first.

"My name is Warden."

"Ah, yes! Will you be seated, Mr. Warden? Excuse me a moment."

The man stepped to a door, tapped, opened it and disappeared. Next instant he returned.

"Will you go right in, Mr. Warden? Thank you."

MR. WARDEN went in. Instead of the figure he expected, he found himself facing an entirely different man who sat at a flat-topped desk littered with papers. This man was perhaps fifty years of age; Warden guessed him to be an Italian. Black hair

"I am well guarded," Dominetti warned.

just touched with gray, a high brow of extraordinary width, the whole face tapering down to a pointed, intolerant chin; but the most remarkable feature was the eyes.

These, instead of being, dark, were of a light and vivid gray, affording a singular and striking contrast with the black hair and swarthy skin. They were filled with a most astonishing vigor; these eyes fairly burned into Warden, giving him full and sufficient warning of what energy lay in the brain behind them.

"Good afternoon, Mr. Warden. My name is Dominetti," and the speaker bowed slightly in his chair. "Will you have the kindness to be seated? I desire a little chat with you."

"Eh?" Warden was taken off guard. "But I thought—"

Dominetti smiled, and this smile lifted his thin lips in an oddly menacing fashion.

"You thought, perhaps, that Mr. Solomon was here? He is not, I assure you. Come, my dear sir, let us chat quietly and frankly.

I assure you that Miss Tully is unharmed and is close by. If you like, you shall speak with her presently."

Warden blinked, sat down, tried to get himself in hand. Such a meeting as this was the last sort of thing he had expected; but the mention of June Tully's name served as a bracer.

So—instead of Solomon, the mysterious Dominetti! The man who, according to North, was the cleverest scoundrel in Europe. And North had warned him that Dominetti probably knew all about him by this time.

"A cigar?" Dominetti extended a silver box, and Warden found himself accepting a weed—of most exceptional quality, as the bouquet proved. "Come, let's be comfortable! I suppose you think Miss Tully was kidnaped and all that. Quite the contrary, I assure you. She was met by a friend of mine, was brought to this hotel, and has received every consideration."

"May I ask," said Warden, gathering himself together, "by what right—"

Dominetti lifted one tapering, slender hand.

"Right does not enter into the matter, Mr. Warden," he said impressively. "May I ask whether you have accepted any position with my very good friend, Mr. Solomon?"

"No," said Warden.

"Excellent. I should regret to be compelled to deal with you as one of his agents. Since you can act merely as a friend of Miss Tully's, that is very good indeed."

Dominetti lighted a cigar reflectively. The perfect poise of his manner, his absolute restraint, indicated all too clearly his actual power.

"See here!" exclaimed Warden, rallying. "You can't get away with this sort of thing in a place of this character, Dominetti. One word from me—"

"Give the word if you like," and Dominetti smiled at him.

WARDEN STARTED to his feet, and turned to the door. It swung open to his hand; beyond it, in the outer office, he saw two men standing. Each of them held an automatic pistol, covering the doorway.

Warden halted, and, slamming the door swiftly, faced Dominetti. Behind and above the seated man was an open panel in the wall. Framed in this panel was a man's face, and the blued steel muzzle of a weapon looked down upon Warden.

"Melodrama!" snapped the American angrily. "You know you'd never risk a shot!"

"Try it," said Dominetti, puffing at his cigar with an air of quiet good humor. "But I advise you not to try it, my friend. Instead, sit down and chat, as I requested. I am well guarded, I assure you. Force will not serve you; diplomacy might."

Warden repressed his anger. "What's the idea of all this stage-setting?" he demanded.

"Precaution. I desire you to do me a service," returned the other, politely. "Will you be seated, and listen to me?"

Warden sat down.

"It is unfortunately the case," went on the Italian, "that I am blamed for many things of which I know nothing. What you have been told, I do not know; but I understand that if anything goes wrong in this part of the world, it is laid at my door. Let me assure you that all this is extravagant. For example, Miss Tully arrived here last night. She carries something which I wish to obtain. I asked her for it, and she refused. Good! She was not molested. I am now asking you to obtain it from her. She carries the document in question in her hand bag. As you can see, if I were the terrible creature some persons think me, nothing were easier than for me to rob her. Instead, I ask that she hand over this document, and she will then be at liberty to accompany you, whither you wish."

Warden listened to this amazing speech with an odd sensation of belief. The thing was incredible, yet he felt it was true. At the same time, he knew there was some excellent reason behind it all. He had been brought here, then, to make June Tully prove false to her trust?

"Bah! It's an absurdity—it's childish!" he exclaimed heatedly. "Dominetti, I'm no fool. Come, what's the answer? You don't pull the wool over my eyes for a moment. If you wanted to rob her, you'd do it."

The Italian laughed slightly, amusedly. "Yes? Quite right. But I don't want to, my good friend. To rob a lady would offend my sense of delicacy. Also, it would jeopardize me with the police. There I put my cards on the table. I suggest that you see—ah, excuse me."

The telephone buzzed. Dominetti listened for a moment, then spoke.

"Send him in at once."

He leaned back and waved his cigar at Warden.

"Think it over—I shall be free in a few moments. No, keep your seat. Good day, Mr. Matsura! Come in, come in; we may talk freely before my friend here. Your report?"

A smiling, bespectacled Japanese gentleman entered, bowed, advanced to the desk, and spoke in fluent English.

"There is no doubt whatever about the matter. The man was killed by sound waves."

"Sound waves?" Dominetti frowned. "I do not understand. I was given to believe that this ray was a beam of intense light which could burn any given object out of existence. You know Pearson, the English scientist now in Paris, worked upon such a thing several years ago. Since he has been in charge of the present laboratory—"

MATSURA LIFTED a deprecatory hand.

"Pardon, sir, but you have been misinformed," he said politely. "When you laid the matter in our hands we, also, believed as you. Now we know better. It is not a beam of light which must be sought, but a beam of sound—it may, indeed, appear as light, yet it is sound."

"Explain," said Dominetti curtly.

"If light burns a thing, what happens? Ash results," responded the Japanese. "In the present case, there was no ash. There was nothing. The arm and hand remained, nothing else. The rest of the man had vanished."

Warden's attention was jerked sharply to these words. Could they be talking about that item in the Paris paper? Undoubtedly.

"Besides," went on the polite, evenly modulated voice, "you previously spoke to me about certain discoveries by Loomis of the Johns Hopkins University, which you hoped to place in our hands. Now, Loomis has been working upon sound waves. What is the result of these waves? The limit of human hearing is represented by waves oscillating at the rate of twenty thousand per second. Sound waves of, let us say, twenty times this speed, would destroy living tissue—they have destroyed it in laboratory experiments. They dissolve it into nothing, the very atoms disintegrating. You will observe, the process of burning does not destroy anything; it merely changes form. But these supersonic waves—ah, they destroy, disintegrate!"

"Very well," Dominetti cut in. "I am not a scientist and you are. What I desire is practical results. You know what has been done in Paris. Could you do the same thing?"

"Not without time and experiments," said Matsura.

The Italian frowned.

"There is no time," he said incisively. "Supposing I were to place in your hands the results attained by Loomis! The definite results of his latest experiments?"

The Japanese bowed. "Then we could achieve something, at least—perhaps a great deal."

"Very well. I'll send them to you within an hour."

Matsura clicked his heels and departed.

When the door had closed, Warden found those burning gray eyes fastened upon him with a compellent and disquieting intensity.

"How much of all this do you understand, Mr. Warden?" asked Dominetti.

"Mighty little," admitted Warden.

"Enough, however, to know that I am in earnest, I trust," and Dominetti's gaze narrowed a trifle. "My dear sir, I wish you to see Miss Tully. I wish you to advise her to hand over to me the papers which she carries. Do this, and you and she are free to depart. If you refuse, if she refuses, I shall be very sorry for what will happen. Now, pray, forget anger!" And the tapering hand lifted as Warden was about to speak. "Believe me, my friend, anger is a very useless thing in this world. See her first, talk with her, and then make your decision. Persuade her or not, as you may decide. The matter rests with you."

"Very well," said Warden. "But if you think I can persuade her against her will, I assure you you are very much mistaken."

Dominetti broke into a clear, ringing laugh.

"I believe you!" he exclaimed, almost gayly. "Well, well, at all events neither you nor she can do me any harm, and lean afford to be generous. And remember, my friend: Do not be impulsive! I have had no obvious connection whatever with you or her, remember!"

The warning remained with Warden.

Dominetti clapped his hands, a man entered, and was ordered to escort the unwilling guest to Suite Twenty-four. So Jimmy Warden left the presence of this singular man, little dreaming where and how he was to see Dominetti again, or under what frightful circumstances that meeting with the Italian was to be.

So far as Warden was concerned, this meeting had one very definite result. He carried away a clear-cut impression of the suave Italian as a man of ruthless force; and he now knew past all doubt that what he had considered a fantastic dream was bitter hard reality. Melodrama, perhaps; but most certainly war—war without mercy, as North had said. And, once wakened to this realization, Jimmy Warden girded himself for the contest that he knew was before him.

HE FOLLOWED his guide out into the corridor again, and around to the other side of the hotel. He perceived instantly what this meant. Dominetti had placed June Tully safely enough, probably under guard, but the Italian himself had not appeared in the transaction; if complaint were made, if the police were brought in, Dominetti could not be connected with the affair.

As the guide halted before Suite Twenty-four, Warden's glance swept around. The elevators were not close by, but there was a stairway just across the hall.

A man opened the door, admitted them in silence. Here was an ordinary hotel room, to all appearance. The man was swarthy, alert, inimical. He spoke with a marked accent.

"I have just received instructions," he said, and pointed to a door on the right of the room. "You will knock, please."

Warden went to the door, rapped sharply. Then something leaped in him as one word came in reply—one cool, defiant word in the voice of June Tully.

"Well?"

"It's—it's Jimmy Warden," he responded. For an instant he had found it hard to speak, as though something choked him. "June! Are you there?"

"Oh!"

The quick rising thrill of her exclamation, with all its amazed incredulity, shot through him. She had recognized his voice at once. Then there was the turn of a key, and the door before him was flung open.

She was standing there, staring out at him—and suddenly her hands flew to meet his in swift greeting. The strained lines of her face vanished in quick relief.

"Jimmy!" she exclaimed. "It doesn't seem possible—it's a dream. You've come for me?"

"To talk with you."

He turned, glanced at the two men. The foreigner bowed and gestured. With a nod, Warden stepped into the farther room and closed the door behind him. Here, he perceived, was a small two-room apartment.

"How on earth did you get here, Jimmy Warden?" demanded the girl, drawing back, staring at him as though he were a ghost.

Warden smiled, took her hand, patted it.

"No time for small talk now, June," he said. "Explanations later. Are you confined here?"

"Absolutely, Jimmy," she said, and gestured toward the other room. "Windows locked. No fire-escape. Nothing. You don't know the reason—"

"I know it all," he cut in, and her eyes widened in surprise. "Then there's only one way out of here? All right. Now, what about the papers you're carrying? Can you give them up or must you deliver them?"

Her gaze searched his face for one intent instant.

"You here, of all places—and you know all about it! What does it mean, Jimmy?"

He read the half suspicion in her eyes and voice, and smiled.

"It means that I'm here to get you to Solomon if possible. You suspect me, eh? Forget it." His manner became crisp, alert. "I'll tell you later how glad I am to see you, June; the most important thing now is safety. Dominetti sent me in to persuade you to give up what you carry. If you refuse, well and good; we'll smash a way out somehow. If your letters from Professor Loomis—"

"FORGIVE ME, Jimmy." Her hand caught at his convulsively, and for a moment her eyes closed. "I—I had to doubt everything, every one! I thought I was meeting Mr. Solomon here; oh, you can't realize how clever, how infernally clever, they are! I was warned, too, and that only made it worse for me to walk right into a trap."

"Cheer up, old girl," said Warden cheerfully. "Never mind all that; look ahead, and not back! I walked into the trap myself, and now we have to get out of it. About the papers—"

June Tully picked up her hand bag from a chair and opened it.

"I don't understand their actions," she said, as her fingers moved deftly. "They could have used force, but did not. That man, Dominetti, was very polite—but I'm horribly afraid of him. Here's what they want—just this one letter."

She produced an unsealed envelope, which was addressed to Mr. John Solomon.

"Probably Dominetti feared you would destroy it," said Warden. "And he didn't want to get involved with the police—he hinted as much. Well?"

A sudden glint of laughter broke in her dark eyes as she spoke.

"Well, I happened to write this letter myself," she said. "You know, I was secretary to Professor Loomis. If you think we can get away, we'll turn over this letter to Dominetti."

"Eh?" Warden was amazed. "You're not in earnest?"

"Of course I am!" she exclaimed eagerly. Her voice fell to a low murmur. "Haven't I been alone here since yesterday, Jimmy? I know this letter by heart. I can write out a copy of it, of every formula, of every word! And there's one essential word which makes or spoils the whole thing. Look!"

She swiftly opened the folded letter, and Warden saw a mass of neat typing—from which one word had been cut out of the paper, in two places. He comprehended on the instant.

"My word—good for you!" he exclaimed. His eyes swept the room. "What is there here you must take? Your grips?"

She made a gesture of dismissal.

"Nothing, nothing! If we can get away before he discovers that he's been tricked—"

"Good. Give it to me."

Warden took the letter, went to the door, and flung it open, the girl at his elbow. In the outer room, the two men, who had been sitting smoking, came to their feet. Warden stepped forward.

"Here is the document which Signor Dominetti wants," he said. "First, I must be sure that his word will be kept—that we shall be permitted to depart at once."

The foreigner bowed, and motioned toward the man who had brought Warden here.

"The letter will go instantly," he returned. "Signor Dominetti will telephone to me, and the door will be open. It will be only a very few moments, *signor.*"

Warden nodded. He had to make his decision instantly, and made it. On a table, beside the foreigner, he saw a pistol lying.

"Very well," and he handed the letter to the other man. "Go quickly, please."

He was alert for hidden traps, for unsuspected guards. However, the man left the room, and the open door showed an empty corridor outside. The foreigner flashed white teeth in a smile as he looked at June Tully and bowed.

"You will be seated, yes?" he asked politely. "The wait will be very short."

"Not worth while," said Warden, and produced his cigarette case. He must get the man away from that table if possible. "You have a match, I hope?"

"But yes, *signor.*"

The other produced a box of vestas, lighted one, held it out to Warden's cigarette.

WARDEN'S HAND closed on his wrist, jerked him forward. He fell into a crashing left that knocked him sidewise, stilling the cry on his lips. Another blow, another—cruel blows, merciless, doubling him up in agony—and the man sagged limply to the floor, low inarticulate moans breaking from his lips. Warden darted to the table, seized the pistol there, turned.

"The door, June!"

She was already at the door, throwing it open. They were out in the corridor now; all empty here. Warden caught her arm, and next instant they had gained the stairs opposite and were descending narrow, carpeted stairs, leading down to the lounge and safety. Warden put away the pistol and drew a breath of relief.

"Fooled them! Beat them at their own game! If we—"

Two men suddenly uprose before them at the turn of the stairs—two swarthy figures, astonished, startled, yet closing the way against them. Warden had no time to reach his weapon. He hurled himself on the two, swept them aside, went down with them in a tangled mass.

"On, June!" he cried. "Get a taxi—waiting—"

A fist hammered his lips into silence. Quick oaths, the thudding of rapid blows, the scraping thrust of writhing bodies on the carpeted stairs.

Out of the welter Warden scrambled, just evading the plunge of a knife that drove between arm and side.

Both of them were up now, both of them with knives; June Tully had vanished. Warden gave them no chance to dart in upon him, but caught the knife-wrist of the nearer man, kicked out at the other—a kick that reached the throat, with his weight behind it. That man went down and lay sprawled upon the stairs.

The other gave a cry, and with a twisting plunge wrenched the weapon clear. Warden countered with a smashing blow in the face, and brought up his knee to the stomach—no time for niceties! The Italian groaned and fell backward.

Warden went down the stairs two at a time, unhurt.

As he came to the ground level and strode rapidly toward the street entrance, his brain was hard at work. Now the safety of June Tully was paramount. Dominetti would know the secret was locked in her brain, and would not hesitate to have her killed rather than deliver that secret to John Solomon.

North's office in Chancery Lane? Not at all. Unsafe there, and this would be the first objective of the enemy also. Paris! At Croydon airdrome he could wire Solomon, could have the plane met at Le Bourget. He could wire North, too, for North must have discovered that the letter from Solomon was forged.

There was nothing in sight—no one in the lobby whom he knew. He was outside now, saw June waiting there, anxious, white-faced, beside a taxi. At sight of him, relief sprang into her face, and she entered the cab.

"Croydon airdrome," said Warden to the driver. "And an extra sovereign if you make it in half an hour."

"I'll do me bloomin' best, guv'nor!"

CHAPTER V

THE HOUSE OF SOLOMON

THE RUE Montorgeuil, that very heart of ancient Paris now doomed to extinction under the inexorable law of progress, whereby a city beautiful will ultimately replace a city medieval, was a narrow and gloomily dark old street. Here were crowded, leaning walls, a maze of ruinous buildings, a few old-fashioned residences—most of them long since converted to other uses.

One of these former mansions, two stories about a central courtyard, had in recent years been somewhat restored to its ancient glories, yet remained a place of mystery to all the neighborhood; market gossip said it was occupied by a Russian prince. Great cars came and went at all hours; glimpses were had of servants in strange costumes; not infrequently callers arrived, escorted by agents of the *Sûreté*—heads of state, perhaps, or distinguished foreign visitors.

According to rumor—and a Parisian rumor is apt to be well founded—the old mansion had been occupied after Waterloo by a great nobleman who, taking no more chances on revolutions and guillotines, had connected his residence with the outer world by subterranean passages.

However this might be, all the quarter was looking forward with lively curiosity to the approaching demolition. Within another six months the old landmark would be wiped out, and many strange things were expected to be brought to light.

Upon a warm spring evening—it was the same day that

had witnessed Jimmy Warden's hurried flight to London and return—a crawling red Renault taxi crept up the street and came to a halt before the massive bronze gates of the old house. These gates stood open, and the courtyard was dimly illumined by a single electric light. The chauffeur turned to speak with his fare, then uttered a disgusted oath and climbed out.

He stamped into the entrance and rang the bell of the *concierge*. An old woman came forth and greeted him.

"Sacred name of a species of pig!" exclaimed the chauffeur. "Your pardon, *madame,* I was addressing this cabbage of a foreigner who is in my cab. We seek the residence of one M'sieur Solomon. Can this be it?"

"It most assuredly can," said the *concierge.*

"Then," said the chauffeur, "let some one come and give me a hand with this imbecile, for he is drunk and has fallen and hurt himself, since there is blood on his face. I picked him up outside the Porte de la Vilette—"

"Drive in, then, drive in," said the old dame tartly. "I will have some one help you."

The chauffeur climbed back into his cab and swung the vehicle through the entrance into the courtyard. There, a sudden brilliant light flooded the cobblestones, and two men came out of the house to the cab. Both were Arabs, garbed in loose white robes. They helped the chauffeur get his fare out of the cab, and examined the unconscious man.

"Bruised—and a scratch across the cheek. His nose has bled. Nothing worse," said one of the Arabs, and turned to the chauffeur. "Where did you get him?"

The chauffeur recounted his story—how he was returning from Le Bourget when this man had appeared, apparently drunk, beside the road and halted him. The name and address of Solomon were given. That was all.

"Very well." The Arab pressed a bill into the hand of the chauffeur. "Go and forget it. We'll take care of him."

The taxi departed. The two Arabs lifted Jimmy Warden and carried him into the house.

WARDEN OPENED his eyes to a vision of luxurious surroundings—soft lights, thick rugs, walls adorned with bizarre ornaments and weapons. A man was bathing his face. Another was holding a drink to his lips.

Warden swallowed deeply, and looked around.

"Where am I?" he exclaimed. "Solomon—"

"Solomon Effendi awaits you, Mr. Warden," said one of the dark-faced men. "You are safe; if you are able to walk, come with me."

Warden rose, repressed a groan, and staggered after the Arab.

A moment later he found himself in a rather small and very plain room. It contained a few chairs, a large desk, and upon the floor a magnificent old Shiraz rug. At the desk sat a pudgy little old man whose round face was quite devoid of expression; the mild blue eyes looked at him with a placid and childlike gaze. Then things swirled around, and Warden felt himself lowered into the depths of a large armchair.

"Take it easy, Mr. Warden," said a wheezy voice. "There ain't nothin' like takin' of it easy, as the old gent said when 'e kissed the 'ousemaid. You're all right, and werry 'appy I am to see you a settin' 'ere. I'll make so bold as to go on with me work, if you don't mind."

"But I must tell you," cried Warden desperately, trying to struggle up.

"Don't do it, sir," came Solomon's voice. "I know all about it already. Take it easy."

Warden relaxed, giving way to a resigned helplessness. Gradually his senses cleared, and things took shape before him. Solomon was speaking with one man and another who came in and went out, but in a strange tongue—Arabic, thought Warden.

Light came through a large crystal pane set in the ceiling. It was a queer and ghastly illumination, yet pleasant enough.

Under its radiance, all reds became purples, and Warden, looking down at his hands, saw that his skin was an unearthly yellow. A violet ray light of some sort, he concluded. Odd that it should be used for lighting; yet, why not?

His attention centered upon the little man at the desk, and wonder possessed him. The appearance of Solomon was anything but impressive. Yet that pudgy face, those blue eyes so curiously lacking in any expression, were singular in the extreme. From beneath a Basque *beret* gray wisps of hair escaped at odd angles. The man's clothes were rumpled, as though slept in recently, and he was sucking at an old clay pipe, which smelled most vilely. All in all, a helpless old man in appearance, yet possessed of a certain poise, a certain nameless restraint and quiet assurance, which grew upon the observer.

A buzzer sounded. Solomon dismissed a man speaking with him, and took up the telephone receiver from the desk.

"Oh! It's you, Mr. North!" he said. "Werry 'appy I am to 'ear from you, sir. Mr. Warden, 'e just got 'ere—yes, all by 'imself, just like that. I 'opes as 'ow you ain't got no more bad news, sir?

"What's that again? Well, sir, if I was you I'd leave the London office to run itself, and get back 'ere. Things is mortal bad, Mr. North; I don't rightly know what's a going to 'appen, for a fact. You won't 'ave Yusuf to-morrow, neither. He went out to meet Mr. Warden and Miss Tully, and they up an' got 'im, just like that. Yes, sir. In the St. Ouen clinic now, 'e is, 'is shoulder dislocated and 'is leg broke. They took the car and went on with it to Le Bourget. Comin' back, they threw Mr. Warden out and went off with Miss Tully. No, 'e ain't 'urt to speak of. You ain't 'ad no word from Berlin?"

A SUDDEN trace of excitement showed in Solomon's eyes, and he caught up a pencil. "What's that again, Mr. North? Dang it, sir, you're sure o' that 'ere date? Werry good. You get back 'ere on the night plane, sir. Good-by."

Solomon pressed down the hook, keeping the receiver to his ear, and spoke rapidly.

"Get 'old o' Mr. Newton at Rome, and get 'im quick."

Putting down the instrument, Solomon picked up a plug of very black tobacco and began to whittle at it with a case knife. Suddenly Warden started, and his hand went to his pocket. He drew forth a crumpled sheet of paper, on which were penciled words.

"Here! She said—give you that. It's complete."

He leaned forward and put the paper on the desk. Solomon picked it up, glanced at it, and whistled. Then he pressed a button; an Arab appeared at the doorway.

Solomon gave him the paper, and spoke in French.

"Take this. Take Ahmed ben Zain with you. Use my own car, and deliver this to M'sieur Pearson at the laboratory. Telephone him you are coming, so he'll expect you. If you fail, do not return here, for shame will be upon your head."

The Arab saluted with dignity and departed.

The buzzer rang, and Solomon took up the receiver.

"That you, Mr. Newton? Werry good. You pay sharp attention, sir, this 'ere is most important. Grand Duke Basil, now at Berlin, will be in Paris on the twenty-fifth. You get up to the Chigi Palace right away, sir, see the Duce 'imself, and tell 'im that 'ere fact. Tell 'im Baron Yamanaka is a goin' to be in Paris at the same time; comin' from London, 'e is. That lets the cat out of the bag, sir—now we 'ave something to work on. All right, sir, you do that. Good-by."

Laying down the instrument, Solomon sighed wheezily, tamped the whittled tobacco into his clay pipe, and struck a match.

"Now I can 'ave a bit o' rest," he observed between puffs. "A bite to eat might do us both a mortal lot o' good, Mr. Warden. Don't you go to talkin' now. A man as asks questions gets less 'n he asks, I says. Food and sleep, that's what you need, sir."

Solomon pressed a button, an Arab appeared, and departed with an order. Meantime, Jimmy Warden stared at the singular little man. Was it true that Solomon had just sent an emissary to Mussolini in person? Fantastic!

The thought of June Tully tugged at him, wrenched at him. She was gone, then; Solomon knew about it, and sat here doing nothing! They had taken her with the car. Warden had been dragged out and flung in the ditch, all in a moment's time, without a fight, without a chance to do anything! Then, to his astonishment, Solomon spoke as though reading his very thoughts.

"She's all right, Mr. Warden—they won't 'urt 'er none. I've been discoverin' a lot o' things, as the old gent said when 'e fired the 'ousekeeper. To-morrow you and Mr. North can take things in 'and, so to speak. Now we'll 'ave a bit o' grub and talk about somethin' else."

An Arab entered with a tray and set dishes on the desk. Solomon addressed him.

"Tell Hassan to bring in the coffee when it's ready. You take the Hispano car and go to the Hôtel de Choiseul, and fetch Prince Sergei Romanoff here at once. If he's not there, find him, and bring him. He'll come."

WARDEN NOTED with some surprise that when speaking any other language Solomon seemed to have no trouble with his aspirates, yet with English the cockney twang was unmistakable. Now, at a gesture, Warden drew a straight chair up to the desk, joined Solomon at a most appetizing repast, and speedily felt in a better frame of mind.

"I expect as you know Prince Sergei?" asked Solomon.

Warden nodded. "I know who he is, of course. Grand Duke Basil is the direct heir to the Russian throne—or is so accepted by most of the exiled Russians. Sergei has a pretty good claim himself, and has a minority following. No love lost between them, I understand. Basil seems to be a Romanoff of the old type, conservative, high-hat, autocratic—and some bad stories are told about him. Sergei isn't so bad."

"That 'ere Grand Duke is a mortal bad egg, sir—just like that," observed Solomon between bites. "True, 'e's got a lot o' money and a lot o' backin', but 'e ain't me choice by a good deal, not 'im! Mr. Warden, who's the most powerful man in Europe to-day?"

Warden shrugged. "No two ways about that, Solomon. The Duce."

"Make it John, sir, make it John," said the little cockney. "I'm John to me friends, sir, and werry 'appy I am to 'ave you in the number. We'll 'ave some real Arabian coffee— Ah, there's Hassan now!"

Another Arab entered, placed coffee before them, set out cigarettes, cigars.

When he was gone, Solomon leaned back in his chair and sighed wheezily. "I ain't as young as I was, Mr. Warden, or I wouldn't be a settin' 'ere dependin' on other men to be 'elpin' of me! No, sir. But age is a werry mysterious thing, as the old gent said when 'e up an' kissed the 'ousemaid. Now, sir, about that 'ere Mussolini—the Duce. If 'e was to up an' back the Grand Duke, we'd 'ave another Russian czar—but 'e won't do it. And why? 'Cause 'e knows that 'ere Grand Duke is a treacherous dog, just like that. The Duce 'as 'is enemies, Mr. Warden, but 'e 'as 'is friends likewise. If I do say it as shouldn't, 'im and me are werry good friends, sir."

Having delivered himself of these amazing words, Solomon sipped his coffee and pursued the topic, his mild blue eyes dwelling tranquilly upon Warden.

"I don't 'old with no Bolsheviks and such, sir, and neither does Rome. This 'ere new Italy is a great country, and it's all for doin' of things right and as they should be. It don't straddle the fence to wait and see who's goin' to win, like England and France, and it don't 'ave no truck wi' bloody murderers for the sake of policy. What would 'appen, sir, if so be as Rome was to back this 'ere Sergei Romanoff?"

"Well," and Warden smiled faintly, "Mussolini would have the wrong cat by the tail. And he wouldn't have much influence in Russian affairs."

"Oh, werry good, sir!" A wheezy chuckle broke from Solomon. Somewhere a bell sounded very softly. "I expect this is 'im now, and if you'll be so good as to listen, sir—"

"One minute," interrupted Warden. "About Miss Tully?"

"In the mornin', sir," and Solomon held lip his hand in restraint. "She ain't come to no 'urt, upon me word. Oh, come in, prince! I'm werry 'appy to see you lookin' so well. This 'ere is me friend, Mr. Warden. Hassan, coffee for Prince Sergei. Make yourself at 'ome, your 'ighness, and we'll 'ave a bit of a talk between friends, so to speak. There ain't nothin' like friendship to break the ice, as the old gent said when 'e kissed the new 'ousemaid."

Prince Sergei laughed amusedly as he bowed to Warden and took a seat. He was a man of forty, his features deeply lined, grave, yet capable of great animation. If his face held no great strength, it did hold a kindly dignity and a promise of high possibilities.

"I suppose you have some news, eh?" he observed in English. Hassan was setting coffee before him, and holding a match to his cigarette.

"More or less, your 'ighness," said Solomon.

WARDEN OBSERVED that Solomon's manner seemed habitually deferential, almost apologetic; it afforded a strange and striking contrast with the words that sometimes came from his lips. And always his wide blue eyes were innocent, devoid of expression; save for an occasional twinkle, they seldom changed.

"Excellent," said the prince, half idly, half in alert expectancy. "Your man brought me here on short notice, Solomon. I left a lady waiting."

Solomon took up his plug and began to whittle tobacco. For some reason. Warden tensed. The moment was electric, charged with tremendous things. He marveled at his own feeling.

"Yes, sir," said Solomon. "That's werry true o' princes, your 'ighness. There's always a lady waitin'—to spoil the course of 'istory, just like that."

The prince stiffened, his eyes struck out sharply. Warden,

despite weariness, despite stiffness and bruises, was suddenly jarred into acute suspense.

"What d'you mean?" demanded Prince Sergei.

"I means," returned Solomon, whittling very carefully, "as 'ow your own fate and the 'ole bloomin' destiny of Russia is a goin' to be settled in this 'ere room, inside of 'alf an hour. Ten minutes ago I got the clew to the 'ole blessed thing in me own 'ands—and I'm ready to talk business, your 'ighness."

"Mon Dieu!" ejaculated the Russian. "Are you serious?"

Solomon chuckled. "There ain't nothin' serious in this 'ere world, I says, except maybe bein' born into it. 'Ere you be, sir, all shipshape and Bristol fashion—" and taking a box of wax vestas from the desk, he began setting out slips of wax, the while he went on speaking.

"First off, 'ere *you* be, your 'ighness. Over 'ere is Grand Duke Basil—and who's with 'im? Some o' the old nobility. A predominant party in Germany, ready to back 'im. Chief of all, Signor Dominetti."

"Dominetti? That Italian prince exile?" The Russian's voice was acid with contempt. "Of what use is he? How can he help Basil?"

"First off, wi' money," said Solomon. "Second, with influence. This 'ere blackguard 'as a 'old on a lot o' people, your 'ighness—blackmail. Your brother Nicholas is a payin' 'im or 'is agents a thousand francs every month."

"Nicholas—that boy? Impossible!" exclaimed the prince, but the color drained from his face as he spoke. "Well, well. What actual help can he give Basil?"

"Political 'elp, financial 'elp—and a weapon," said Solomon earnestly. "A machine, a death ray, that can sweep men and things out of existence."

"You mean, like that English invention—the one that never worked?"

"Just like that, sir," said Solomon. "Only better. This 'ere works. Now, then, besides Dominetti—who else? Japan. When

Grand Duke Basil attacks with German 'elp from the west, Japan throws 'er armies into Siberia, attacks from the east. When Basil is made Czar, Japan takes part o' Siberia, to keep. It's a werry good bargain for Japan, your 'ighness. If you— Dang it! Excuse me a minute, sir."

At the buzz. Solomon picked up the telephone and spoke. For a moment he listened. Then:

"Now, 'old on a minute! This is you, Patterson—in Constantinople? And Sotheby was killed in Angora. All right. If you 'ave the information, let me 'ave it, mortal quick, sir. Yes—Kemal Pasha 'as signed the agreement? And 'e supports Basil by attacking Russia from the south, seizing the Crimea? Yes. And what's 'is ruddy terms—oh! So 'e's a sendin' Fakri Pasha to Paris to meet Basil 'ere, eh? Werry good, sir."

Solomon hung up. Prince Sergei was intent, wide-eyed, staring.

"ANGORA ATTACKS Russia from the south—at a price!" murmured the prince. "What does Basil promise?"

"I don't know yet, sir," returned Solomon. "But there you be. And the brains behind the 'ole blessed thing is Dominetti. Let Basil win Russia, and everybody gets a slice. Once on the throne, 'e supports Dominetti and the royalist party against Mussolini, and disrupts Italy to get them back in power there."

Prince Sergei nodded. Warden, however, suddenly perceived a ray of light. He had already begun to suspect that this amazing little man was a very active Fascist partisan—and now the suspicion became conviction.

"So you're acting for the Duce, John?" he blurted out. Solomon chuckled wheezily.

"Yes, sir, I am—just like that," he returned. "And now, your 'ighness, I'm ready to talk business; if so be as you'll 'ear me out."

Prince Sergei took a fresh cigarette, leaned back in his chair, nodded.

"Speak," he said quietly. "If I am put on the throne of Holy

Russia—what part of her throat do you want to cut, you and the blacksmith's son who rules Italy?"

The bitter words drew no expression from Solomon, who was lighting his pipe.

"You ain't on the throne yet, sir," he returned. "Basil would barter away 'alf o' Russia in order to 'ave the other 'alf. You won't. Just 'ere behind you," and his hand went out to the wax vestas on the table, "is, first, the Nationalist government in China."

"Disrupted into factions, weak, helpless!" sneered the Russian.

"The Duce, and Italy," went on Solomon, unheeding. "Munitions, men, power, floodin' into Rumania, where the veterans o' Wrangel's army are a waitin' for you, sir. No barterin', no waste o' time, no danged negotiations—a quick, sharp stroke wi' fifty thousand men straight up at Moscow and Leningrad! While Basil talks, you take Russia! Fifty thousand men in two weeks' time, your 'ighness; a fleet of airplanes, a flood o' tanks, mobile artillery—and this 'ere machine that sweeps men and things away into nothin'!"

Now, staring at Solomon, the Russian's keen features were lighted by a flush, his deep eyes kindled into fire; the words, the vision, swept him into momentary exaltation. Then a cold bitterness came back into his gaze.

"All this needs money," he said slowly. "Italy may provide much, but she cannot provide money."

"I can, your 'ighness," said Solomon quietly. "I can turn over to you fifty million dollars to-morrow—and obtain a credit of a billion."

There was momentary silence. Prince Sergei caught his breath, staring hard. Warden, too, looked at this pudgy, unassuming, blank-eyed little man who puffed a clay pipe and spoke the incredible. Yet Sergei seemed to find it not so incredible.

"And you? And Italy?" asked the Russian in a low, tense voice. "Your pound of flesh?"

"Mine? Repayment of that 'ere money, without interest. Italy's? The destruction of communism in Russia. That's all, your 'ighness. But you 'ave to decide 'ere and now, to-night! On the twenty-fifth Basil comes 'ere from Berlin. 'E meets Baron Yamanaka, the Japanese ambassador to London, and the 'eads of the Russian Imperial Council."

"Basil—here! In Paris!" exclaimed Sergei. Then a sudden passion flamed in his face and voice. "And you—and Rome— you ask nothing more? No Russian territory? Bah! Are you, then, philanthropic fools?"

"Perhaps, sir." Solomon reached out to the telephone. "You know the voice of the Duce?"

"I have met him, yes," assented the prince, suddenly very pale.

Solomon picked up the receiver. "Get me the Chigi Palace—I want to speak wi' the Duce 'imself. Right off."

ABSURD! WARDEN stirred in his chair, not believing what he heard or saw. That this pudgy little man should seek Mussolini over the air, should demand instant speech!

"It is madness! It is a dream!" said Prince Sergei, his eyes wide. Solomon made no response. Abruptly Warden recalled the former conversation with Newton, evidently the agent in Rome. Could it be possible, after all? Was the Duce, there in Rome, awaiting just such a call as this? Was the Fascist party, that bitter enemy of Bolshevism, ready to back this man?

"Yes, sir," Solomon broke into quick speech. "This 'ere is John Solomon, sir. Prince Sergei Romanoff is werry anxious to 'ave a bit o' speech with you, sir, if so be as you 'as the time—'Ere you be, your 'ighness."

He held out the instrument. Sergei, like a man in a dream, took it, hesitated, spoke in Italian. Warden knew the language well enough to follow his words, but was too lost in amazement to care about them. Either this was a colossal bluff or else—or else it was history in the making, history, cooked up like broth by this pudgy little man with the wide blue eyes!

Then, presently, Solomon had the instrument and was listening, while Prince Sergei sat back and regarded him fixedly, nervous, utterly astonished, yet visibly convinced. And when

Solomon finished his talk and leaned back again with his stained clay pipe, the Russian drew a long breath and stooped forward, placing his two hands on the desk.

"Very well, my friend," he said in a solemn voice. "You have—you have convinced me. It is true. And my answer is—*yes!* I accept!"

"Werry good, sir." Solomon opened a drawer of his desk and brought forth a *dossier* of papers. "The agreement is 'ere, all ship-shape. But there ain't a word to be said about it, mind that—not until you're in the field, leading that 'ere army to Moscow!"

Sergei nodded, leaned farther forward, began examining the papers.

Jimmy Warden knew in his heart that it was no dream, that it was no fantastic conception, but an excellent plan mapped out in cold reality. Sergei was the idol of the old Russian army, a stern but just man, a born soldier. With an army of fifty thousand men, with no lack of equipment, with a terrible and unguessed weapon, he could cut Russia in two, before the Reds could awaken to their peril; he could seize Moscow and Leningrad, he could gather around him all the shattered, dormant elements of old Russia.

So, sitting there in the bare little room, which still held undreamed secrets for him, Warden saw the papers signed, saw the two men shake hands, found himself bowing to the stately Russian—and then was alone again with Solomon.

"So that's that, Mr. Warden." Of a sudden, he looked aged and tired, drawn, a great weariness in his eyes. "That 'ere is the one man who can turn the trick. And now, sir, if I was you I'd get to bed. We'll 'ave a talk in the mornin', you and me and Mr. North. And I could do with a bit o' sleep meself. I ain't as young as I was, as the old gent said when 'e kissed the 'ousemaid."

So Warden found himself led away by an Arab; led to a steaming bath, a careful massage by expert hands, a downy bed into which he sank. For the moment, remembrance of June Tully was gone from him amid the rush of greater, more incredible things. For the moment only.

Yet, as he fell asleep, all his wonder died away and was gone in cold sanity. After all, when it came down to facts, just how much reliance could be placed in this man of mystery, John Solomon? As pitted against Dominetti, for example? Warden realized clearly enough that this whole great game was being played between these two protagonists—and where lay the strength of Solomon?

As a matter of fact, he had none. Money he might have, yes; but Dominetti had money, too. Solomon's men, his agents, his organization—all were obviously being smashed to bits right and left. He had none of Dominetti's virile strength and unscrupulous energy.

"But he has a brain!" thought Warden. "Yes, a brain—and what good will it do him? Dominetti has gone beyond him, has circled Russia with potential enemies, has secured backing in every way—and what has Solomon done? Nothing, except talk with a man sitting in the Chigi Palace."

And, upon despondency, with the thought of June Tully tearing at him in cruel despair, Jimmy Warden fell asleep in the house of John Solomon.

CHAPTER VI

THE FIGHT OPENS

"TELL ME about Solomon—who he is," said Warden. "I suppose you can talk now."

North laughed. The two men were at breakfast together in a huge oak-paneled dining room, whose painted ceiling showed nymphs and graces disporting themselves in the most florid Empire style. Solomon had not yet joined them. North had come in during the night, and looked exceedingly fresh and fit. Warden, except for a few bruises and a scratched cheek, was quite himself.

"There'll be more than talk doing to-day," returned North. "What happened last night?"

Warden grinned. "Ask Solomon. Enough to make me damned curious."

"Huh! You're not talking, eh? All right, Sherlock." North chuckled as though enjoying himself. "Our friend is just plain John Solomon; there's no other like him. He's an old man with one foot in the grave. You know what Aeschylus called old men? Dreams left wandering in the day. That's him."

"You're a liar," said Warden cheerfully. "Come across."

"Not much to come across with," returned North. "Seriously, I understand John has spent most of his life in Arabic-speaking countries. He's immensely rich, so far as actual money goes, and he's still richer in his friends and connections. You've heard of Sir Basil Condax, the Greek, who married a Spanish princess before the war, and who was said to make and unmake thrones and republics—lending money, selling munitions, throwing a huge mass of wealth into the stock market at critical times to further his own string-pulling? I understand that Solomon wiped him out a few years ago and since then has been enjoying himself—in the interests of peace rather than of war. I've seen some queer things happen in this house. But here's the gentleman himself. Morning, John!"

"Morning, gents," said Solomon, from the doorway. He came into the room, walking a bit stiffly, and took the chair held back for him by the deft white-clad Hassan. "Werry 'appy I am to see you lookin' so fine, both of you. If I ain't mistook, we'll 'ave a 'ard day ahead, as the old gent said when 'e caught the butler a kissin' of the 'ousemaid."

"Just who was that old gent of yours, John?" demanded North. Solomon wrinkled his face into a smile.

"That 'ere is a secret, sir. Wouldn't do to make it public. Well, Mr. Warden, I expect as 'ow you're a thinkin' about Miss Tully? As soon as I get a bit o' food, sir, we'll 'ave in a few reports and such, and unless I change me mind, I'll leave 'er in your 'ands, with Mr. North a helpin' of you."

"Oh, you will!" said North dryly. "And what about other things, John?"

Solomon's blank blue eyes twinkled at him.

"You'll likely find out, Mr. North, as 'ow there ain't nothin' more important than this werry matter o' Miss Tully, just like that."

So saying, John Solomon went on with his breakfast, unhurried. The other two men sat in silence before this placid unconcern; North was frowning slightly, as though puzzled and uncertain. Jimmy Warden, to his own surprise, found his doubts of the previous night swept away in the presence of the little cockney. Then, abruptly, North turned to him.

"YOU MIGHT as well understand one thing, Warden," he said grimly. "This man Solomon uses men like pawns on a chessboard. He drives ahead to his aim, he sacrifices you or me without a thought or a care—his whole concern is in the final checkmate. Isn't that so, John?"

"No, sir, it ain't," said Solomon, and he glanced at North with a startled hurt in his gaze. "Leastwise, you don't look at it rightly. It ain't that at all. You take Dominetti now. What's 'e doin'? Piling up a score, that's what! Providence is a werry mysterious thing, Mr. North, and men like 'im don't take it into account, which is a mortal bad error to make. If so be as you makes a mistake and one o' Dominetti's men puts a bullet into you, that ain't me own fault, is it? A man pays for 'is mistakes, says I—"

"And you don't make any," cut in North, half angrily.

"No, sir, I don't," said Solomon with simple earnestness. "If so be as Yusuf 'ad kept 'is wits about 'im last night, 'e wouldn't be in 'ospital now. If so be as Mr. Warden 'ad watched 'imself, 'e wouldn't ha' been caught nappin'. Ain't that true, Mr. Warden?"

"Yes," said Warden, reluctantly.

"Then," and Solomon rose, "let's be a gettin' to work."

The three men passed to the blank little office of Solomon, whose desk was heaped with papers. Opening a drawer, Solomon took forth a long-cuffed gauntlet and then pressed a button. He handed the gauntlet to Warden, as the room was filled with that unearthly violet-ray light.

"If so be as you'll put this on, Mr. Warden, we'll make a mark on your wrist, so me men will know you as one of us. Or—wait! Dominetti knows that 'ere mark. No, we'll let it go. There's no use temptin' the enemy."

Warden returned the glove, and remembered the Seal of Solomon that had appeared to be burned into the wrists of North and Fisher. Solomon carefully whittled tobacco, filled and lighted his pipe, and began to go through the papers on his desk.

"This 'ere light," he observed, sorting the papers into neat piles, "is a werry good thing for an old man like me. Keeps 'im young, it does. Well, Ahmed ben Zain?"

A tall Arab appeared in the doorway, touched his hand to

brow, lips and breast in reply to Solomon's greeting, and spoke briefly in Arabic. Solomon leaned back in his chair.

"Werry good, Ahmed. Bring 'im in."

Warden saw North stir expectantly, and felt a swift tenseness in the air. In the doorway appeared a bound man between two Arabs. The prisoner was a small rat-eyed man, his face vicious in the extreme, and he burst forth in speech which showed that he was an American.

"What do you mean by this, huh?" he exclaimed. "Just because I made a mistake and got into the wrong house—that ain't nothing. You can't hold me on no charge, understand?"

Solomon did not reply, but looked blankly at him, and he fell silent. Ahmed stepped forward and laid a number of articles on the desk, evidently coming from the pockets of the prisoner; a jimmy, a large roll of American bank notes, a revolver fitted with a silencer, and a glass flagon, sealed with wax and filled with a colorless liquid. Solomon took up this flagon with a show of interest and picked at the wax with his nail.

"Fer God's sake lay off that!" cried out the prisoner. "That—that—"

"Yes?" Solomon laid down the flagon. "I suppose this 'ere would bust and there'd be an explosion and fire, most like. So Dominetti give this 'ere to you, did 'e?"

"Never heard of him," said the prisoner sullenly.

Solomon made a gesture. The prisoner was shoved into a chair and sat there like a trapped animal, alert, waiting. Ahmed stepped to the one window of the room, set high in the wall, and drew a blind across it. Solomon touched another of the buttons on his desk, and the glare of light faded slightly in the room.

North, who seemed to know what was going on, looked at the blank wall behind the desk, and Warden followed his gaze. So did the prisoner—and then a choked cry of incredulity burst forth, and was silenced.

THERE ON the wall appeared a picture, silent, moving, life-size.

It swiftly grew and took form. A man—the prisoner—was standing before a desk, at which sat another man. Warden repressed a start; this second man was no other than Dominetti in person. Dominetti looked up, his lips moved, and the prisoner assented. Dominetti handed him a flagon, apparently the same which lay upon Solomon's desk, and spoke warningly about it. The prisoner nodded with scornful unconcern and pocketed it. Dominetti handed him a silenced revolver, and a roll of money. The picture faded abruptly.

"It's a damned lie!" cried out the prisoner, his features ghastly.

"Take 'im away," said Solomon, with a jerk of his head. The man was dragged out of the room, leaving behind a trail of obscenity and curses.

Warden looked around. In the walls were set two crystal panes, like that overhead from which came the radiance, but there was no sign of any motion picture camera. He met the gaze of North, and the latter smiled.

"Startling, eh? Yet it's logical enough, Warden. You'd have to get Pearson to explain it in scientific terms—he's in charge of our laboratory in Auteuil, and this is one of his pet toys that John has turned to use. Take a man, place him in that chair, make the contact, and get his brain working on a certain subject—and the pictures in his brain are flung on the wall."

"Simple," said Warden ironically. "But how?"

North shrugged. "How is television worked? What is electricity? What is life? Ask me something easy. Pearson was working on a method of recording thoughts on a film, and found that up to a certain point, with a certain type of person, thoughts are pictures, images. His devilish machine—it's in the next room—makes some application of the infra-red rays, and other light-effects Pearson has discovered; it digs the pictures out of a man's brain and throws them on the wall here. It works about twice in five times—often there's only a blur. Pearson himself is afraid of the damned thing, doesn't know what effect the rays have on the human subject, and wouldn't perfect it or carry his experiments farther. John took over the contraption, and isn't worried about what might happen to the chap in the chair."

"I'd be werry sorry to use it on either o' you two gents," said Solomon, sorting out his papers again. Warden stirred uneasily.

"Do you mean that this man was sent here by Dominetti?"

"Just like that, sir," and Solomon nodded. "You've talked wi' Dominetti 'imself?"

Warden assented, and found North eying him with new interest.

"What do you think of 'im, sir?" demanded Solomon placidly.

"About as dangerous as they make 'em," said Jimmy Warden. "Those light gray eyes of his—well, they're bad. There's power in them, but not a good sort of power."

"Right you are, sir," assented Solomon, and relit his pipe. "Now we can get down to business, gents. First off, about Miss Tully."

"You know where she is?" broke out Warden eagerly.

"Yes, sir, and she ain't comin' to no 'arm. Now, 'ere's a report on Halsey, who engineered her abduction."

He handed Warden a typed sheet, and North leaned over to scan it with him. However obtained, the information was concise and to the point:

> HALSEY, FRANK. Alias: J.H. Frank.
> Gentleman Hall
>
> Age 42. Education, Harvard. Family, good. Adept at stock market rigging, high-class confidence work. Promoted General Finance Corporation, Western Oil, etc. Prosecuted and convicted in 1923, served three years; sentence commuted good behavior. Indicted twice, but failed conviction. Ability, very high. For past two years has conducted Chicago office as agent of Dominetti, handling large stock transactions through Middle West. Twice named as correspondent divorce actions. Has twice been in Europe, recently.

"AND JUST where does he come in on this deal?" asked Warden.

"Right now," said Solomon, "you'll find 'im at Dominetti's villa in Boulogne-sur-Seine. 'Im and that 'ere Russian, Glazunoff. Miss Tully's there, too. This 'ere Halsey is interested in 'er, so to speak. I'm werry much afraid, gents, as 'ow Dominetti is a fixin' to 'it me 'arder yet—and if I was you, Mr. Warden, I'd do me best to get on the inside o' that 'ere villa. You 'ave a werry good chance o' makin' it, sir."

"How?" Warden frowned. "Break in? Or as a spy?"

"You and Mr. North can fix that up, if so be as you're disposed," said Solomon.

Warden laughed harshly. "Oh, I'm disposed all right!" he said. "Why not let me appear as an interested party—say, as the agent of Prince Sergei?"

Solomon regarded him with a fixed expression, the blue eyes very wide.

"Dang it, sir—now we're a gettin' somewhere! I'll 'ave a letter 'ere in 'alf an hour, authorizin' you to treat on 'is behalf, just like that! And you can sell 'im out or do as you danged well please, yes, sir! If so be as you're a good liar, all werry fine—and 'avin' been a diplomat, I'd be werry sorry indeed if you couldn't tell a lie, Mr. Warden."

There followed a half hour of detailed discussion, Solomon meantime telephoning Prince Sergei for a letter appointing James Warden as his agent.

What was more to the point, Warden learned also that he and North would be flung entirely on their own resources.

"It's you gents as is fightin', so do it in your own way, says I," he observed. "I'll take on Dominetti me own self when the time comes. Dang it! I'm werry much afraid as 'ow that 'ere man is a fixin' to strike at Pearson and 'is laboratory in Rue Jasmin."

This was the second time Solomon had voiced the same fear, and warden looked at the pathetically absurd little figure with a sudden blank dismay. This man—against Dominetti! It was ridiculous. Solomon, for all his brain, was old, cautious, slow; his organization was paralyzed. Opposing him was a virile, powerful man.

"I'm a goin' for a little trip out o' town," said Solomon, wheez- ily. Hassan appeared and said a few words, producing a letter. Solomon handed it to Warden. "There you be, sir—and if I ain't mistook, something werry interestin' is 'appenin' in the court- yard."

Such was their farewell. Warden and North reached the courtyard, where a car was awaiting with Ahmed ben Zain as chauffeur. At one side, a huge truck was standing, and from it a number of porters were carefully lifting a mammoth packing case.

"What the devil is that, and what did he mean?" asked North, irritated.

Warden shrugged and got into the Hispano. Later, however, in the moment when John Solomon was utterly broken, trapped, facing destruction, Warden was to recall the incident.

CHAPTER VII

"FOLLOW THAT CAR!"

"**D**O YOU know where Dominetti's villa is located?" asked Warden, as the Hispano wound through the Paris traffic and struck into Rue St. Honoré. North nodded.

"Yes. I want to take you past the laboratory on the way. I think we'd better separate. I'll leave you the car and establish myself at some place in Boulogne. We can meet each morning at a certain time; we'll see. Got any notions of your own?"

"Nary a notion," said Warden cheerfully. "If you and I are in charge of this particular business, go ahead and line things up as seems best to you."

"I don't savvy our friend John a bit," returned North thoughtfully. "Why is he going out of town now, of all times? Why is he putting us on this sort of errand? Take it from me, feller, this Solomon knows a lot more than he says, and he plans ahead pretty well. I've heard that he actually foretells the future and makes his plans accordingly—which is all rot. But we'll see on the way out."

Ahmed nodded back in response to North's instructions, and bowled along by way of the Trocadero and Passy, presently turning into Avenue Mozart and sweeping down the Auteuil hill to the Metro station at Rue Jasmin. He turned off upon this short and newly built-up little street, and slowed to a crawling pace.

"There you are."

North pointed ahead to a building on the left. It was a most peculiar structure—two-storied, and massively built of stone, apparently with no windows on the ground floor. Located on a corner, it was built out to the sidewalk and gave an impression of being a solid stone block. Behind was a walled garden.

As they turned and went down the street to the avenue again. Warden noticed that the one door in the building seemed to be made of heavy brass. A carriage entrance broke the wall of the garden and was closed by massive and unpierced gates.

"It was in this street that the arm was found?" asked Warden.

North nodded silently.

The car whirled on to the Auteuil gate, halted for gasoline check at the barrier, and went on out toward Boulogne. Warden was by no means unfamiliar with Paris, and knew that this once elegant residential suburb had of late years become more and more occupied by huge factories, so that now its old beauty was gone. Its streets and grog-shops had been invaded by Algerian and other foreign workmen; it was now a hotbed of communism.

They turned into Boulevard Jean Jaures, and after a couple of blocks Ahmed slowed down.

"There's the place, on the right," said North. "The high wall with the house at the right end. It's a splendid old villa, I understand, though like all the rest of these places, it doesn't look up to much."

Nor did it. In common with most of the street, this house was largely blank wall, the lower windows protected by heavy iron grillework. To the left of the house extended a garden wall, broken only by gates, which stood open at the moment, giving a glimpse of a garden with trees and fountains, and a huge Mercedes car standing ready to leave.

Then they were past. Ahmed went on to the corner of the Avenue de la Reine and halted. North indicated a café terrace across the street.

"Let's drop over and have a drink. Good place."

They walked over to the café and settled down at a table, the terrace being unoccupied at the time. After a waiter had taken their order, North lighted a cigarette and spoke.

"Warden, I haven't a ghost of a notion what to do—we'll simply have to see what turns up, and act accordingly. To break into the house and take Miss Tully away is out of the question. For one thing, French law is pretty liberal. Get into a man's place, or into his garden, and he can pump you full of lead—and usually will do it, too. Besides, don't forget this point: we're by no means sure that Miss Tully wants to be set free."

"HUH?" WARDEN stared at him, startled by the implication of these words. "What are you driving at?"

North shrugged. "She's no helpless jointed doll, is she? To be honest, I'm not sure just what I am driving at, but I know one thing—John Solomon never tells anybody just what's in his head. Don't be surprised at anything that turns up. For all we know, he may have been in communication with Miss Tully already. I do know that when he goes out of town, he usually expects hell to pop. But don't think he's running away. When the popping is going on, he'll show up in the middle of it."

Warden sniffed skeptically. "It's all mud to me, anyhow. We don't know what's going on, we don't know what to do—"

"I'll tell you what to do. Follow a hunch, every time!" said North. "We play hunches in this game, mister! Near as I can figure the thing out, Solomon gets the best men he can find, then expects them to use their heads. He backs 'em up to the finish, but he never has any strings on 'em."

"What about his organization getting smashed?" demanded Warden.

"Mistakes. You heard him. We can't make mistakes, that's all. Got a gun?"

Warden shook his head.

"You'll find one in the right-hand door pocket of the car, with a couple extra clips of cartridges. Carry it and use it."

North was suddenly crisp, concise, authoritative, as though he had settled on a scheme of action. And so he had, as his next words evinced.

"Now, I'll go to a little hotel around the corner and get me a

"So long, folks," Halsey called as
he stepped into the coffin.

room, savvy? I'm pretty well all in—didn't sleep any too much last night, and I've been on the go. So I'll rest up. At ten in the morning and five in the afternoon I'll be sitting right here over an *aperitif,* and if you get wise to anything or need me, show up."

"And meantime?"

"Follow your nose," North grinned, lifting his glass. "Here's luck!"

Warden drained his glass and rose. "Then I'm off."

"Eh?" North's brows lifted. "Just like that?"

"You bet. No use having a perfectly good car and chauffeur loafing on the job—and I just happened to remember the car standing at the villa. Can this Ahmed do the chase act?"

"Try him. I never found any of Solomon's Arabs who couldn't do what was wanted in a pinch. Go along, then, and here's hoping you have luck! But I doubt it."

Warden nodded and strode off to the car. Ahmed ben Zain swung down, and as he held the door open Warden addressed him.

"Do you speak English? No?" He switched to French. "Well, you recall the villa we passed around the corner, where a car was standing ready to leave? Drive back that way. If the car's still there; pull up in front of a shop."

"Oui, m'sieur," Ahmed replied.

The car hummed into life. Warden waved a hand at North and a moment later was turning along the main thoroughfare of Boulogne. A glance at the villa showed the gates still open, the car still there, a chauffeur at the wheel. Only a matter of moments, then, if the driver was ready to depart.

Ahmed turned in at the curb, and Warden, leaving the car, stepped into a plumbing shop and passed the time of day very frankly with the proprietor.

" I A M an American, *m'sieur,* unacquainted in the neighborhood. Perhaps you would know of any private hotel which I might lease, near by—a place something like that very comfortable-looking villa across the street. Eh?"

The plumber shoved his mustaches out of the way and responded genially enough:

"Alas, *m'sieur,* I am desolated! Only three days ago I heard of a very good villa just beyond the church, but now it is gone. It is difficult to secure a house at this season, *m'sieur.* That one across the street belongs to M. Hamelet, and is leased by an Italian prince. Perhaps, if I hear of anything—"

Warden laid down a ten-franc note and a card, on which he wrote a fictitious name and address. At least, the plumber would not lose anything. A warning honk of Ahmed's horn came to him, and, shaking hands in the cordial French manner, he left the plumber and returned to the car. The big Mercedes which he had spotted was just coming out of the villa gates and was turning in the direction of the church.

"Follow that car!" said Warden as he hopped in.

The Mercedes swung past, but another car intervened, and Warden could not see whether it was occupied or not. Looking back, he saw the gates of the villa being closed by two men, and realized that Dominetti must have servants in plenty. Then Ahmed was off, tooling the Hispano into an ever increasing speed.

Past the church, on into the Bois, sweeping through the pleasant, endless vistas of trees and water at sixty miles an hour. Then in at the Porte Dauphine and on to the Étoile.

Warden had completely lost sight of the car ahead, but Ahmed never faltered, and swept down the Champs Elysées to the Rond Point. A sudden swerving turn, and Warden saw the Mercedes ahead, rounding into Avenue Gabriel.

Ahmed slowed down and spoke back through the open window.

"The Marché aux Thimbres, *m'sieur*. He is getting out."

"Good," said Warden. "You know the Café Marigny, just down the street? Wait near there."

The Mercedes had, indeed, turned in at the curb, and from the car was stepping none other than the agent, Frank Halsey. Here at the corner of Avenue Marigny was the only place in Paris where unlicensed peddlers could concentrate freely—the Stamp Market, where a corner beside the Theater Marigny and the puppet-shows of children's delight was given up to the national indoor pastime of Frenchmen—the collecting of stamps.

Here, in the outdoors, beneath the widespreading trees, the king of hobbies held sway twice a week, rain or shine. The ground was lined with rows of tables and portable booths where postage stamps were displayed; other peddlers, usually with valuable wares in pocket containers, circulated among the throng. Two out of three of these merchants were foreigners; a large percentage were Armenians, or Russians, who had seized upon this form of business since the war days.

Between sidewalk and street moved the crowd. Here little iron chairs were rented, the booths being confined to the space inside the sidewalk, and men sat by the hour, chatting or putting over deals. Some were of magnitude, also—the largest philatelic dealers in France circulated here, either personally or through agents. To this point also came clerks with the envelopes of their firms' foreign mail, heirs and boys and women with stamp collections to sell, people who had turned up old letters.

The crowd was fascinating enough. A fair proportion were boys, but the majority were men of all ages—distinguished old characters with ribbons at their lapels, younger men who stole an hour from the office, even some women. The Café Marigny, a block distant, catered with eagerness to this trade, and on market days was always crowded to capacity by the overflow from the stamp bourse.

WARDEN, MOVING through the throng, presently picked up his man. He was curious to see what business Halsey would have here, for such a type would certainly not be a collector of stamps and would not be interested in the small profits of such a business. He was confident that he himself was unknown to Halsey, except by description, so he had no hesitation in trailing his quarry closely.

It was soon apparent, in fact, that Halsey had no interest in postage stamps. This tall, distinguished looking man with piercing dark eyes and aristocratic features, was obviously an American, and was eagerly approached by vendors. He waved them all aside, passed curiously but negligently among the booths and tables, and appeared to be sauntering around to kill an idle hour.

Warden, whose French tailored clothes were less readily marked, was scarcely bothered by the ambulant peddlers.

Strolling along in the tightly packed crowd as closely as he dared behind Halsey, Jimmy Warden observed his quarry halt abruptly before a little booth, presided over by an ancient crone whose straggling gray locks and hardbitten face were at singular contrast with her occupation. She was, at the moment, engaged in making a ten-centime deal with a pair of schoolboys, but Warden saw her flash a look at Halsey, and fancied recognition in it.

Mr. Halsey began to study her wares with evidences of absorbed interest. Mr. Warden, moving up close by, took one of the beldame's smaller albums and turned the pages slowly, examining a stamp here, another there, laying aside a few as he went on.

The old woman dismissed the boys and turned to Halsey and Warden. For a moment she stood jotting down the price of the stamps selected by the latter. Presently Halsey spoke to her, in English.

"Tell Victor I'm bringing a client to-night at seven."

The old crone flung him a leer—a knowing, significant glance.

"Good," she said. "We have moved since you were here last, *mon ami.* Fifty-six Rue Jacob. Is it the old game?"

Halsey laughed. "The same," he said. "But be careful. Wait for the *liqueurs.*"

"Naturally," she returned. "Victor is at the café now, if you want to see him."

Halsey nodded and moved away.

Warden closed the album, took the envelope of stamps he had selected and paid for them. He edged his way out of the throng, caring nothing further about trailing Halsey. He had learned what he was seeking, and a good deal more than he had expected. And yet—there was the man Victor! Halsey would go to the Café Marigny, beyond a doubt.

Jimmy Warden chuckled to himself as he made his way across the street and started down the wide sidewalk under the great trees. Luck was breaking his way, for once.

Halsey had been in Paris before this trip, obviously, and knew the old crone and her precious Victor. He was on his own errands this morning, not those of Dominetti. And Solomon had said that Halsey was "sweet" on June Tully. Therefore, whatever this place in Rue Jacob might be, it was a fair gamble that the "client" Halsey was taking there that night, was none other than June Tully herself.

"It's a good chance, anyhow," thought Jimmy Warden cheerfully. "And if I were to meet friend Halsey all alone in the dark— that would be just too bad!"

WARDEN SAW Ahmed ben Zain with the car at the curb, but passed him with a brief nod and turned in at the café, already largely filled with patrons, books of stamps, catalogues. Warden took a corner table whence he could command a view of the place, then settled down over a Rossi.

He had plenty of business of his own to keep him engaged until evening. Whether Yusuf had taken care of his grips from Le Havre, he did not know; in any event, they would be safe enough. However, he had only the clothes he stood in, and this meant making purchases. Solomon's house was closed to him, evidently, so the best plan would be to get a hotel room for the night, if he needed it. And there was North to be met at five o'clock, too.

Presently Halsey strode into sight, entered the café and went to a swarthy man who sat behind some albums at a center table. This man, disfigured by a large red scar across the mouth, rose and shook hands in surprised recognition.

Halsey sat down, and they fell into talk, low-voiced, eager. Halsey produced a wallet and counted out some yellow hundred-franc notes.

Having secured all he could hope for, Warden paid his score and left. He went to the car, and as he slammed the door the Hispano rolled away. Ahmed knew his business.

"See anything of the Mercedes?" asked Warden.

"No, *m'sieur*. It went away."

"All right. Go down Rue Jacob and let's take a look at number fifty-six. Then we'll think about lunch—getting on to noon."

Ahmed struck across the Alexandre III bridge to the left bank and swept up along the quays. Rue Jacob was a short, famous little street between St. Germain and the Beaux Arts—a dingy abode of publishers, booksellers, cafés.

Watching the numbers narrowly, Warden was astonished to find that fifty-six was one of those bizarre places which catered to the night life of the quarter. "The Abode of Bad Spirits" was its ironic name; the windows and doors were decorated to represent the fires of hell. It was closed at the moment, and probably would not open until the evening.

"Place St. Michel and luncheon," Warden said to his driver. "Then we'll do some errands and get back to meet M. North at five."

During luncheon Warden determined to stake everything on his conjecture that the "client" to whom Halsey had referred was June Tully, and that Halsey was bringing her to the Abode of Bad Spirits that evening. Why? No answer. How could she be brought if she were a prisoner? No answer again.

However, there was something in the air. Warden had a hunch, and meant to play it hard.

In the course of the afternoon he replaced necessary toilet articles and a few clothes, did an errand or two, wrote a letter at the bank, and obtained a room at the Hôtel Vignon behind the Madeleine.

Following the obvious example of North, he resolutely shut Solomon out of his mind—clearly enough, they must temporarily discount any assistance from the little cockney. He tried to pick up information regarding the Abode of Bad Spirits, but could learn nothing of any consequence about the place—it was one of a hundred tourist traps.

At five o'clock Warden was sitting on the terrace of the little café in Boulogne, when North came striding up and plumped down at the adjoining table.

"Well, how's everything?" Warden inquired.

"Mad. Utterly mad and impossible and restful." North laughed. "I've slept up and feel fit as a fiddle—with nothing to do. Tried to reach John, but the phone wouldn't answer—he's kept his word and shut up shop. How about you?"

"Oh, I've been on the jump all day," and Warden recounted his experiences. Two elderly Frenchmen were the only persons in sight, so talking seemed safe enough. After he had finished, North made shrewd comment.

"This bird Halsey is pulling something on his own hook,

feller, and you've stumbled on to it fine. I have a man at Le Bour-get, and I've wired London; Dominetti is still there. I imagine Halsey and that chap Glazunoff are running things here for Dominetti. This cabaret is not so good—I've heard of it once or twice. Suppose I show up there alone around seven or eight to-night, eh? I'm known to Dominetti's crowd, of course, but I don't think any one is trailing me; still, we'll play safe and keep separate. Then they'll be watching me and not you. By the way, you should have a lady to make you look like an innocent tour-ist."

"I hope to have one before the evening's over," said Warden grimly.

"Nope; I know a better trick than that."

North took out pencil and paper, jotted down a name and address. He signed his name, drew the Seal of Solomon beneath, and gave the paper to Warden.

"Sophie Haller—she has a perfume shop in Boulevard Haussman near the Galeries Lafayette. She's one of our outfit, and can take care of herself in a fracas. Go to Sophie. Tell her you want her to go to dinner with you. She's good company. If there's any fuss, I'll take her off your hands and leave you free to act."

Warden assented, and five minutes later was on his way to the Boulevard Haussman.

CHAPTER VIII

THE ABODE OF BAD SPIRITS

A FEW MINUTES past seven saw Jimmy Warden and his companion, a vivacious lady of thirty odd, with false blond hair and a steely eye, seated in the Abode of Bad Spirits, giving a very good imitation of a tourist and his Parisian sweetheart.

The aspect of the place had changed with evening. Like many such resorts, the general note of the interior was rather cheap at first sight. The door attendant and waiters were all masked green devils, of small size—none of them over five feet in height. There was a narrow central dining floor running down to a dancing space, where an orchestra of six green devils made weird but rhythmic music. On either hand were semiprivate booths, each of which was emblazoned with the name of a fallen angel in glaring red neon tubes, and the curtains to each booth were decorated with the likeness of a bad spirit rising from the flames of hell.

Walls and ceiling carried out the analogy in a riot of colors, while the lights, of a vivid and uncompromising green, gave the whole place a rather ghastly appearance.

At the far end, to the right of the orchestra, was a large statue of a scarlet and grinning Mephisto, pointing with mute invitation to a large doorway whose curtains bore the title *"L'Enfer"*—Hell.

In small details, calculated to impress tourists, the general idea was carried farther still. Salt and pepper shakers were in the figures of devils; the plates and china were decorated with crudely obscene shapes; each table bore candles set in skull-and-crossbones holders, and so forth.

What really gave the place its convincing touch of grotesque and bizarre oddity was the small size of the waiters, who scurried about, made odd squeaking noises as they spoke, and conducted themselves like spoiled children. These masked and horned little green figures were, as Sophie Haller murmured to Warden, abnormal products of the slums of Paris, though two or three were jockeys who eked out a living in this fashion.

"There is M. North," said Sophie.

Warden looked around to see North, alone, led by a dancing green devil to a table in one corner. The head waiter, who was a statuesque figure all in red, unmasked but made up to the part, went to North's table and stood for a moment in talk. North was laughing as he replied.

"They've recognized him," murmured Sophie, "They don't know me, luckily. And who is this coming in now?"

"My party," returned Warden.

Half the tables were occupied, largely by tourist parties, and most of the booths on either side were filled. The couple now entering were met with great ceremony, and their wraps taken. Halsey looked more handsome, more distinguished, than ever in his evening clothes, and with him June Tully!

Warden blinked as they came forward, conducted toward a booth close by, marked with the name of Beelzebub. Was this June, in shimmering green evening wrap, or some one else? He had expected to see a shrinking, hesitant girl, compelled by force; instead, she was gay, laughing, as though having the time of her life and enjoying it thoroughly.

They passed close. Warden, staring, saw her glance sweep around; saw her eyes meet his gaze squarely—and detected not a hint of recognition in her face as she passed on.

"Name of a dog, wake up!" came the sharp admonition from Sophie Haller. "Don't stare like a fool, man! What's the matter?"

"She didn't know me!" muttered Warden. "She's drugged!"

"Bah! Where were your eyes?" retorted the lady. "She knew you well enough—her hand moved, gestured to you—and you were looking at her face! Use your wits in this game, my friend. Don't you see she's playing a part?"

Warden grunted disdainfully. He saw nothing of the sort. He did see the Beelzebub curtains drop behind Halsey and June Tully, and anger rose in his eyes. But he kept quiet.

PROMPTLY AT seven-thirty, and not until then, was the dinner served; the doors were then closed until the next "show," which took place at nine. The reason for this was to become obvious later.

Halsey and his companion were installed in their booth—deeply upholstered on three sides—when the tall Mephisto head waiter, none other than the scarred Victor, pushed aside the curtains and bowed deeply to Halsey.

"*M'sieur,*" he announced in sepulchral tones, "I bear a summons. His Highness, Prince Lucifer, demands speech with you in private. If you have an evil conscience there is yet time in which to depart."

Halsey glanced at June Tully and laughed.

"Excellent! You'll excuse me for a moment?"

He followed Victor across the floor to a doorway, and next moment the two men were in a private room, the office of the restaurant. Victor closed the door.

"*M'sieur,* there is a man here," he announced. "One M. North, an agent of that accursed Solomon. I recognized him at once from the photographs supplied to us all. He is alone. If you think he is on the trail of you or—"

"No," said Halsey, frowning a little. "In any event it will do them no good. She will disappear. You might have this man watched and taken care of in case he attempts anything, and point him out to me as we return."

"Very good, *m'sieur.* And a little behind you, as you entered, came in two men, Chinese or Japanese. I think they looked hard at you."

"Oh!" said Halsey thoughtfully. "I must see them, by all means."

They returned to the floor and passed among the tables. North was pointed out, and then Halsey came to a halt as, at one side, he sighted the two Chinese. One of them was Dr. Lee, who rose and bowed very politely, but without noticing Halsey's extended hand.

"Good evening, Mr. Halsey!" he said with a peculiar irony. "This is, indeed, a very pleasant surprise! You could do me a great favor, if you will."

"Yes? Glad to do whatever I can," said Halsey, puzzled by Lee's manner. "What is it?"

"Return to me the envelope which you took from my papers," said the Chinaman calmly. "The one containing a letter in Chinese—which cannot possibly do you any good."

Halsey stood stock-still. The two men looked one at another. The second Chinese had not risen, but was quietly smoking as though not understanding the conversation. Something in the calm, assured air of Lee put any thought of denial out of Halsey's brain.

"Well?" he said with a steely bravado. "And what if I refuse?"

Dr. Lee shrugged lightly.

"Ah," he murmured, "in that case, of course, I am quite help-less. I have remembered that cup of broth, I have put conclu-sions together—and I found a cigarette stub in my cabin. One of those English cigarettes which you like so well. You would make things much easier for me, and possibly for yourself, if you would return that letter."

"Is this a threat?" demanded Halsey sharply.

"By no means," returned Dr. Lee, his face very bland. "It is— shall we say—an endeavor to do you a favor, my friend."

"Oh!" said Halsey, not quite comprehending the menacing irony. "Well, save your breath, doctor. The letter has been passed on to the right hands, and you'd better not try any tricks, let me tell you—either now or later. Especially not in this place."

S O , W I T H a slight bow, Halsey passed on. Dr. Lee returned the bow, sat down again, and transferred his attention elsewhere. There was no suggestion, not even an undercurrent, of menace or ill feeling.

Halsey returned to the Beelzebub booth and fell into gay conversation with June Tully. At her suggestion the curtains were opened and left back to afford a view of the room. A few moments later she was on the floor with Halsey, dancing. In passing the table of Dr. Lee, she exchanged a hand clasp and a word of greeting with the Chinese, but once more encountered the look of Warden without recognition.

Dinner was served—an excellent dinner, interspersed with dancing. June Tully danced only with Halsey. Warden approached her once, as though to ask a dance, but she coolly turned her back and he sheered off.

In each booth was a telephone. It happened that, midway of the meal, the buzzer in the Beelzebub booth sounded, and as it did so a devil outlined in neon tubes came to life against the wall. Halsey picked up the instrument from its stand.

"Yes," he said. "This you, Boris? Anything new?"

"Nothing much," replied a voice, vibrant with exultation. "Except that we've got Pearson. Got him right here."

"Oh! Very well, then—keep him until I get back," said Halsey. "Better wait for orders in regard to him, hadn't you?"

"Not necessary," was the response. "Matsura just got in from London to question your little lady. We may turn our attention to Pearson. He's a weak sister, you know—one of these erratic genius chaps with no backbone and a lot of brain. He's not hurt to mention, and he's scared to death already. When will you be back?"

"In an hour. The car's waiting."

A soft laugh sounded. "Right! Good luck to you—and to her!"

The tables were cleared, and orders were taken for coffee and *liqueurs*. Then Victor stepped out to the center of the floor, doffed his long-feathered Mephisto's cap with a sweeping bow, and addressed the company in broken English—although he could speak that language perfectly when he so desired.

"Ladies an' gentlemans! Before ze coffee is served, you will kindly accompany me to ze lower regions. Wiz me you shall haf no fear of ze bad spirits, for you are under ze special safeguard of His Satanic Majesty. Ready! You will form in single file, if you please, and you will follow ze little devil Nicephoro. Behold!"

And turning, Victor pointed. The large red statue of Mephisto was suddenly illumined in a bath of scarlet light, the eyes flashed fire and leered at the company, and the curtains of Hell were drawn back to disclose the arched mouth of a stairway that descended to parts unknown.

The company formed up with great laughter and wine-induced jests ringing on all sides. One of the little prancing green devils took the lead, some hilarious spirit suggested forming the lock step, and the long procession wound toward the mouth of the stairway. Among the first were Halsey and June Tully.

Amid the confusion no one observed that Warden had disappeared from sight, though Sophie Haller was in line, with North directly behind her.

LITTLE BY little the file wound down the steps and vanished. When half were out of sight, Victor appeared, sending the green-devil waiters scurrying; coffee and liqueurs were placed about the tables as ordered. Victor himself, tray in hand, approached the Beelzebub booth, whose curtains were now drawn.

He stepped inside the curtains and set down his tray. Upon it were two long glasses of coffee, and two small glasses of cognac. He placed them carefully, turned—and came to a paralyzed halt. At his left, just inside the curtains, sat Jimmy Warden.

"Eh? Eh? What's this, *m'sieur?*" exclaimed Victor.

Mr. Warden held up his hand in restraint. He was busy with pencil and paper.

"So!" he observed, then glanced up. "Eh? You, Victor? What do you want?"

"Name of a name!" ejaculated the astonished Victor. "You know me, *m'sieur?* What do you here?"

"Is that your business? Go and ask M. Halsey, if you like." Warden folded and refolded the note he had just written, and tossed it on the table. "Go! Do you wish to read the note, also?"

Now the amazed Victor saw that here was some one who knew Halsey, who was leaving a message for him—undoubtedly, one of the right crowd. So, not to be himself suspected of too much curiosity, Victor retreated with dignity.

Instantly the curtains fell. Warden seized his imitation note, pocketed it, and then changed the position of the two cognac glasses—placing each where the other had been.

Then, swiftly, he was out in the dining room and catching up with the tail of the procession. He was in time to tag on with the last as they wended in beneath the arch and started down the winding stairway.

Jimmy Warden chuckled to himself at thought of the booth with June Tully's wrap marking her seat, and the cognac glass before her place. Sophie Haller had needed only the details of his story to outline precisely what Halsey had in mind; for it appeared that the Abode of Bad Spirits had a certain reputation in the underworld, and had seen the finish of more than one Beaux Arts career.

She intimated, indeed, that the *Sûreté* was watching the place closely, for the general clean-up of Paris instituted by the present prefect was no bluff, and M. Chiappe was after the tourist traps with all the heavy artillery of the prefecture.

"We've spoiled one little game, anyhow," thought Warden, "and gosh, how I'd like to see what happens after Halsey puts down the wrong drink!"

He was still chuckling when the stairway ended, and he found himself crowded with the others in a large underground room, probably a former wine cellar.

The place was pitch dark, except for a glowing red ball of light which was tossed from one to another of three little green devils, who accompanied their play with weird shrieks and laughs, while women drew closer to their escorts and shuddery cries of anticipation went up.

Abruptly, with a loud yell, one of the devils flung the red ball at the ceiling. It shattered, sent flames scattering about—and on the instant appeared the figure of Mephisto-Victor, all lighted in scarlet from below.

So strong was this light that it permeated the entire chamber, and showed, standing against a wall behind Victor, a massive stone coffin. Mephisto struck it with a trident which he held, and a luminous greenish light played on the coffin.

"A little entertainment which has been arrange' for you, my friends," declaimed Victor. "To show you ze power of His Majesty. Will you, over zere, kindly step up? You will not be hurt. We will kill you and bring you to life again—zis way, if you please!"

His trident darted out at Halsey, who stood in the front rank of spectators. There was a gasp from those around, then Halsey laughed and obeyed.

"I'll take a chance, Mephisto," he said cheerfully. "I'm so heavily insured, anyhow, that I won't have any luck."

THERE WAS a general laugh, and Halsey was placed inside the stone coffin, which stood on a raised step. He waved his hand at the spectators.

"So long, folks! If I don't come back, I'll see you later—there'll be a hot griddle ready for you all!"

There was another laugh. Suddenly the red light was cut off; Halsey was seen standing there, illumined by the greenish radiance playing around him. This died down and down into almost complete blackness, in which only his cuffs and his white shirt-bosom were revealed—then, all of a sudden, a woman uttered a gasp, and another cried out. "Look—look— his head—"

The head of Halsey had become a grinning skull—which moved slightly.

"Now he is dead!" proclaimed the voice of Victor, exultantly. "Now you see all ze pretty bones—"

A faint scream, a chorus of gasps. Where Halsey had been was now a skeleton, articulated, moving its hands. Halsey spoke whimsically, and the jaw of the skeleton moved in unison with the words, provoking fresh cries from the women, to whom the X-ray effect was ghastly enough.

"You folks seem to be getting more excitement out of this than I am—"

"Stop it!" cried out a tourist in startled alarm. "By the eternal, this is going too far—stop it! My wife's fainted!"

For some reason these words started a burst of laughter. In the midst, the lights were suddenly turned on, flooding the place with illumination—and the skeleton in the coffin was Halsey, indeed. He stepped forth, grimacing, and Mephisto swung up his hand for silence.

"Now back for ze coffee and *liqueurs,* my friends, and zen out you go, all of you!"

Warden looked for June Tully in the crowd. He had arranged with North and Sophie that any one of them who might be close to her, should breathe a warning about the *liqueur.* He saw that Sophie was close beside her, North a little distance off.

Victor had halted Halsey and was speaking rapidly to him. Warden saw Halsey's eyes sweep over the crowd and come to rest on him, with an expression of surprise. So Victor was telling him about the note!

Warden ignored the man, made his way to Sophie Haller, and they awaited their turn to ascend the stairs. North had slipped ahead. An instant later, Victor came to Warden and bowed, with a flourish.

"*M'sieur,*" he said in French, "if *madame* will pardon me and will excuse you, would you have the great kindness to give me a word in private?"

"Certainly," said Warden, surprised at the request, but finding no animosity in the man's words or air. "Another gentleman, perhaps, wishes to speak with me?"

"*M'sieur* has divined it," and Mephisto bowed. "There is a little room here at one side, if *m'sieur* will follow me. Your pardon, *madame*—I myself will escort you to your table."

Jimmy Warden followed his guide to a small, bare room separated by a curtain from the main chamber. He suspected that Halsey was curious and wanted a word alone with him.

"In two minutes, *m'sieur*," said Victor, and vanished, to hasten the crowd's departure.

Warden lighted a cigarette, patted the automatic in his coat pocket, waited until the shuffling feet and laughing voices had died down, and heard the music of the orchestra strike up a lively tune overhead. He put forth a hand to the curtain—then swung around at a slight, scraping sound. Somewhere beside or behind him a door had swung open. And all the lights had been switched off.

SWIFT AS thought, Warden dropped to the floor, heard an oath and a rush of something through the air, and flung himself at the curtain.

"Missed him, imbecile!" rasped a voice.

Warden was in the dark outer room now, but a body collided with him, caught at him; he rose, feeling hands tearing at his throat. Some one else rammed into him.

"All right, let the fool have it!" came a sharp order.

Abruptly, his assailants loosed their grip, fell away. Warden was left standing there alone. A sense of imminent peril held him paralyzed for a moment. There was utter silence all around.

What were they waiting for—to get his position? His hand crept inch by inch to his pocket, found his automatic, slipped it out.

Still silence. A minute passed, interminable with suspense. Warden breathed softly, naturally, heard nothing. He was certain now—they were only waiting to locate him. Good! Then let them have it, if they wanted it!

His left hand slipped up to his necktie, worked out his scarf pin, a heavy gold dog's head. He flipped it between thumb and finger, and it fell somewhere with a rattle. Instantly there was a spat of fire, then another two sharp, metallic sounds! Silenced revolvers, no doubt. A bullet ricochetted from the stone walls, with a thin whining scream.

Warden did not move.

Silence again; then a low voice in words he could not catch— some slang phrase. The stillness was jarred suddenly by noises from the floor above, the scraping of feet, the rise of voices. The company, then, was leaving.

Warden was considering, not merely his present situation, but his get-away. To escape by way of the stairs and the cabaret above was probably hopeless; yet there was no other egress from the cellar—or was there?

He recalled the little room whence he had just come, the scrape of a door; these other men must have come from some passage, then! And beyond doubt they had left the door open. He must try to find that curtain.

Besides, there was North upstairs. A shot would warn him, must warn him.

Venturing a careful step, then another. Warden reached out; yes, as he had thought, the curtain was within touch. Again a low voice, taking advantage of the upstairs noise.

On the instant, Warden fired—shot after shot, bullets plunging through the darkness, automatic spitting red flamespats, the barking roar of his shots filling the darkness with volleying echoed sound.

Whether his fire were answered, he did not know. He heard a man scream, but was already plunging through the curtained way, feeling for a door beyond. He came to it, collided with a man, fired point-blank into the unseen body and heard it fall heavily, the man groaning in the blackness.

Whither the doorway opened, he did not know, and could see nothing. He jerked at the door and it swung shut, heavily. Feeling for a hasp, he found a bar and shot it home. A moment afterward men were trying to open it from the other side, in vain.

Warden struck a match, saw that he was in a stone-walled passage, and discerned an electric switch on the wall. He touched it, and light flooded the passage, which turned a sharp comer ahead.

Warden stood motionless for a moment, found the extra clip he had brought along, and reloaded his pistol. Surely, he thought, the firing would bring any one who might be at the end of this passage! Yet no one came. Behind him was a pounding at the door, yet ahead of him all was silent.

Warden turned, looked at the heavy plank door, and deliberately placed a shot through it, waist-high. The pounding ceased. From the other side of the door came a thin sound that might have been the cry of a stricken man. Warden chuckled softly.

"Looks to me as though somebody were paying—and not Solomon's men this time!" he reflected. Then he started swiftly, alertly, along the passage.

CHAPTER IX

INTERROGATION—
ORIENTAL STYLE

TWO MEN sat in a very ornate library—the library, indeed, of Dominetti's villa in Boulogne. One of these men was Boris Glazunoff, tall, slender, sallow-skinned, with vivid black hair, sharp eyes, handsome features, and the air of a man of breeding. The second man was short, spectacled, smiling—the same Matsura, who had recently been in London.

The room in which they sat was on the west side of the house, its large bay window overlooking the garden. Now the blinds were closed; a double door at the far end opened on a small conservatory, filled to the very roof with all manner of flowering plants. A few bookcases stood about the walls, loaded with books in half a dozen languages.

In the center of the room was a large flat-topped desk, looking rather out of place among the other furniture, which included a Buhl table and secretary, massive chairs of carved oak and needle-point in the Louis XIII style, and a massive black oak receptacle built into the wall. The door of this last stood open, revealing shelves of various tobaccos and liquors.

Several solemn French portraits adorned the walls, and the ceiling was painted in graceful geometrical patterns. The room showed what the house was—the home of a wealthy family of a past generation, taken over and put to new uses.

Matsura sat at the desk, poring over papers under a desk-lamp. Boris Glazunoff was comfortable in a deep leather chair, smoking and sipping a drink that stood beside him. He looked lazy, very much like a snake basking in the sun.

"Clever trick," observed Boris. "So Dominetti got the letter, eh? And it had the one essential word cut out. Strange that you couldn't supply the word, Matsura."

"You are a scientist—and you looked blank when I showed it to you," said Matsura with a polite smile. He tapped the paper under his light; the same letter which June Tully had yielded up. "I conjecture that it must be a word of seven letters. It is a disk of some metal—I know not what."

"Cross-word puzzle without the crosswords, eh?" Glazunoff laughed quietly. "On the super-sonic wave proposition?"

The Japanese lighted a cigarette and leaned back.

"Yes. You followed that line of research, I understand? The audible limit of vibrations is, as you know, around forty thousand per second; this is sufficient for echo-detectors as used by the British and United States navies, but we must double or triple this number of vibrations. So far, nothing better suited for the purpose has been found than Langevin's slice of quartz rigidly held between two electrodes of three-centimeter steel."

"Exactly," drawled Boris. "Place your sandwich in contact with the water, with its controlling circuit—an electric spark exciting the oscillations. All very well for deep-water work, but the most fascinating point about it is that the sound-beam kills all the fish it touches. To make this beam kill men—well, it would need vibrations of a quarter of a million per second. Slight difficulty, eh? Did Loomis manage it?"

THE LITTLE man at the desk spread his hands.

"Apparently, yes—and Pearson has managed it, too. We know that instead of the 'sandwich,' as you call it, vacuum tubes can be used; but what can be used as a resonator, except the quartz slice? There's the rub. In this letter, Loomis thrice mentions a disk of—what? This disk vibrates in an oil bath on the principle of Wood's disk, with which four hundred thousand vibrations can be attained. Loomis speaks of the disk as being created by the fusion of two disks, with the vibrating axis as the shortest dimension. Therefore, metal must be meant."

"Quartz can be fused," suggested Glazunoff.

"Quartz is not the word here; it contains seven letters—I have measured the cut spaces, very carefully, and the typewriting is most even throughout the letter."

"Well, we should know to-night from one or the other," and Boris shrugged. "If Halsey were not infatuated with that woman, I'd have had it out of her before this. Let him I slip her the drug as he intends, and by the time she's been back here for an hour, she'll have lost all her will-power and resistance."

"She is a bright woman, and very dangerous," said Matsura suavely. "So you say she has not fought, has not tried to get away, but instead has made herself agreeable? And she went with him to-night quite willingly? Then look out for her, my friend."

Boris laughed. "Oh, I warned him, but the fool is infatuated. He can take care of himself, just the same. If she's playing him, he'll be playing her in another hour or so. She'll give him what he wants, and she'll give us what we want—"

"And so will Pearson," said Matsura. "In fact, I prefer making a man talk by force, to getting the information from the brain of a woman whose control has been broken by that damnable concentration of *cannabis indica!*"

A hint of passion shook Matsura's suave voice.

"Hashish itself is bad enough," he continued. "This concentrated product is devilish. My friend, a brain is a sacred object, a thing more delicate than any man knows. A crime against the brain is frightful to contemplate! Once thrown off balance, once the will is destroyed, who can be sure of any result? She might speak the truth, she might not. She will certainly be abnormal for a couple of days."

"Whereas, dealing with a suffering man, you know what you're getting, eh?" Glazunoff laughed and lighted a fresh cigarette. "Well, you have the night before you; and the moment you get what you want out of Pearson, my men are ready to work.

We'll put his little laboratory where it belongs—and whoever happens to be there, goes with it. You and your brain worship! That's because you're all brain yourself."

"Thank you for the compliment," purred Matsura. "It is a pity to destroy that workshop. Undoubtedly we should find experiments there, valuable papers, most interesting."

"Get inside if you like—I prefer to die otherwise," cut in Glazunoff, and rose. A faint bell had tinkled. "There's Halsey now, I expect."

Matsura put his papers together. Boris poured himself a fresh drink and went to the bay window, pushing aside the heavy velvet, silk-backed curtains. The beams of a car's headlights showed, just entering the garden—two men standing by the open gates.

"Halsey," and Boris drew the curtains again. "How long before the drug works on her?"

"That depends on the strength used," said Matsura. "An hour, perhaps less."

They waited, watching the entrance of the room, which opened upon the main hallway of the house. Presently voices were heard—men's voices, low, urgent, excited. Into the room came no woman at all, but Halsey, walking like a man drunk, supported by his chauffeur.

"What the devil!" exclaimed Glazunoff. "What's wrong, Halsey?"

"Dunno." Halsey lowered himself into a chair. His aristocratic features were blurred, his mouth slack, his eyes vacant. The chauffeur turned to Glazunoff.

"I DO not understand it, *m'sieur*. He was all right when he got into the car, with *ma'm'selle*. We were turning into Rue Remusat when she rapped on my window and said M. Halsey was ill. I stopped the car and found him like you see him now. As I was trying to revive him, she disappeared—went running into that café at the corner of Rue Mirabeau. If I had followed and brought her back, there would have been trouble; a couple of agents were at the corner. So I brought *m'sieur* on here."

"The devil!" said Glazunoff. Matsura had come to the side of Halsey and was examining him attentively. "What happened in Rue Jacob? Anything?"

"As we left, yes," replied the chauffeur. "It sounded like shots, muffled. There were a number of agents and plainclothes men from the *Sûreté* outside, too. Probably a raid of some sort. However, we got off before it happened."

Matsura looked up. He was smiling—that strange smile of the Oriental whose enjoyment of cruelty is supreme.

"I believe this is a most delicious joke, Boris," he said. "Halsey has taken the drug himself—you comprehend?"

Glazunoff swore. He caught Halsey by the shoulders and shook him savagely.

"Wake up, you fool!" he said, slapping the sagging face. "What happened, eh? Speak!"

Halsey looked up, vacuous, eyes rolling.

"Everything happened," he drooled, his head lolling again. "Man there—North—and 'nother man wanting to see me—Dr. Lee—"

His voice passed into a meaningless mumble.

"Let him be; it's useless," advised Matsura. "So our Chinese friend Lee was there, eh? I wonder why? Hard to make anything of this, my friend. And the woman is gone. Therefore, I suggest that we lose no time in getting to work on Pearson. We'll need both your big Russians."

"Right."

Glazunoff turned to the chauffeur, addressed him in Russian, and the man departed after a smart salute. Halsey remained limp in the chair, eyes open, but apparently insensate. Matsura looked at him and shrugged.

"He will be asleep until some time to-morrow—and of no use for a couple of days more. Better have him put to bed and out of the way."

Boris pressed a wall-button, and another man appeared, who was given the necessary orders. Boris returned to his neglected drink, Matsura returned to the desk. Within five minutes Halsey had been carried away—and into the room came Pearson, between two Russians of huge size. In their hands Solomon's English scientist looked like a pygmy.

He was a fairly small man, of singular appearance. His ill-assorted features and body suggested abnormality; from the high brow, the face tapered to a weak mouth and chin, which could be stubborn, but not strong. The eyes were wide-set, but now an expression of almost ungovernable terror was stamped in the whole face—aided by a large purplish bruise on his right forehead. His gaze fastened on Glazunoff, and he cringed; but it was Matsura who addressed him.

"Well, Mr. Pearson, I have come all the way from London to discuss a small matter with you. You do not know me, but that is quite immaterial."

MEETING THE suave, implacable gaze of those slightly oblique eyes, Pearson shivered. Then, with an effort, he gave tongue.

"I won't!" he cried out in a shrill voice, and made a ludicrous attempt to break from the grip of his two guards. "That devil there tried to make me tell—I won't! I know what it is you want, and you'll never learn from me!"

Matsura smiled.

"So we do not need to—how do you say?—beat about the bush, eh? That simplifies everything, my dear Pearson. You know, I have great respect for your researches, which I have followed in my own poor way for several years. You do not know me, perhaps?"

"Yes, I know you," said Pearson in his thin, high voice. "You're Matsura—the chap who was expelled from the University of Tokyo four years ago, and who went to Leningrad. And so you're working with Dominetti now, are you? I suppose you'll sell him out to the Bolshies, and make yourself a nice fat pile out of it!"

Matsura's eyes glittered—perhaps because Glazunoff gave him a glance and a lazy laugh.

"Come!" he said with less suavity. "You know what I want, my friend. You have found it, just as Loomis has found it; undoubtedly, his discovery improves upon yours."

"It does not!" cried out Pearson in sudden violence. "Loomis is a fool. He uses an oil bath, when he should use one of crude petroleum! And his fused disk is no better than my simple disk, when its curves are cut with care—"

He checked himself, glared at the smiling Matsura, conscious that he had nearly given away the secret.

"Perhaps, perhaps," said the Japanese. "And this disk is made of fused—what?"

"Damn you!" cried Pearson, the veins in his forehead swelling with passion. "You'll never know that, you yellow barbarian! Ah, that went in, did it?" A shrill laugh of triumph burst from him, as he saw how the shot told. "Ha, barbarian! You know the eye-film test, do you? How the rudimentary eye-film of reptiles is found only in the races most removed from all civilization— how it is found more frequently in Japs than in any other race? And what does that prove?"

Matsura responded to this childish, spiteful shaft in terrible manner.

"It proves that you will tell me the word I want to know," he said, "or you will suffer agony unbearable. You!" His hand swept up at the two Russians. "Tear the legs out of his body!"

The command was curt, carrying the lashing bite of a whip. It drove into Pearson, silenced his gibes, sent pallor creeping across his face.

The little Englishman tried to struggle—fought, kicked, bit. The two big Russians laughed, and a word passed between them. One of them caught Pearson about the shoulders—his arms were tightly bound behind his back—and held him thus, in a viselike embrace, motionless. The second man plucked up one leg, then the other, took one kicking leg in each hand, and with scarcely a visible effort began to force the two legs apart.

PEARSON CRIED out, madly, fell into oaths and foaming blasphemies, writhed and fought vainly in the grip of the two Russians. Then, abruptly, he fell silent and still; all his force, all his energy, was flung into resisting the ruthless arms that slowly wrenched his two legs wider and wider apart. His body trembled, quivered with the strain, sweat streamed from his pallid face, his eyes were distended, his mouth clenched.

"Stop!" commanded Matsura. The Russian checked himself, looked up. "Come, my friend, this is your last chance, remember. Save yourself and tell!"

"Go to—hell!" gasped Pearson.

"Proceed," said Matsura calmly.

The silent struggle was renewed. Again the legs of Pearson, bent upward at the knees, stiffened in every nerve and muscle, striving against the pressure of the huge hands of the Russian. Suddenly the Russian laughed, as he felt those strained sinews give to the pressure. A despairing cry burst from Pearson, then shrilled up into a wild, awful scream of agony.

"Stop!" commanded Matsura. "Quickly, Pearson! The disk?"

"Crystal!" wailed the tortured man. "Crystal, you devil!"

Matsura motioned to the Russians, gestured with his hand. They departed, taking the groaning, sobbing Pearson with them. Matsura sat motionless, an expression of stupefaction in his flat, spectacled face. Glazunoff lifted his glass and drank, then laughed softly.

"Crystal! Your word of seven letters—crystal!" said Boris, half mockingly. "The same thing you've been using—another name for quartz!"

Matsura started, shook his head.

"No," he said. "Fused, remember! Two disks fused into one. It can undoubtedly be cut and mounted so the vibrating axis lies along the diameter of the crystal; but there the frequency would be reduced with the ordinary crystal. With the fused disk—who knows? Worth trying. What about Pearson?"

"Is he of any further value?"

"No," said Matsura, with a slight frown. "We have his secret—no evasion this time. Alive, he is a menace to us. There's no telling how much he has discovered, for he must have been working on some protection against the ultrasonic waves."

Glazunoff touched the wall-button. A servant appeared.

"Send Signor Neri to me."

Presently a man appeared—a dapper Italian, who entered the room with a bow and stood waiting. Glazunoff went to the desk and scrawled on a sheet of paper the words, in Italian:

"Death to all traitors and enemies of Fascism!"

He handed the paper to the Italian, and sank back again in his chair.

"Take one of those Fascist knives," he said, "and this paper. Put the knife into the heart of the man Pearson, pinning this paper to him. Take the body in the large car out to the Bois, and leave it near the lake. Understand?"

Signor Neri bowed and departed.

"NOT BAD," commented Matsura, with a trace of admiration. "A Fascist murder—the victim an Englishman. There will be complications, eh?"

"Exactly," said Glazunoff. "That is Dominetti's idea throughout. You'll recall the riots not long ago when the French consulate at Livorno was mobbed? And a dozen other such incidents. This will react on London, of course. Our friends in Rome will be kept busy for a fortnight at least. And the twenty-fifth is only three days away, now."

"Very neat, all of it," said Matsura, with a complimentary intake of his breath, Japanese style. "And now, please—I have what I wanted. I must return to London at once. Will you telephone Le Bourget and have a special plane ready?"

Glazunoff shook his head.

"Against orders," he returned, taking down the telephone, and calling a number. "That has to be done by Baron Calvi—regular routine in this business. Hello! Boris speaking. Put me through to Baron Calvi, please."

There was a short wait.

"Boris speaking," pursued the Russian suddenly. "Report Halsey has been drugged, apparently by accident; safe in bed, but useless for a day or so. I secured the Englishman Pearson to-night and he was interrogated by Matsura; his body will be found in the Bois in the morning. We have found what we wanted—yes, the missing word. Matsura wishes to return to London immediately by air; will you have a machine ready? I'll send him out to Le Bourget. Orders?"

Glazunoff listened, then laughed.

"Yes, everything's in readiness. Santone is awaiting the word from me now. Very well."

He pressed down the instrument rack for a moment, called another number.

"Is this you, Santone? Boris speaking. Everything all right? You can go ahead whenever you choose—say, within an hour. Be sure and leave that Fascist pistol somewhere near the place— shoot it once or twice first."

Glazunoff replaced the instrument, took a fresh cigarette, and regarded Matsura with lazy insolence.

"Well, you have heard the orders, you have seen things set in motion; to-morrow you will hear the news of what has happened. Do you do these things better in Japan, eh?"

"I fear not," confessed Matsura politely. "In Japan, my friend, we have very efficient police."

"So does Paris," Glazunoff chuckled as he rose. "But we are superior to police. Come along. Get your things and we'll be off. I'll run out to Le Bourget with you."

"And leave the place with no one in charge? Remember Halsey—"

"Bah! We have men enough on watch, never fear! Ready?"

"In two minutes," returned Matsura.

CHAPTER X

SECRETS

JIMMY WARDEN, alone in the passage beneath the Abode of Bad Spirits, had not the ghost of an idea whither the passage led. Beyond, in the glow of occasional electric lights, lay the sharp turn; gaining this, he found ascending stairs that twisted off to the left. Still no one in sight.

"It's a cinch this leads somewhere," he reflected, "and evidently well out of this joint into some other underworld hole. And with these birds, whoever shoots first and talks afterward, comes out on top. So go ahead. James, and keep your eye skinned!"

The stairs ended in a door, of modern but massive construction. Gingerly opening this, Warden found himself facing a dark corridor, with a streak of light showing from beneath a door to the right. He entered the corridor, closed the door behind him, turned the key in the lock, and went on toward the thin streamer of light. He came to the door, listened, then stepped sharply to one side.

The heavy tread of a man was coming to the door. "Fools!" said a voice in Italian. "Shots, police in the street, devil knows what next—why aren't they back?"

The door swung open, and a man came out into the corridor. Warden had not the least notion where he was, or who might be in that room. A shot here might ruin everything unless it were needed—and it was not needed.

Standing to one side, he glimpsed a tall, thin figure, the delicate features of a poet or artist; then his fist crashed home to the angle of the jaw. The unfortunate Italian never knew what had hit him. He went down and stayed down, but the noise of his fall brought no one else.

Warden glanced into the room, found it empty, then turned to his victim. He dragged the limp figure into the light—only to rise, after a moment, soberly enough. In falling, the man had been hurled headlong against the wall, and some projection of the stones must have smashed his skull like an eggshell.

It was one thing to shoot a man, hot-blooded—another to kill him in this fashion. However, any feeling of regret Warden might have had, vanished swiftly enough once he considered the place in which he now found himself, and the recent activities of the late unknown.

The room proved to be large and long, two windows at the far end, no others. A long central table was loaded with a multitude of things, and illumined by two low-hung lights. The walls, run to the ceiling with shelves and cupboards, displayed many bottles in sight—at first glimpse, Warden thought the room some sort of laboratory. He went to the table and looked at what the Italian had evidently been doing—making up tiny packets of a white powder from a large glass jar.

Warden smelled it, crumpled it between his fingers, tasted it—and the meaning of this pleasant occupation broke upon him. Cocaine!

Then, recalling what the man had been saying, he strode quickly to the windows at the far end, pushed aside the curtains, looked out. The room was above the street, on the second floor— and several doors away from the café. He saw a crowd in the street below, caught the glitter of uniforms, but could make out no details.

Satisfied that the Bad Spirits were in good hands, he left the window and gave more particular attention to his surroundings. He had, at least, some little time before the former occupants of this place would return—and he was curious.

HE DROPPED into a chair, lighted a cigarette, and surveyed the long room with more attention; which, as it proved, was more than deserved. The burden of the table alone was most interesting.

A telephone stood close at hand. Aside from the apparatus of the snow merchant, one entire end of the table was piled with books, many of them open; books, chiefly, dealing with state documents—many of them rare and expensive works. The other end, about which several chairs were grouped, with a debris of cigarette butts, as though recently vacated by the gentry whom Warden had encountered, afforded more puzzling field for surmise.

Here were papers, letters, one of them half-written when interruption had come; some official stationery of the Paris Prefecture, and a large seal, also of the Prefecture—most astonishing stuff to be located here. A rack of pens and ink, a revolver fitted with a silencer—a cumbersome and lengthy weapon—and two curious keys strung on a piece of wire, completed the inventory.

"Hm!" reflected Warden, frowning a little. "The chap who was writing the letter dropped those keys on it—probably when he and his friends got the summons to come and get me. We might have a look at the letter."

Suiting actions to word, he pulled over the paper; the writing was in Italian, which Warden could read better than he could speak. When he had deciphered the unsigned and unfinished epistle, he sat staring at it blankly, startled beyond measure by its implications:

INSPECTOR LEBLANC:

At six in the morning a car will be awaiting you—not at your door, but at 51. Rue de Provence, just around the corner. It will contain a package. You will enter the car and be driven to the apartment of the man Ivan Vassilovitch, 42, Rue Theophille Gautier.

You will be in full uniform and will enter openly in your capacity as inspector of the *Sûreté*, taking the package with you. Ivan Vassilovitch is at the moment alone. You will shoot him, then place the contents of the package in his desk—the die in one drawer, the forged thousand-franc notes in another. You will then make your report that he attempted to resist arrest.

It is suggested that you report that Armand encountered you to-night and gave you one of the forged notes, stating that the man Ivan had changed it this afternoon with him. Armand will swear to this. You desired to question the man Ivan before making official report.

There the letter ended.

Warden blinked, then thoughtfully extinguished his cigarette. Leblanc, an inspector of the *Sûreté*, detective bureau of Paris, was evidently in cahoots with this precious gang; had probably furnished the note paper and seal of the Prefecture. As for this killing—

"The devil!" ejaculated Warden, sitting up. "Ivan Vassilovitch—why, that's Prince Ivan Salinoff, the grand old man of the aristocrats, the uncle and chief backer of Prince Sergei! Great Scott, that throws the whole damnable thing wide open! They murder Ivan, and they have the goods on him; forged bank notes, a life offense! They'll implicate Sergei somehow, and perhaps get him expelled from France. Sweet little system, this! This Armand is some merchant who'll back up this yarn by swearing that Prince Ivan changed one of the notes with him. The whole damned gang must be Reds!"

HE CAREFULLY replaced the letter as he had found it, glanced at the others, saw they were in Russian and beyond his powers. Then he rose to his feet and gave the walls a closer scrutiny. He paced up and down excitedly, wondering what he could do here, what he should do.

The shelves in sight held books, office equipment, odds and ends—nothing of any interest to Warden. He opened one of the cupboards, passed to the next; clothes, uniforms of various kinds, probably disguises. Then he halted. The next cupboard door revealed no clothes, but the front of a massive, old-fashioned wall-safe or cupboard, probably installed when this by-no-means-modern house was built.

What lay beyond this front of steel? Secrets, undoubtedly; Warden's hands clenched as he stood looking at it—how could he get past that barrier? Suddenly he started—he had observed that there was no combination lock here, merely a rounded knob for hand-grip, with a keyhole above and below. He tried it; the thing was locked.

Turning, he strode back to the table. Was it possible, indeed? Could the two keys so hastily dropped there—

Feverishly he tried them, found that they fitted the two locks. Already his whole scheme of action lay before him, half-formed, yet only awaiting the clarification of details. He knew that here he had only himself to depend on; Solomon was beyond reach; he had no idea where to find North.

If he could get out of this room and this house, well and good. The plotters would not suspect that he had possession of their secrets. The dead man lay in the corridor, certainly; but dead men told no tales. And if nothing here in this room was touched, they would think he had killed the man and fled.

If he had time! This safe might hold greater secrets than the mere life of a Russian prince, however important he might be.

The steel door swung open.

Warden saw before him a number of compartments or large drawers, none of which was locked. The face of these drawers was handsomely finished in inlaid woods, and the affair was obviously the relic of a generation when such things were most expensively done, but without proper regard for the wrong hands.

Pulling out a big drawer at the bottom, Warden discovered a large, heavy wrapped package, on which was penciled the name "Leblanc." This, then, was the promised packet of forged notes

The Italian never knew what had hit him.

and die. The companion drawer to this seemed to hold nothing but a mass of papers. Warden passed on to the smaller drawers.

These would have richly repaid an agent of the *Sûreté*, but yielded nothing of interest to Warden. There was a good deal of extremely valuable jewelry, with packets of thousand-franc notes which might be either real or forged; there were letters in Russian script, whole packets of them; and Warden remembered what Solomon had said to Prince Sergei about the blackmailing affairs of the grand duke. However, these meant nothing to him, and he completed his examination without finding anything which appeared worth the taking.

As a last resort, he returned to the mass of papers in the large bottom drawer. He lifted them out—then halted, transfixed by sight of the large envelope lying below. Upon that envelope was printed the seal of the United States, and the words:

DEPARTMENT OF STATE
Confidential

Jimmy Warden drew it out, left the papers where they were. He had never seen this word "confidential" so employed, but there were plenty of things in the diplomatic service of which he was beautifully ignorant. How had this envelope and its contents come here?

EXCITEMENT GRIPPING him. Warden took from the unsealed envelope a remarkably handsome booklet of a few pages bound in tooled morocco—a document specially bound. He opened it, then, thunderstruck, carried it over to the table for examination beneath the lights there.

For five minutes he scanned the surprisingly brief text of this document, looked at the signatures of the President, the Secretary of State, the Italian and British statesmen who had affixed seals and signatures. Then, appalled, stunned, Warden lighted a cigarette and fought for sanity. The thing was preposterous, incredible—yet here was the proof under his hand, an original of a treaty.

A secret treaty—which, made public, would blast France into uproar, revolution, war! Stocks would crash, finances would be brought low, armies would be set on the march—

"How in the name of all that's holy, could the President have signed such a thing?" thought Warden. He seized the signature page, scrutinized the seals and writing there, laid the bound document down again. "It wouldn't be legal unless ratified by the Congress—yet there it is—and these precious scoundrels have one of the originals!"

The pact was brief enough, concerning only the chance of war between Italy and France. In such an event, Great Britain and the United States bound themselves to close the Suez and Panama Canals, and the Straits of Gibraltar, to all ships of the belligerent countries. Very innocent on the face of it—but meaning that France was cut off from all colonial troops, that her navy in the Atlantic and Mediterranean was separated, that her stocks would go smash, her credit be broken, at the very outset of hostilities!

Suddenly Warden wakened to the situation.

Time must be growing short—they would be back here now at any moment. He closed the drawers and the safe, locked it, darted back to the table. There he dropped the keys again on the letter, replaced everything very carefully just as he had found it all. The treaty in its envelope he thrust into his side pocket, where it fitted snugly. A last glance around to make certain—

The telephone rang sharply, insistently.

Warden, already in the doorway, stepped on out into the corridor, then paused in the darkness there. The body of the Italian lay behind the open door, invisible. Why not answer the call, see who was on the line? It was tempting but the envelope in his coat pocket forbade any risks. They must not suspect this was gone. Undoubtedly it had been stolen from a courier, perhaps from an embassy.

"Damn that phone! Hey! Why in hell don't youse guys answer it?"

At the voice, at the words. Warden whirled around—then swiftly shrank aside behind the open door, as far as possible. Another door had opened on the corridor. Now, cursing, a man came into sight, shuffling into the lighted room, hurrying toward the table and the ringing telephone.

Even from a rear view, Warden could not mistake the symptoms—the ghastly complexion, the jerky movements, the twitch to hands and nostrils. A hophead, and an American at that. The man snatched up the telephone.

"HELLO!" HE snarled. "Yeah, this is Red Farrow speakin'—aw, can that stuff, will ya? Talk United States! No, there ain't nobody here, not a one. Who the hell are you? Oh!" His voice changed slightly. "Glazunoff, huh? Well, looks like I'm all alone. I dunno. I been asleep and just woke up."

Mr. Farrow looked astonished.

"Who, me? Well, I s'pose I can, sure. American girl, huh?

Green and silver... Yeah, don't worry; any girl from home stands out on these here streets like a sore thumb, believe me. I don't see where these French dames get off—they don't none of 'em ever wash except with perfume, and they ain't never heard of razors—huh? All right. Go ahead."

Red Farrow looked sulky, but listened. So did Jimmy Warden. He knew at once they were speaking of June Tully, from that description, "green and silver." Farrow made a response now that confirmed it.

"Got away from Halsey, huh? Then she's a slick one, feller—any skirt who can slip that bird deserves a medal! Sure you want her croaked, do you? Get me right, now! I don't want no come-back on this from Halsey, see? All right. Now, where's this here street—sure to be dark and empty, huh? Gimme the name of it; spell it out so's I can show it to a taxi driver, M-o-n-t-o-r-g-e-u-i-l—my good gosh, that ain't a name, it's a Chinese curse! All right. I'll get right up there. You say she'll be makin' for thirteen what? *Bis?* What the hell's that? Same as 'and a half'? Well, all right. Yeah, they's a gun right here on the table. But you mind, now—Halsey's got to be fixed, see? I don't want him takin' me for no ride, not him! All right."

Red Farrow hung up. Then, evidently, he saw the cocaine bottle and little twists of paper for the first time. An incredulous chuckle broke from him; rising, he pocketed all the twists that had been prepared, then dumped out half the contents of the jar into another sheet of paper and wrapped it up carefully.

"If this ain't luck!" he muttered.

Jimmy Warden, watching through the crack of the door, repeated the chuckle and the exclamation, but strictly to himself.

Red Farrow proved to be a rat-faced man, very thin and stooped, but sharp and alert in his motions. He helped himself to a liberal sniff of the white powder, then he took up the silenced gun and examined it. Once more Warden found himself tempted—and once more the envelope in his pocket gave him caution. One dead man might be found out in the hall, but he would have to shoot to be rid of this snowbird; and he did not want to shoot.

He wanted Red Farrow to show him the way out of here. Ahmed ben Zain would still be waiting, in the square before the church.

Some five minutes afterward, Mr. Farrow descended a short flight of dark stairs, pushed open a door, and emerged on the street—not the Rue Jacob, but a tiny little street behind it. He walked jauntily along, whistling cheerfully to himself, and did not abate either his whistle or his strut when two strolling agents turned a corner ahead and stood there under the light as he approached. He did, however, come to an abrupt halt when something touched him in the back—touched him very hard.

"UP, RED!" cracked Warden's voice. "Stick 'em up!"

Mr. Farrow obeyed. Warden called to the agents.

"*Messieurs!* Here is a dope runner—his pockets are full of cocaine, and he carries a silenced revolver. He is an American crook who is probably wanted. With great pleasure I turn him over to your care."

Mr. Farrow was promptly taken in charge and pinioned, despite his voluble curses, by one agent, while the other drew Warden aside and requested explanations, papers and passports in no uncertain tone of voice.

Warden, as North had instructed him, gave his name and the address of Solomon, producing a card and writing down the address. Somewhat to his surprise—even though he was long past surprises where John Solomon was concerned—the agent bowed politely and made no further requests. He accepted a cigarette, however.

"Do you, by any chance," said Warden, holding a light, "know one Inspector Leblanc of the *Sûreté?*"

"But of a certainty, *m'sieur,*" said the agent. "He is one of our officers, the most efficient. He spent some years in Italy and knows the Italians very well. He was largely concerned in the happy outcome of the Garibaldi incident some time ago—you may recall it?"

"Perfectly," said Warden. "Well, I advise you to look after this rascal; you may find that he has a record and is wanted in America."

The agent laughed.

"If so, America will be disappointed for some years to come, *m'sieur*. We in France are much less gentle with the peddlers of cocaine than you in America."

Warden bade the agent good night, and walked away. Clearly enough, the name of John Solomon was quite well known; but at that, no one who handed over a crook whose pockets were stuffed with snow would be too seriously questioned as to himself.

"Mr. Farrow is silenced and put out of the way; good!" thought Warden, and patted his coat pocket. "They'll probably think he bumped off the Italian, grabbed all the snow in sight, and lit out—it'll be several days at least before he gets in touch with any of the gang or they discover where he is. Which, if I may say so, is pretty neat work, James! Now we'll see if our car is waiting—and we'll keep an eye on Rue Montorgeuil ourself. So June got away from Halsey, eh? Good for her!"

Jimmy Warden did a little whistling on his own hook, as he emerged before the old church of St. Germain and discovered that the Hispano was still awaiting him.

CHAPTER XI

INSPECTOR LEBLANC

"GO TO the house of Solomon Effendi," said Warden to the Arab, "and wait in front of it. I expect some one to come there."

Soon they were purring up the quay to the Pont Neuf, then plunging into ancient Paris—a silent, medieval city at midnight, with its narrow streets; the madly hurtling taxicabs of daylight hours were gone now, pedestrians were few, everything was deserted and empty.

They came into Rue Montorgeuil and drew up before their destination. The great bronze gates were tight shut, not a light was visible.

At Warden's order, Ahmed ben Zain got out and pressed the button by the gates, but no answer came. No one opened.

Warden sat in the car where he could see the street in both directions. Would she come? Beyond doubt; the enemy were right enough in thinking so, and having heard the orders. Warden knew that for June Tully it was now a question of life and death indeed. He laughed softly.

At least, she had got away from Halsey—perhaps North had helped. But no! She was supposed to be alone, evidently. No matter; she was free, and therefore safe for the moment.

Upon Warden descended that comfortable, dangerous sensation, that feeling of everything being for the best and working out right, if only left alone. Perhaps Solomon's talk of "Providence" was not unjustified.

If North could only be reached—but that was impossible. Warden patted his pocket and thrilled to the feeling of the envelope there. What was he to do with this invaluable thing, at this time of night? It was well worth going to the Embassy, of course; yet he was more concerned with June Tully.

The signatures on that document, the text of it, had left him with a sort of stupefaction; the tremendous weight of responsibility had staggered him. It was literally true that in his pocket lay the course of history.

Publicity of this treaty would mean eruptions in France— riots, consulates attacked, furious outbursts in the Chambre des Deputes and the Senat, a government overthrown, perhaps revolution. International upheavals would follow, inevitably.

Dominetti was behind it, of course, and this nest of crooks was certainly headquarters for some of Dominetti's organization; they might have photographed the treaty already—but that would not be like publishing the actual document, having the original on view. No, they were checkmated now thanks to Jimmy Warden and luck!

"Voilà, m'sieur!"

The windows of the car were a little blurred; a thin, fine mist had begun to fall, hardly a rain, yet sufficient to wet the cobbles of the street. The reflection of a car's headlights was glinting against the glittering street—a taxicab, slowly crawling along, the chauffeur craning out to examine numbers.

Warden got out of the car and waited, and the taxicab came to a halt ten feet away. Fully visible in the glare of the headlights, Warden stepped forward—and heard a quick cry.

"Jimmy Warden!"

June was out of the taxicab, greeting him with a joyous eagerness that could not conceal her vivid relief.

"Pay him, Jimmy, please!" she gestured to the bearded, grinning chauffeur. "I picked him up away down in Auteuil, and I haven't a red cent—I was sure Solomon would arrange it."

"Our friend John has shut up shop," said Warden. "You climb into my car, and I'll settle the bill, then we can talk things over."

THE TAXICAB departed. Warden got into the Hispano, told Ahmed to await orders, and took June Tully's cool, firm fingers with a quick grip.

"Congratulations!" he said. "I don't know how you managed it, but—"

"I don't know how *you* managed it!" she broke in, laughing excitedly. "Listen, Jimmy: in that cellar some one whispered to me not to touch the *liqueurs*—I think that woman who was with you. Who is she?"

"A lady supplied by Solomon," said Jimmy Warden. "What do you care, anyhow? You wouldn't even look at me."

"I didn't dare," she cut in quickly. "I was afraid they'd spot you if I did. And when we got out, Halsey must have drunk the wrong cognac."

"He did; I changed the glasses on him," and Warden chuckled. "What happened?"

"He went to sleep in the car. I stopped it, and hopped out and ran."

June Tully broke into a peal of laughter which gave warning to Jimmy Warden. She had been through a lot that night, and must be under a tremendous reaction now.

"Then, after a wait in a café, I got that taxi and came here. You say Mr. Solomon isn't around?"

"Nope. He's out of town," returned Warden. He went on to make the situation clear as regarded himself and North, but did not detail his adventures of the night. "What you had better do," he concluded, "is go to a hotel and stick around until Solomon shows up."

"But listen, Jimmy!" she broke in. "I've no money, nothing! I came over here to take a position with Solomon—"

"And you hit right in the middle of a thunderstorm," said Warden. "You've got to take shelter until it blows over, that's all. As for money, forget it. I'm not broke, and so far as I can see, North has an unlimited expense account, so you'll be well taken care of. And let me tell you something pretty definite: Halsey may like you a whole lot, June, but Dominetti doesn't. You know that scientific formula or whatever it is—therefore, the orders are out to shut your mouth so you can't give it to Solomon. There was another gent expecting to meet you to-night—"

He went on to tell of Red Farrow and what had happened to that gentleman.

"Now," he finished, "the minute Dominetti learns that the damage is done, he'll forget all about you. I'll make it my business to see that he's informed of it, too. All straight so far?"

"Yes," she rejoined. "But, Jimmy, it's sort of hopeless! I don't know what's going on or just what I can do."

"Well, right now I'm going to land you at a hotel," said Warden. "They know me at the Hôtel d'Angleterre, and will take you in without baggage if I vouch for you. I have a date with North to-morrow morning at ten—this chauffeur, Ahmed ben Zain knows where it is. I've got to use the car earlier in the morning, but it will be at your hotel at nine thirty and you can trust Ahmed to the limit. Ahmed! Pay attention. I'll speak French for your benefit."

The Arab, in the front seat, slid back the dividing window and listened.

"At nine thirty in the morning, you be at the Hôtel d'Angleterre," said Warden. "Send up word to Miss Tully's room that you're there. Take her to where M. North awaits me, at the café in Boulogne. You understand?"

"Perfectly, *m'sieur*," said the Arab.

"Good. Go to the Hôtel d'Angleterre now."

THEY STARTED off through the misty rain. June Tully sat silent, her face showing a look of hesitant perplexity as the street lights flashed past. Warden, meantime, was determining his own course. He wanted sleep first, for he had to be up and about at an early hour if he was to put over the coup on which he had set his heart. Since the whereabouts of June Tully was now unknown to Dominetti's men, she was in security—and was a safer agent than any one else.

From his pocket Warden took out the envelope, and laid it in her hand.

"Here, June; this is a far more precious secret than the letter from Loomis," he said soberly. "Take care of it, and give it to North in the morning, if I don't show up. I'll be there if possible, but you never know what'll develop. Tell him he'd better take it right to the Embassy and get rid of it; he'll understand after he looks it over."

"But where will you be?" demanded the girl anxiously.

"Lord knows!" Warden laughed in his cheerful manner. "I'm off on the trail of something interesting. If I don't show up in the morning, I'll be there in the afternoon. Tell North, and he'll know I'm busy. The main thing with me, young lady, is your safety; that's why I'm in this whole game."

She was silent for a little. Then, unexpectedly, without the least warning, he felt her crumple against him, sobbing.

"Oh, Jimmy!" she cried, as his arm went around her. "I—I'm not so silly, as a rule, but I've been afraid—it's just the reaction. I tried to play a part with Halsey—tried to make the best of things, and smile, and make him think I liked him—but it was terrible! And the other men there—that horrible Glazunoff, who looks like a snake! At first, when he came aboard the boat and said he'd been sent by Solomon who was in London, I believed him. But he frightens me. He just isn't human. I know that awful things have been going on in that house, too—I don't know what. I could feel it in the air. And now, to have you show up when I needed you most—is just too much—"

Warden patted her shoulder.

"Those are sure welcome words, June," he exclaimed happily. "You'll have another chance to say 'em, too, when you're sure of what you're saying. Lots of chances! Everything's coming out all right, so you buck up and get a good night's sleep, and to-morrow you'll be able to do some shopping, and get clothes and things. There's our hotel now; rather, yours. I'm staying at a place down near the Madeleine."

It was not difficult to see that the girl was on the verge of a breakdown, and small wonder. However, she pulled herself together, and was smiling when the hotel porter opened the car door, and she descended with Warden. As he was known at the hotel. Warden had only to present his card and explain that *madame* could not get her luggage until the morrow; and in a very few minutes the matter was arranged.

"Good night, young lady—pleasant dreams, and sleep hearty!" Warden smiled into her level eyes and marveled at their regained poise. "See you to-morrow; and above all else, keep that envelope safe. Good night!"

"Good night, Jimmy—and thanks for everything," she returned simply.

Warden returned to the car and paused before getting in.

"To our hotel, Ahmed," he ordered. "Grab some sleep, and show up at five thirty sharp—not a minute late. Understand?"

"Perfectly, *m'sieur.*"

"Have you a gun?"

The Arab's teeth flashed. "Two, *m'sieur.*"

Warden laughed as he got in and the car rolled away. He had good reason for laughter; June Tully safe, a night's work of triumph behind him, the enemy outwitted and hoodwinked at every turn, a keen, sharp game waiting him in which he held all the trumps—yes, he had every reason for exultation!

"This Dominetti gang isn't so confounded terrible," he reflected, as he alighted at his hotel and went to his room. "I've put it over on 'em from the start, with considerable aid from the goddess of luck. And in the morning—"

IN THE morning, with a thin rain falling and promising to continue for a solid day or two, Warden dressed and found the Hispano awaiting him at the door.

"Go to 51, Rue de Provence," he told the alert Arab. "Stop there and stay close at hand when another car shows up. You might drop by a café on the way, for a cup of coffee and a roll, but make it snappy."

The street in question, in the old section behind the Hôtel des Ventes, was not far away, and at a quarter before six Ahmed halted the car at the proper number. This was an old building now converted into rooms and offices. Except for an occasional truck or cab, the street was empty at this hour.

Warden, keenly expectant, enjoying with every fiber of his spirit, the desperate game upon which he had embarked, left the car and was standing smoking at the curb when he saw the big Mercedes of Halsey approaching.

He waved his hand, and the Mercedes drew in behind his Hispano. The chauffeur was a trim, swarthy Italian, who regarded him with open suspicion until Warden spoke.

"Orders to intercept you, my friend!" said Warden cheerfully. "We just had word that Signor Dominetti is coming by special plane from London and will reach Le Bourget in an hour. You're to meet him there, and I'm to take care of Leblanc and his little errand in Rue Theophile Gautier."

The Italian gaped for an instant.

"Eh, *m'sieur?* And who are you?" he stammered, taken aback by mention of these names.

Warden waved his cigarette with a smile. "I? Oh, a mere American—a friend of M. Halsey. By the way, is he still asleep, eh?"

The chauffeur grinned, and flung aside any further suspicion.

"You heard about that, eh? *Diavolo!* They say he sleeps like the dead! He hasn't heard a thing yet about the work in Rue Jasmin."

"In which he and I are one," returned Warden. "What work?"

"That accursed house, or laboratory, or whatever it is," said the Italian. "We blew the back of it to hell and burned the rest, last night. And the Englishman there is lying in the Bois now, unless they've found his body. To-morrow's newspapers will have some furious denunciations of the Duce, I promise you! All the work of these abominable Fascisti, and so forth. Well, I'd better be moving if I'm to make Le Bourget on time, eh"

"Yes," said Warden. "Wait—take a message to Signor Dominetti or Halsey or Glazunoff, no matter which. Say that the American girl has reached protection and has told all she knows to Solomon or his agents."

The Italian's brows lifted. "So they didn't get her, eh? I thought Basil was a fool, to trust it to them. He should have used surer men. Right, comrade—until soon!"

And with a wave of his hand he threw in his gears. Ahmed, who had listened impassively, touched Warden on the arm; his eyes were wide.

"You heard, *m'sieur?*" he said in a low voice. "About the laboratory in Rue Jasmin?"

WARDEN NODDED. Clearly enough, Solomon's predictions had been fulfilled—Dominetti had landed a blow, and a heavy one. If some such thing had been foreseen, why had not Solomon guarded against it? But perhaps he had—no doubt, indeed, he had taken precautions. Dominetti had simply got ahead of him.

"Drive past that way from here," he said to Ahmed. "In any case, there's nothing we can do. Ah, there's our man now! I'll give you the address when I land him safe."

A smartly turned out figure had turned the corner—the figure of an inspector of the *Sûreté*, in full uniform, carrying a parcel. Ahmed got behind the wheel, while Warden strode forward. At sight of him, Leblanc paused, then came on. He was a wide-shouldered little man, with enormous mustaches which lent him the deceptive air of fierceness so coveted by the hirsute Frenchman. Warden saluted him cheerily.

"Good morning, Inspector Leblanc! It is for you the car is waiting, no doubt?"

"But of a surety, yes," returned the officer, his eyes very sharp on Warden. "And you—"

"M. Warden, an American, a friend of M. Halsey," said Warden. "I'm to take you to Rue Theophile Gautier, *m'sieur*. May I relieve you of that package?"

"A thousand thanks." Leblanc was affable at once, and turned over the package to Warden as he entered the car. "You are, then, one of—"

"One of many," and Warden laughed. "Ahmed! To 42. Rue Theophile Gautier; pass by Rue Jasmin, and show M. Leblanc what has happened during the night."

As the car rounded into Rue Lafayette and headed for the Etoile, Leblanc turned in some surprise.

"What has happened? What mean you, *m'sieur?*"

"Another Fascist outrage," Warden grinned. The other broke into a laugh of comprehension as he accepted a cigarette.

"So! That is interesting, very. These accursed Fascists! They have ruined Italy."

"Entirely," agreed Warden, keeping his gravity with an effort. "Poor Italy! You spent some years there, I believe?"

"Five years, *m'sieur*. My family is of Italian origin," said Leblanc.

Eying the package, Warden sniffed in contempt. It still bore the penciled name of the inspector—crude work! His disdain for these conspirators increased as he reflected on the ease with which he was handling this very ingenious but poorly managed murder plot. How Dominetti had attained such a terrible reputation was more than he could comprehend, if this affair were a sample of his work.

They bowled along at a fast pace through the Étoile and out toward Passy. Leblanc said nothing, but smoked in silence; from time to time he directed a quick glance toward Warden, as though puzzled by the activity of this American.

AT LENGTH they were descending the grade of Avenue Mozart, but on reaching Rue Jasmin, Ahmed merely turned in past the Metro entrance, then applied his brakes. Looking down the short street, all three men saw that it was blocked by a crowd and by fire apparatus. Where the laboratory had stood was now only a smoking heap of ruins, with two gaunt fragments of wall standing high in air.

"No use going on there, Ahmed," said Warden.

With a nod, the Arab swung around the Metro curb, crossed the avenue, and started down Rue Ribera. Then Leblanc pointed to a café at the far end of the little street.

"Before we go farther, my friend," he said, "let us stop there. To tell you the truth, I received the instructions rather late, and my *concierge* did not bring my morning coffee. A *café fine* would, I believe, materially assist the campaign."

"By all means!" said Warden affably. "Two, if you like!"

He gave Ahmed the order to halt at the café, and as they approached, saw that it was one of those places catering to the trade of taxi drivers—a *rendezvous des chauffeurs*. Three cars stood before it, and as the Hispano halted. Warden was not astonished to find four or five men clustered at the tiny bar inside. As he was opening the car door. Leblanc checked him.

"One instant, *m'sieur*, is it possible that you are aware of my errand?"

Warden nodded, as he met the dark, piercing eyes.

"But naturally," he returned. "If you have need of any assistance—"

"Oh, not at all! Come, then, let us descend."

They walked together into the café, the assembled chauffeurs eying the inspector with evident hostility. Leblanc passed to the rear end of the bar, and ordered a *café fine*, then turned to Warden with a slight smile beneath his huge mustache.

"You do not perceive the joke, *m'sieur?*"

"Eh?" Warden's brows lifted. "The joke? What joke?"

"Why, just this, *m'sieur!*" Leblanc grinned and dug an elbow into his ribs. "The excellent jest—the fact that you did not read the postscript to that letter, which was not written until later! I shall let you read it, presently."

And, as Warden was striving to comprehend the meaning of these words, as he was groping with startled senses for realization, as he became conscious of the malice and grinning triumph in the leering features of Leblanc—the sky fell upon him.

He reeled and dropped, not even hearing the swift, sharp scream of Ahmed, in the car outside.

CHAPTER XII

A FOOL TOURIST

WHEN WARDEN opened his eyes, he found himself tied very efficiently to a chair, and sitting in the back room of the café, as the casks and racked bottles testified. Two men in chauffeur's cap and dust-robe sat smoking languidly and regarding him, as they chatted in slang phrases.

"He's awake," said one. "Go tell the pretty officer."

The other slouched out, and in a moment Leblanc came into the room. He stopped, looked at Warden with a grin, and cocked his head on one side.

"Well, well! A good hit, Scorpion," he observed approvingly. "Didn't even draw blood, and yet it knocked him cold. You're an artist, my boy. So, M. Warden, you appreciate the nice little joke, eh? We'll have to let you read the postscript to that letter here, it'll keep you quiet while I go to knock off that rascally Russian. Give him a drink, one of you, and keep him quiet until I come back. Where's that chauffeur of his?"

"Emile took him and his car—drove off with him," said one of the two. "To Boulogne, I suppose."

Leblanc nodded. From inside his tunic, he drew forth a letter, opened it, and spread it on a cask just to one side of Warden, so the latter could read it at leisure. Then, with a mocking salute, the inspector departed.

One of the two men came with a glass of vile cognac and held it to Warden's lips. The fiery stuff was invigorating; Warden's head cleared, despite the dull aching pain from the blow behind his ear, and he pulled himself together.

Fool that he was! Had the whole thing been a frame-up, then? He cast his eyes on the letter, and found it to be the same unfinished epistle that had lain on the table the preceding night. Now, however, it had been finished, with a postscript written in another hand. The words of it burned into Warden's brain:

> P.S. These orders have possibly been read by an American, one M. Warden; we cannot be certain of it. We have taken measures to safeguard you in any emergency. If Coccini meets you in the morning, all is well. If Warden or another meets you, then take him to the café at the corner of Ribera and La Fontaine and he'll be attended to properly. We want to get hold of this Warden if possible. He is the kind to play a lone hand, so we may be able to gather him in and also dispose of the man Ivan.
> Dictated by the chief, taken down by E.C.

The "chief"—that must be Dominetti! Then the wily Italian must have come back to Paris during the night. Or else Glazunoff was the chief. Impossible to say.

Fool! Warden's eyes closed and he cursed himself and his folly bitterly. His scheme had been simple and good—to accompany Leblanc to his destination, then put a pistol to his head, identify himself to the Russian by means of the letter from Prince Sergei, have Leblanc collared by the police—a full *exposé*, which would involve a police raid on the room in which Warden had made such astonishing discoveries.

Now, this was all wiped out. They had not been sure about his having entered that room, but they were taking no chances— and as a result, he had fallen slap into the pit which he himself had digged.

"I was pretty cocky, sure," thought Warden bitterly. "Took 'em for a pack o' fools. Huh! I walked right into their hands."

Well, it was done and no help for it. The most important thing of all was that June Tully was safe. She could not join North unless Ahmed took her to the café; Warden recalled now that he had only mentioned the place casually, depending on the Arab to take her there.

Thus, if Ahmed also had been trapped, as seemed most likely, June Tully could only remain at her hotel and await some word—and only Warden knew where she was.

THIS RECOLLECTION made him twist in his seat, wrench at his bonds, uselessly. Luckily, he had given her what money he had—three or four thousand francs. The two men watching him grinned at his struggles, and one of them spoke mockingly.

"This bird has remembered something, what? Let's see what's on him, comrade. Emile got whatever pickings were on the chauffeur and the car—it's our turn to pluck this rooster while we have the chance."

The other nodded. Warden made no resistance, said nothing as they came to him and went through his pockets. These words had shown him that Ahmed ben Zain was also trapped, and he knew the worst. There was only one streak of good luck in the whole wretched business—that impulse that had caused him to give June Tully the treaty.

Finding themselves only scantily rewarded for their work, the two grumbling rascals left Warden's papers alone, but took his other possessions and divided them, squabbling over his watch and scarf-pin and cigarette case.

"Skip with them," said the Scorpion, suddenly giving up the argument. "There's plenty of time before Leblanc can get back. Run down to the Chat Noir and sell the lot, and get back here; we'll divide the loot, and if you tell any lies about it I'll find them out. Then, if this bird squeals to Leblanc or the chief, we won't be caught with the goods."

"Brilliant, my old one!" was the response. "Back in half an hour."

The Scorpion was a man of fifty—a yellow-haired Norman, heavily built, crafty of eye, with a sour and greedy visage, but intelligent above the average of his ilk. His companion gone, he settled down to read a folded newspaper which he produced from his pocket.

"You're losing time," said Warden suddenly. The other looked up, scowled, then regarded him attentively. "True, I had no money on me—but money can be obtained, my friend. That is, in exchange for a service."

The Scorpion grimaced.

"No, no, my little one!" he growled. "Pinched you are, and pinched you stay. I have an unfortunate prejudice, me, against waking up in the morning to find a knife in my back, and St. Peter beckoning me forward."

Warden chuckled. "At least, give me a cigarette, and a cup of coffee. After all, we might do business."

"Not if it involves your liberty, my fat one! That's final."

The Scorpion rose and went into the café, returning with a glass of black coffee. This he aided Warden to drink, following it with a cigarette and a light. The man was avaricious enough, plainly so, but stood in healthy fear of his associates. Bribery might accomplish something, but winning freedom was out of the question.

"Come, let us consider the matter reasonably!" said Warden, between puffs. "You're a man of sense, and you know the certain advantage of having five thousand francs, cash, in your pocket. I can provide the cash, if you provide the pocket. Eh?"

The Scorpion folded up his newspaper, put it away, and chuckled.

"I like you, my American—what a pity that you're on the other side of the fence, you and your dollars!" he said. "I'd make some money out of you if I had the chance; but me, I do not like to take risks with our crowd, you comprehend."

"Naturally not," agreed Warden cheerfully. "You can't set me free; that's understood. However, there are other ways of earning money, less riskily. Let's see, now. What about the delivery of a letter at ten o'clock in Boulogne?"

"Hm! All things are possible, with the saints aiding," said the Scorpion cautiously. "But in my estimation two letters are better than one."

"Why two?" asked Warden.

The other man grinned.

"The first, to deliver five thousand francs to bearer. The second—what you like."

WARDEN LAUGHED, then reflected swiftly. North was undoubtedly, by this time, trailed by Dominetti's agents, therefore small harm would be caused by revealing his rendez-vous. This rascal might never deliver the message at all—here was a risk that must be run. If he did deliver it, then much would be gained.

"Very well," said Warden. "Give me pencil and paper."

The Scorpion grunted. He produced a stub of pencil and a few sheets from Warden's own notebook, and laid them on the cask within reach. Then, passing behind Warden, he began to unfasten the knots of the rope.

"Don't turn around, my friend," he warned. "I'll be sitting in the corner behind you, and one move out of your easy chair will get you plugged."

"Right," said Warden, recognizing that the man would take no chances whatever if he made one false motion. Any attempt at escape would be rank folly.

He felt the rope loosen, and next moment his arms were free. He took pencil and paper and wrote two notes:

> NORTH:
> Pay the bearer five thousand francs for the delivery of a second message.
>
> J. WARDEN
>
> NORTH:
> Have been pinched with Ahmed. See that you don't make any mistakes likewise. If I don't return. I bequeath you my gold-headed cane and my debts; kindly pay my account at the

Hôtel d'Angleterre. The bearer is a good fellow, but look out
you don't meet him on a dark night.

WARDEN.

"All right," he said.

The Scorpion came up behind him. For an instant Warden
considered taking a long chance, but one hand held a pistol to
his neck while the other arranged the rope around his arms and
drew it tight. Then, swiftly, the Scorpion took the rope in each
hand and knotted it, and the chance was gone.

"Now let's see what we've produced," observed the hulking
rascal, picking up the two notes. "This ought to beat the *Prix
Goncourt*, eh? That is, for cash results. Hm!"

"You read English?" said Warden, seeing the Scorpion looking over the notes.

"Why not? Don't you read French, my little one? Well, these
look all right to me—you're a smart one, and no mistake! Whatever you wanted to say, you've hidden it well. I don't think the
chief would find this worth any five thousand balls."

"No," said Warden dryly. "He certainly wouldn't get anything
out of it, so it'll pay you to play straight with me. Who's the
'chief'—our friend Glazunoff?"

The Scorpion nodded, carefully folded the notes and pocketed them, then resumed his seat and his newspaper. So far as he
was concerned, the affair was finished—except for the delivery
of the notes. Warden described North, and gave the location of
the café, and the Scorpion nodded again with great unconcern.

If the message were not delivered, no damage would be done.
If North got it, he would at once seize on the mention of the
Hôtel d'Angleterre and a little investigation there would put
him in touch with June Tully.

This much accomplished, Warden relaxed in his chair and
breathed more freely. He now knew that Glazunoff wanted
him alive and unhurt, probably for questioning, so he was in
no immediate danger. The loss of the treaty would probably
go undiscovered for some little time, and in any event June

Tully would take care of it. If she failed to reach North, and if Warden did not return, she would probably take it to the Embassy herself.

"She will, too; she's the kind that doesn't need words of one syllable," thought Jimmy Warden. "So we might as well make the best of things and not worry. They've got me, but that doesn't mean they've won much!"

THE SECOND man came stamping in, and jubilantly exhibited a sheaf of hundred-franc notes. A folding board and a pack of cards were produced from the front room, with another drink all around in which Warden was included most generously, and the two rascals settled down to pass the time comfortably and profitably.

"I came back by Rue Theophile Gautier," said the second man, as he shuffled the cards. "There was a crowd around Number 42, and Leblanc was strutting about with a gang of his accursed agents. He must have bumped off the old Russian neatly."

"He's a neat worker," commented the Scorpion. "But he knows too much. If he went against us, he could turn us all in."

"And if he did that, my old one," said the other complacently, "he'd have a knife sheathed in his belly inside of two hours— which he knows very well. So save your worry, and let's begin winning some of your money."

Warden's jaw set hard at this information. Prince Ivan murdered! And it was his own fault that the plot had been put through. He realized, bitterly enough, just what John Solomon had meant by his talk of "mistakes." If he had turned over his information promptly to the prefecture, instead of trying to play the game himself, then—

"Then I wouldn't be sitting here, and a better man would still be alive," he concluded morosely. "Wonder how long this will keep up?"

The same thought was in the mind of the Scorpion, who gestured to the prisoner.

"Any orders about him? What did Leblanc say?"

"Emile will bring back instructions," said the other carelessly. "Otherwise, we wait till Leblanc shows up."

"Well, I don't wait longer than nine, me," announced the Scorpion. "I have to pick up my accursed Englishman at nine, remember. He's too good a meal-ticket to lose."

The other gave him an envious look.

"You're a lucky dog, Scorpion! To have a fool of an English tourist engage you for three hours every morning, and at a flat rate, too! These English tourists don't tip. When you take this *saligaud* around and show him the sights and act as guide, and don't have to depend on an English tip, I call that luck!"

"You well may," said the Scorpion complacently, and twisted his mustache. "That's what comes of speaking English, my friend. He's a fool, like all Englishmen, but he pays well and asks only that I show up promptly and take him over a different route every morning. He lives in that *pension* up the street, and he has money, too. Well, to work!"

The precious pair fell to their game. Presently, at another interval, the second man gave the Scorpion a crafty look, and winked.

"You say this Rosbif is a fool, and has money? Listen, my old one! What's to hinder, eh? You and I—that is to say, if he carries enough to make it worth while—"

The Scorpion became vehement, incensed, furious.

"What, propose such a thing to me? Is it, then, that I am not a man of honor? Devil take you for a rogue! My Englishman drinks with me in cafés, I tell you. He trusts me. He is a fool, but he knows that I do not make a fool of him. Name of a dog! He's always buying a drink. He likes cafés, bars, every little rendezvous. True, he is an Englishman, but all the same we are friends. And my honor is my honor."

"Obviously," said the other with heavy sarcasm. "And you are touchy about it, eh?"

"Besides," went on the Scorpion, without heeding the interruption, "you remember that our instructions from the chief are very clear. We are to be ready for orders at all times, and we are not to engage in any little enterprise on our own hook. If we do, then we are lopped from the pay roll. It would not be wise to forget these instructions."

"That is true," said the other more soberly. "But when I see some of these tourists and how they disregard good money—I tell you, my mouth waters!"

"Wipe it on your cuff, then, and get on with the game," said the Scorpion rudely.

THE GAME progressed, while Warden sat watching the two men. His bonds were not too tight, and he was in no great discomfort except from the blow behind his ear, which had caused a blinding, swirling headache.

He perceived that these men and their recent companions were, so to speak, on the outskirts of Dominetti's "mob." Probably they had never even heard the name of Dominetti. They were used for such purposes as the present one, looked up to Glazunoff as the *patron* or boss, and were very little, if at all, acquainted with the general business of Dominetti and his agents. Except for the salient fact that they had a most healthy fear of getting a knife in the back.

Suddenly there came interruption—a voice from the café.

"Name of a name! Where's every one, Ignace?"

"In the back room," was the response.

The card game instantly ceased. The two players exchanged a significant glance and swept out of sight the piles of blue and yellow bank notes. Evidently they did not care to have their wealth observed.

A man strode in, leaving the swinging door half ajar. The Scorpion looked around.

"So, Emile!" he exclaimed. The newcomer was, like the others, an obvious chauffeur. "You landed that fellow, eh? No trouble?"

"Not a bit." Emile turned toward the outer room.

"Ignace! Give us a *fine* all around! And honest Martell, too; none of your rot-gut! I've got the cash, me."

"Then you'd better split with us," suggested the Scorpion. "You got some pickings from that car, did you? Excellent."

"Go to the devil," said Emile, with a glance at Warden. "You've got the pickings off this bird, so forget it. No, no! *Ta bouche, toi!*" he cried furiously, as the Scorpion seemed about to argue the matter. "Forget it! We draw a hundred francs each for the job. One of us has to stay here with this chicken until noon, and gets an extra hundred. The chief will send for him at noon. Now, then, which of us gets the extra hundred?"

"I'm out of it," said the Scorpion, with a shrug. "I've got my steady—three days, now, I've run this Englishman around, and he stays for another three weeks, at least. Me, I stick to him."

"Then we'll draw cards for it," said Emile to the third man, who readily assented.

The cards were spread out, with much wrangling and furious discussion in the eloquent and passionate Gallic manner. The proprietor, Ignace, entered with a tray of drinks and stood looking on with interest; he was a big fellow with a scarred chin and curled mustaches. At length it was settled, Emile winning the lucrative honor of remaining as Warden's guard until noon.

Another man came stamping in and joined the party. He, too, was a chauffeur, and ordered a drink added to those on the tray. Ignace went to fetch it.

"WELL, LEBLANC turned the trick like a good one," announced the new arrival, in a low voice. "I was just up there and stopped for a bit of talk. They say he plumped two slugs into the old Russian. Wish he'd do it to every damned Russian taxi driver in the city! An honest Frenchman hasn't a chance to make a living these days, what with Russians and Serbians and these cursed—"

"Get to business, now!" growled the Scorpion. "What happened up there?"

"Search me, little one. It seems the old Russian was caught

with forged notes; or they were found. He drew a gun and Leblanc popped him off. That bird probably planted the forged notes; remember the package he was carrying?" The speaker grinned. "Clever fellow, Leblanc! He'll draw down a fat wad from the chief for this job, and from the other side he'll get promotion and what not! That's working it both ways, eh? Ignace! Where's that cognac?"

Ignace came in, leaving the door ajar. The outer room was empty.

The men stood about, sipping their cognac and discussing Leblanc's cleverness. Warden was given a drink with the others—and he did not miss the appraisal in their eyes, the lack of humor, the half-pitying manner. They had no fear of talking freely before him. They were quite certain as to his ultimate disposition, evidently.

So interested grew the discussion that none of them heard a step in the other room, or a voice lifted in English.

"Dang it! Ain't there no one around?"

Warden stiffened. Impossible! Yet he seemed to recognize that voice. The speaker rapped on the bar with his knuckles. The Scorpion looked around through the doorway, then sprang to his feet.

"Name of a name—it is my Englishman!…'Allo zere, my friend! I am coming, me!"

He started for the doorway. There, however, looking in upon the room, stood a pudgy little figure, whose blue eyes rested blankly upon Warden for an instant—checking with their lack of all recognition the cry that came to the American's lips. Then the Scorpion caught the little man by the arm and propelled him out of sight.

"Zis is ze good luck, my friend!" came his voice. "I was on ze point of going to your *pension*. Come, ze old bus is here outside. But we will not drink in zis place. It is no good—"

The voices died out, and they were gone. But, for an instant. John Solomon had stood there looking in upon the back room—

John Solomon, the "fool English tourist" who was the Scorpion's meal ticket!

CHAPTER XIII

AN IMPRISONED ENVOY

NOON APPROACHED.

Since Solomon and his unsuspecting guide had departed, James Warden had been sitting there with no other companion than the brutish taxi driver, Emile—a man who talked not at all, grunted when addressed, and played interminable solitaire when he was not reading old newspapers.

The shock of seeing John Solomon here had at first inspired hope in Warden, but this gradually died away. Solomon had looked at him and departed without a word or gesture probably no less astonished to see Warden sitting tied to the chair than was Warden to see him.

So this was the Scorpion's sucker "tourist!" Then, instead of being out of town, Solomon was hiding in some little *pension* near by. Why? And why had he engaged the Scorpion for three hours of aimless driving each morning?

"Ask me something easy, James," said Mr. Warden to himself. "Does John know that his Scorpion taxi driver is one of Dominetti's gang? Probably not—but he knows it now. As North says, there's no earthly use in trying to account for anything Solomon does, so we might as well give it up. And since he saw me here, he knows I made a mistake; and that probably settles my hash so far as he's concerned. He could send a couple of his Arabs to set me free, or tip off an agent of the *Sûreté*—but will he?"

As time drew on, it became sadly evident that Solomon had

done and would do nothing of the sort. Surely the little cockney could not be actually in hiding! Yet so it seemed.

Noon arrived. The outer room was filled with men, workmen and chauffeurs. Steps sounded, and into the room came a gentleman who swung his stick indolently and eyed Warden with a fleeting smile. It was the man whom Warden had encountered in the lounge of the Savoy in London. Emile came to his feet.

"Good day, M. Glazunoff," he said. "Here is your friend, awaiting you."

Glazunoff nodded. "So I see. M. Warden, this is scarcely a good place for quiet conversation. I suggest that you give me your parole to come with me peaceably, and we shall then not have to use force."

"To the Boulogne Villa?" asked Warden.

"Exactly."

Warden gave his assent. He had, as a matter of fact, no choice in the affair; to refuse would only be to make his position worse. It was not difficult for him to understand June Tully's fear of this man before him—this pallid creature of unemotional mien and reptilian eyes. The suggestion of inhumanity about Glazunoff was a clear enough index to the man's cold cruelty.

"Loose him," Glazunoff said to Emile, and paid the latter his wage. "Then, while he comes out to the car with me, keep close with your gun. Shoot at his first move to get away."

WARDEN STOOD up and stretched leisurely as the ropes fell off. Except for his sore head, he had suffered no ill effects in body.

"Parole as far as the villa, then," he said cheerfully. "I hope you have a good luncheon awaiting me, Glazunoff. I'm hungry."

Glazunoff's thin lips twisted.

"Men don't complain of our hospitality," he said with dry significance. "A cigarette?"

"Thanks."

Warden walked out of the place at Glazunoff's side. Behind him came Emile. The big Mercedes was waiting in the street.

Solomon's startling arrival, the message to North—these things had given Warden more hope than he dared admit. Now, in the open, he sent sharp glances around. If some one were on watch, if they knew he was departing and could trail him to the villa, things were not, after all, so desperate! Yet his heart sank as he swept the vicinity. The two streets were empty. Not a soul was in sight.

"Fool!" he told himself as he got into the car at the bidding of Glazunoff. "Fool! Of course nothing's in sight. Would North be standing out on the street corner? If any one's on the watch they'd be under cover."

None the less, he knew he had made a mistake—and he knew Solomon's calm verdict on those who made mistakes. From this moment, he definitely abandoned hope, so far as any help from the outside was concerned.

Glazunoff sat beside him in silence as the big car whirled out to the Auteuil gate and along the wide avenue fringing the old moat. Emile had not accompanied them. The Russian was taking no chances—he kept his hand in his coat pocket, and watched Warden narrowly. The latter turned to him, as they came to the church and swung into Boulevard Jean Jaures.

"With whom am I dealing in this affair?" asked Warden casually. "With you, with Halsey, or with Dominetti?"

"Dominetti is in London," said Glazunoff. "Halsey is in bed—as you probably know. So it seems that you are dealing with me."

"Good!" Warden smiled, as he met the unwinking, cold eyes. "So Halsey's in bed, eh? He never knew I had switched the glasses on him, eh? He shouldn't make such mistakes."

Glazunoff made no response.

Two minutes later they turned into the open gates of the Dominetti villa, and the gates were swung shut as the car halted. The Russian touched Warden's arm.

In a frantic rage the Russian struck Halsey.

"Let me warn you," he said quietly, "any false motions would be most unfortunate for you, M. Warden."

"Thank you," said the former diplomat. "I shall make none, I assure you."

He examined his surroundings with keen interest, as he alighted and followed Glazunoff into the house; the two men who had opened and closed the gates came close behind him.

The gardens were rather large—graveled paths, a fountain, fruit trees and a vegetable plot in the rear, the blank wall of a large apartment house closing in the opposite side. The house entrance was upon the gardens—a small postern gate in the wall gave access to the street. The house itself was large, of three stories.

A S   H E passed into the entrance hall, Warden noted the inner doors, the holes in floor and ceiling whence came steel rods into the doors when closed—like many such houses built after the communist troubles, the place was a regular fortress.

The hall went on to a large stairway. On the right was a small salon and a dining room. On the left were the kitchens and the library-conservatory, into which Glazunoff led the way. At a glance Warden took in the room and the glass flower-house beyond—the fine old furniture and portraits, the large flat desk with its modern appurtenances, and the massive black oak wall cupboard with its shelves of bottles and tobaccos.

Glazunoff gestured to the two men who had followed, and they remained at the door on guard. Russians, Warden thought. Going to the desk, Glazunoff seated himself, lighted a cigarette, and glanced over some papers before him.

"Make yourself at home, Mr. Warden," he said with dry irony. "It is a pleasure to deal with such a man as you. Here, I assure you, there need be no fear that the drinks or cigarettes are drugged. Be comfortable; when I have disposed of a few details, we shall take up our affair. Until then, we need not be unfriendly."

"Perhaps not even then," said Warden lightly. This shaft at a venture drew a sharp, swift glance from the Russian.

"No? Well, we shall see. Take the big chair there, help yourself to drinks or smokes, and pardon me if I neglect you for the moment. Ivan! Any report from M. Halsey?"

"Asleep, excellency," said one of the men at the door.

"The Arab who was brought here?"

"Has refused to talk, excellency."

The eyes of Glazunoff flashed with a singular light. A slight color came into his face, denoting inward passion, then died into a colder, more vivid pallor. As brown-skinned men turn black under stress of emotion, this man turned a more terrible white. He was on the point of giving some order when Warden, inexpressibly horrified by the revelations of this inhuman face, intervened in his quiet, cheerful fashion.

"Your pardon, Glazunoff—it's no use to torture the poor chap, you know. He'll not talk, and indeed knows little. Let me suggest an alternative. On what point do you wish to interrogate him?"

For an instant the piercing, snaky eyes bored into Warden.

"In regard to Mr. Solomon."

"Very well. Let's dispense with useless cruelty. I'll tell you what I know about this Solomon, if you'll pass up poor Ahmed."

Glazunoff nodded. "Very well."

Taking up his desk telephone, the Russian put in various calls, referring from time to time to the papers on his desk. Nearly all the conversation was in Russian, of which Warden knew not a word; a brief talk in Italian revealed nothing of the slightest interest. Then came a call for Glazunoff. The Russian listened frowningly, and his eyes went to Warden, to whom he put a brief aside question.

"Do you know anything about a man, an American, named Red Farrow!"

Warden nodded. "At the *Sûreté*, I believe. At least, I handed him over to two agents last night. He carried a large quantity of snow."

Glazunoff flashed white teeth in a smile, spoke into the instrument, then laid it down, not on its rack, but on the desk. Rising, he went to the large oak cupboard, poured himself a drink and took it back to the desk. He sipped the drink and eyed Warden appraisingly.

"MY DEAR chap, you seem to have made yourself most obnoxious." Glazunoff said pleasantly. "I, for one, do not quite understand your connection with our business. Why, for example, did you send us word this morning that Miss Tully was in safety? Why did you so violently take her from the Savoy in London? If you are not an agent of the man Solomon, who are you?"

"So far as Miss Tully is concerned, I'm my own agent," said Warden. "I sent that message this morning so you'd know she had delivered her information and so you wouldn't issue further orders to murder her."

Glazunoff set his glass down suddenly. "Very well conceived! However, your solicitude was needless. We have no further interest in her—unless we except the personal interest of Mr. Halsey. He is, unfortunately, a stubborn gentleman where ladies are concerned, so I cannot I answer for him. Was it on her account that you went to the Abode of Bad Spirits, last night?"

Warden puffed at his cigarette.

"Partly, yes," he responded after a moment. "I understand that Halsey was Dominetti's chief agent here, and wanted to have a talk with him. Instead, I was attacked—therefore, I attacked in turn."

"And fell into a pit, eh?"

"So it seems." Warden helped himself to a Dubonnet and resumed his seat.

"Hm! I understand," said Glazunoff, "that you are not an agent of Solomon. Yet his men serve and aid you, and you use one of his cars. Suppose you make your position a trifle clearer, my friend."

"Gladly. I have been trying to find Miss Tully. Solomon offered his help. That is all."

"Oh! And this Solomon—where is he now?"

The American shrugged. "How should I know? He said he was going out of the city." As Warden spoke, it occurred to him that Solomon had probably expressed the exact truth for Auteuil was a suburb, though in reality a part of Paris. "His house has been closed up, I can't reach him, and when he'll return I can't say."

"Your interest in things, then, has ended—now that Miss Tully is safe?"

"So far as she's concerned, yes."

"Let us see," resumed Glazunoff. "You obtained entrance to a certain room last night. You read a letter half written there. This morning you took certain action in regard to what you had learned. How do you justify this, Mr. Warden? It was not on Miss Tully's behalf that you met Leblanc, certainly."

"Not at all," agreed Warden cheerfully. He still had a card, a trump card, which might change the whole course of the game. "Leblanc was ordered to remove a certain gentleman, who was a friend and supporter of Prince Sergei. Naturally, I had to intervene."

"Eh?" Glazunoff looked astonished. "I fail to see the connection. Do you know Sergei?"

Warden laughed. "Of course. How could I be representing him without knowing him?"

"You—representing him?" There was no doubt about the Russian's surprise. "This is most amazing, I must say. In what way do you represent him?"

"In regard to certain events which will transpire on the twenty-fifth in three days," returned Warden calmly. He felt in his pocket and produced his letter of authorization. "Your men did not take my papers, fortunately. Here is a letter—my credentials."

BORIS GLAZUNOFF was stupefied for a moment, evidently. He took the letter, read it over, scrutinized the signature, then returned it.

"Nobody dreamed this," he said slowly, his gaze on Warden. "Sergei has refused to discuss affairs with any of us, has refused to consider any terms. Why, then, should he empower you to do so?"

"Ask him that, not me," said Warden. "Perhaps he thought that his affairs were in such bad shape I could not do them any harm. At all events, I'm authorized to discuss terms with you, or with Dominetti—you understand, I can deal only with the head of affairs—and to report those terms to Sergei."

Glazunoff nodded, his eyes narrowed, reflective.

"Hm! Yes, he'd do it that way," he said, a trace of exultation in his voice. "Instead of coming here personally, he'd send you—and save his face. Well, this somewhat alters my intentions toward you, Mr. Warden. But—ah!" He glanced up, suddenly startled. "You spoke of the twenty-fifth—the day after to-morrow. To what do you refer?"

Jimmy Warden looked a trifle bored.

"Come, come, my dear Glazunoff—are we such children? Surely we can lay our cards on the table and play an open game. Both of us know exactly what is to transpire here on the twenty-fifth. Prince Sergei knows it. John Solomon knows it. I must say that your Signor Dominetti has hit some ruthless blows—to the best of my knowledge, he has practically wiped out Solomon's organization, whatever it was. Sergei doubtless knows this, also."

"Eh? And is ready to talk terms, is he?" Glazunoff's pallid features lighted up. "Come, he's showing sense. Just how far, Mr. Warden, are you acquainted with the negotiations now under way?"

Warden gave him a curious glance. Why was the man taking this tone?

"Do you prefer being a child, Glazunoff? Well, then, be a child. I know all about your negotiations and your plans—from your agreement with Baron Yamanaka to the treaty between Italy, Great Britain and the United States which you expect to publish. The question is whether you—or, rather, Signor Dominetti—think it worth while to deal with Prince Sergei through me, or not."

Somewhat to Warden's amazement, the Russian seemed nothing short of paralyzed by these words. Warden himself was playing the game, no more. He had no instructions from Solomon, and he had no actual right whatever to conduct himself as an emissary of Prince Sergei—except in so far as it might save his life. In effect, he was acting absolutely in the dark.

A N D   N O W , suddenly, occurred a startling thing. There was no third party to the conversation; but, abruptly, a third voice spoke in the room—a voice which Warden recognized at once.

"Am I to understand, Mr. Warden, that Sergei is ready to treat with us?"

Warden started. Then, catching the peculiar half smile on the face of Glazunoff, he repressed his astonishment.

"I do not talk with persons I cannot see," he returned coldly.

"You are in no position to dictate," came the response, in the voice of Dominetti. "I am speaking from London. If it is worth while, I shall come over and see you personally. Is Sergei ready to treat with us?"

"Naturally, since I am authorized to discuss the situation with you."

"And where did you learn of the treaty you just mentioned?"

Warden smiled to himself. He had the whip-hand there.

"Must I repeat that I prefer to see with whom I speak?"

"Very well, Boris! Hold this man until I arrive to talk with him. Exert every effort to locate Solomon; inform me when you succeed. Matsura is coming over to-night with certain instructions; give him every coöperation. That is all."

"Very good," said Glazunoff, and put the telephone on its rack. He looked at Warden and waved his hand.

"I understand that our friend Solomon works miracles—well, we make use of science!" he observed placidly. "Hidden microphones, a connection with the London office, and it is very simple. Dominetti hears all that transpires in this room, when necessary."

Warden wondered what Boris would say did he actually know what sort of miracles John Solomon worked—but he did not voice his thoughts.

"Very well, then. And what about luncheon?" he asked. Glazunoff laughed a little and rose.

"Excellent! You consent to be our guest, then?"

"Naturally. My business lies with Dominetti."

"Understood. And when Sergei hears about his old friend and backer being killed, being caught as a forger of notes—what the devil! Why, the Prefecture will probably ask Sergei to leave the country, eh? He'll be only too anxious to come to terms with us. Yes, yes—very lucky thing you walked into that trap, my friend! So come, I'll take you to your room, and we'll lunch in half an hour."

CHAPTER XIV

THE YELLOW STREAK

THOSE WHO were in Paris last summer will recall the enormous tension which prevailed in political circles at the time, and the tremendous tide of anti-Italian feeling that swept over France.

The rise of the Fascist Italy had for some years been regarded askance, for now Italy threatened the dominance of France in European affairs; but with the various frontier incidents which had recently taken place, the supposed activity of Fascist plotters in Paris itself swept the French people into a frenzy.

A certain portion of the French press had for long been violently anti-foreign—openly distrusting the United States, sneering at American tourists, demanding that Russian refugees leave France, and crying for the expulsion of Italian and other foreign workmen. The near-crisis provoked in the summer of 1929 by the low ebb of tourist money, in consequence of the taxes and petty annoyances visited upon tourists, had frightened all France into treating her visitors with more courtesy; but the rapid succession of outrages made her forget all more practical matters.

Then came the discovery of the English scientist, Pearson— the body found one morning in the Bois, a Fascist dagger pinning to its ribs the flaming words: "Death to all traitors and enemies of Fascism!" This aroused not only France, but England; Downing Street and the Quai d'Orsay sat upon the wires with stern messages. In vain did Rome deny all knowledge of the matter.

The laboratory where Pearson had been working was destroyed by an explosion and fire and later, when the body of Pearson's assistant was recovered, bullets were found in it, and a pistol bearing the Fascist emblem was found in the ruins. The *Gaulois* and the *Quotidien* burst out next day with heated denunciations of Mussolini and Fascism, and half the French press followed suit.

All sorts of rumors ran riot—the King of Italy had fortified the Quirinal, the Crown Prince had been assassinated, Mussolini was concentrating an army on the French border, and so forth—all of them unfounded, but highly exciting to the French mind.

It was amid and because of these circumstances that the great Frenchman, Poincare, issued what was undoubtedly the noblest document of modern history—his now famous "Appeal," which rang across the world within a few hours. Who does not remember those opening sentences of steel, those clanging words of sheer inspiration?

> Fellow citizens! France does not fall to the poniards of conspirators; the sword of our glorious republic is not unsheathed against vile rumor. Twelve years ago, Italy was fighting beside us. Let us remember the brotherhood of patriotism! A passionate love of country is the heritage of the ages. Because a child makes mistakes, shall the entire family be punished? No! Let us be passionate for the right, for justice, for tolerance—not for hatred and warfare and blind savagery!

This remarkable document, followed as it was by the astonishing "open letter" of another leader, Briand, held France stupefied, swaying in the balance, irresolute. And in the days of hesitation, of doubt, of conflicting emotion, the unseen drama that was to determine the fate of half Europe was being played to its finish in the walled villa of Boulogne, and in the rain-wet streets of Paris.

IN THE affairs of men, the accidental ever plays a large, often a crucial, role. And in this drama Jimmy Warden was to take an ever-increasing part, to the surprise not only of others, but of himself as well.

He found his status between that of prisoner and of guest. The upper portion of the house, once composed of very large and luxurious bedrooms, had been cut up into a number of smaller but very comfortable rooms. While his window, which over-looked the garden, was not barred, his door was locked when he was in the room; if the American wished to walk in the garden, it was free to him at all times. He took his meals with Glazunoff, catching no sight of Halsey until the following day at luncheon.

During this time Warden kept his eyes open, but learned little that was new. A good many men were in or about the house—two large, placid Russians who served Glazunoff, the others apparently all Italian. Then there was the smiling, spectacled little Jap, Matsura, who puzzled Warden. Walking in the garden after dinner, smoking, the American saw Matsura arrive, and as he came back into the house, Glazunoff called him into the library and introduced him to the Oriental.

"Mr. Matsura, this is Mr. Warden," said Boris in flawless English. "Mr. Warden is acting for Prince Sergei, as you may be aware, and until recently has been in the United States diplo-matic corps. Matsura is a scientist, Warden—a real one."

The Jap bowed politely. "Of that," he said, "Mr. Glazunoff should be an excellent judge! I am most happy to meet you, Mr. Warden."

To tell the truth, Jimmy Warden was a trifle staggered by this situation. He did not see Matsura again at once; but here, in the house of the enemy, in the midst of a merciless life-and-death game—to experience such treatment, such formality! It left him rather up in the air, but none the less very much on his guard.

His meeting with Halsey, however, quite restored him to balance.

It was noon of the next day when they met. Warden was walking in the garden, waiting for the mess-call, when he descried the tall figure of Halsey approaching and recognized the aristocratic, handsome features. They were a trifle blurred now, as Warden noted with some satisfaction—the effect of the drug had not entirely worn off. Undoubtedly Halsey's normally acute brain was a trifle blurred also, although he came to a halt in palpable recognition.

"Ah—good morning!" he said pleasantly. "You're Warden, eh? I've heard a lot about you."

"Yes?" Warden could not feign any liking for the man, and did not try. "I've heard a good deal about you, too—from Miss Tully and others."

"Oh!" The dark eyes hardened. "Yes, you're the chap who fancies her, aren't you? I'd forgotten that."

THERE WAS momentary silence, ominous silence. Matsura appeared, doubtless to announce that luncheon was ready. Obviously work had gone well with him that morning; he was humming a queer Japanese air as he came, and was looking very happy—this quiet, spectacled little brown man, who soon would be lying there among the flowers!

Glazunoff appeared on the half-round steps of the entrance.

"Come along, gentlemen!" he called.

Still Halsey stood looking at Warden, then lifted one hand slightly, and Warden saw that the fingers of this hand were shaking. Suddenly he realized that Halsey was in the grip of a consuming, although not entirely obvious, passion.

A spasm of sheer fury contracted the man's face for an instant.

"Ah!" he said, as though stifled. "You—you—"

His unspoken words failed. Glazunoff, seeing something amiss, was coming toward them.

Matsura had halted, staring at the two men.

"Be careful, you cheap crook," said Warden quietly. "She's where you'll not lay your filthy hands on her again."

Sharp and swift, Halsey's hand swooped. A pistol appeared.

Warden, poised, flung himself forward before the irresolute hand could press trigger. He gripped Halsey's wrist with one hand, while the other swung in a blow to the stomach.

The two men went down in a lashing heap. Unleashed, Halsey's fury was that of a wild animal; what happened in this brief moment, Warden could not tell. The pistol went off in a smashing, stunning report close to his head, and in blind anger Warden's fist drove in again and again, while he gripped the pistol-wrist.

Then, suddenly, men were upon them, tearing them apart. Glazunoff was there, screaming harsh inarticulate oaths and orders. Warden found himself scrambling to his feet, two men hanging to him. He stood quietly, mastering his anger, staring at the incredible scene before him.

Glazunoff, in frantic rage, was striking Halsey, whose pistol had been torn away by one of the Russian servants. And, at one side, Matsura lay upon his back, smiling at the sky, his right arm encircling a bunch of flowers as though pressing them to his dead breast. That one wild bullet had gone through his brain, stilling its cleverness forever.

After an instant, Glazunoff had himself in hand, stepped back. Halsey was dragged away by two of the men. Warden was released, and Glazunoff, after one glance at the body of Matsura, turned to him. The livid features, the reptilian eyes, were tinged with madness; yet the man's voice was steady and cool.

"I saw what happened," said Glazunoff. "Not your fault, Warden. Oh, devil take all such fools! Dominetti will be furious about this; but it can't be helped. Now I'll have to take on Matsura's work, damn it. Come along to luncheon."

SO THEY went into the dining room, the two of them, and sat at table in strained and terrible silence, until a beaker of fiery vodka had unloosed the tongue of Glazunoff and restored him to himself. Then, cold and deadly, he accompanied Warden to his room and went on down the corridor to another door; his voice came in icy restrained anger, answered by the silky tones of Halsey.

So the matter ended. When, an hour later, Warden encountered Halsey in the corridor, the confidence man was white and shaken, but passed him without a look. Warden smiled grimly to himself; but he did not smile when, returning to his room, he found a summons to join Glazunoff in the large salon below.

Warden entered the room and found Glazunoff at the desk. The Russian beckoned and pointed to the telephone, which was off the rack; at the same time he took down the extra extension receiver and held it to his ear, his gaze intent upon Warden.

"Hello! This is Warden—ah! Prince Sergei?"

"Yes, Sergei Romanoff," came the voice in French. "I wish to inform you, Monsieur Warden, that there is no longer any question of my continuing the course of action decided upon at our meeting with M. Solomon. I wish that you would represent me and reach some agreement with Grand Duke Basil and with Dominetti, along this line."

"Ask if he'll come here," murmured Glazunoff.

"Perhaps you will see Dominetti yourself?" said Warden, who was stunned by this intelligence.

"No, no!" said Sergei sharply. "I shall leave matters in your hands. You understand the situation, I have every confidence in you. I cannot reach M. Solomon, but I am glad to empower you to act for me at the meeting which takes place to-morrow."

"Wait!" exclaimed Warden. "You mean that you withdraw entirely from your agreement with Solomon?"

"Yes," came the astonishing response, in a tone of decision. "For reasons which I cannot go into now, I must withdraw. That is to say, if you can reach terms which seem fitting and proper to you. That is all."

Warden hung up the instrument, sank into a chair, and bit the end off a cigar, while Glazunoff watched him with a glint of triumph in the snaky eyes.

Sergei out of it, abandoning his agreement, refusing to go on with the plan outlined by Solomon—the plan which had every chance of making him master of Russia and a great figure in history! Why?

Then Warden started. How did it happen that Sergei had telephoned him here at this house? Only one answer was possible. North had received the message, Solomon had seen him there in the chauffeurs' rendezvous; Sergei had telephoned to make certain for them that Warden was here. A ruse—perhaps. Perhaps! Yet here were definite instructions, positive orders.

"You don't understand it, eh," said Glazunoff, laughing lightly.

Warden regarded him frowningly. Diplomacy, here; careful words! Caution was needed now, if ever.

"No, I don't," he replied, with an affectation of bluntness. "I was supposed to make some arrangement with Dominetti and Basil, if possible, by which Sergei would throw all his influence behind Basil and share in the successful outcome. But now he's withdrawn entirely. Why? Why give up before the fight?"

GLAZUNOFF LAUGHED again, subtly and deeply amused, it seemed.

"Well," he responded lightly, "for one thing, Basil doesn't care to share his throne with Sergei. For another, he doesn't need Sergei's influence. In fact, Sergei must be out of the way entirely—while he and Basil both live, there can be no agreement. Perhaps you can convince Dominetti that it would be better to throw Basil overboard, and get rid of him, and adopt Sergei?"

"Eh?" Warden flashed the Russian a keen glance. "Would that be possible?" Glazunoff shrugged.

"Ask Dominetti—I can't say! You know how much Sergei would give up, how much he would promise; I don't. If he holds to his childish notions about Russia for the Russians, what use in talking? But I can tell you why he's withdrawn: he's a coward. He's learned about Ivan Vassilovitch being shot, about the forged notes being found. One of the afternoon papers is carrying a big story about the Russian plot to swamp the market with forged Bank of France notes, and is charging that Sergei Romanoff is behind it. The story will be suppressed, provided Sergei withdraws from all further political action. Sergei got this news, and at once telephoned you. Understand? He's out of it entirely."

Jimmy Warden scowled. He perceived now that he had known only a part of the plot—that it went farther, had more ingenuity behind it, than he had supposed. No, it was no ruse. Solomon had hidden himself. Sergei was in a panic, and had quit.

"Damn it!" said Warden angrily.

Glazunoff chuckled again.

"Sorry," he said ironically. "I'll give you a tip, Warden. I fancy Dominetti would be glad to be able to present the meeting to-morrow with a signed statement on the part of Sergei—a statement which could be made public—agreeing to renounce any rights to the throne, and to hold aloof from all political action in future."

Warden started. "Sergei would never sign such an agreement!"

"Well, you heard what he just said, didn't you? And consider your own position. I'm giving you something to work on—a real tip, my friend. Partly for your sake, partly for my own. Let us be frank! You are in no position to dictate to us; make yourself useful, and it will mean a lot to you. On my own behalf—"

Glazunoff paused, blew a thin cloud of smoke, and gestured toward the garden.

"I do not care to face Dominetti when he is angry," he said simply. "The death of this Matsura, who was in charge of certain scientific work, will infuriate him. I should like to balance that with unexpected good news. This little affair with Sergei and Ivan Vassilovitch happens to be one of my own pet schemes. It has succeeded; if Sergei will sign such an agreement as I have outlined, and it can be laid before the meeting to-morrow— well, Signor Dominetti will be pleased! He will arrive in another hour or so, too."

"I see," murmured Warden.

Out of the mental confusion which had seized upon him, the American began to coördinate his thoughts, despairing as they were. He knew well enough that Glazunoff was trying to use him as a tool, yet he saw no better way out of the *impasse*. And Prince Sergei had given definite orders—had broken his agreement with Solomon, was ready to abandon everything. The streak of weakness in the man had come to the top.

"All right," said Warden. "Tell you what you do, Glazunoff. Write out what you want Sergei to sign, give the paper to me. If I reach some agreement in the matter with Dominetti, I can take it to Sergei and get his signature."

Glazunoff nodded.

"You'll not be allowed to leave here, however," he said, "until things are settled. Still, you can always use the telephone—and we can send him the paper! Yes, a good plan. I'll do it."

So it was agreed.

CHAPTER XV

DOMINETTI ARRIVES

JIMMY WARDEN felt an indescribable reluctance to meet Dominetti in any battle of wits, or to go ahead with the course upon which he had entered. Glazunoff sent him a typed sheet, in French, then Warden saw him depart in the Mercedes—probably to meet Dominetti. But for a long while Warden sat reading over those words and realizing what they meant.

The paper was a complete abdication under most solemn oath, by Sergei—an abdication of his possible rights to the throne of all the Russias. Furthermore, not only was it a pledge to abstain from any political action, but it urged his adherents to give allegiance to Grand Duke Basil as head of the family.

No ruse was possible here. If Sergei signed this paper, it meant that Glazunoff's clever scheme had succeeded—he would have completely abandoned Solomon's plan and his agreement with Rome.

"We'll see," thought Warden, folding and pocketing the sheet of paper. "If he signs this, if he throws up a great project, a daring venture, because of a momentary panic—then let him rot! It isn't signed yet, anyhow. The whole thing may be framed up by Solomon to gain time. We'll see."

Boris Glazunoff, meanwhile, was speeding on his way along the outer circle of boulevards for the Porte de la Villette and Le Bourget.

The big Mercedes hummed along smoothly, at a high rate of

speed. It might have been mere coincidence that an enclosed Sunbeam, whose GB license showed that it belonged across the Channel, and whose curtains were drawn, followed the same identical course but some little distance in the rear.

Reaching the Porte, Glazunoff's chauffeur alighted. He did not make the usual pretense of inspecting his gasoline tank, but darted into the little cubby occupied by the Douanerie and came out again, tucking his reëntry ticket into his cap. The Sunbeam was drawn up directly behind the Mercedes, and its chauffeur, a yellow man—possibly Chinese—was at the moment going in for his ticket.

During the momentary absence of Glazunoff's chauffeur, however, something had happened.

Two men had alighted from the Sunbeam. One of them jerked open the left-hand door of the Mercedes, while the other precipitated himself inside and shoved a pistol against the body of the unsuspecting Glazunoff. The first man slammed the door and mounted into the front seat—the car being, naturally, right-hand drive.

Thus, when the chauffeur came back to his place, he looked up, astonished, to see a yellow man sitting there and unobtrusively holding a pistol to cover him.

"Quickly!" said the Chinese in French. "Get up! Drive!"

Helpless, the chauffeur obeyed the order. Once in his seat, a glance into his rear-view mirror showed him a second man seated beside Glazunoff. The Mercedes pulled out and went on along the market-street of La Villette.

INSIDE THE car. Dr. Erh Lim Lee smiled a little as he held his weapon against Glazunoff's body.

"Don't take your hands from your lap, please," the Chinese diplomat said in his low-voiced way.

The Russian looked at Lee with a sort of contempt.

"What? You think that you can get away with a thing like this?"

"I seem to be doing it," and Dr. Lee smiled grimly. "I warned you, my friend! Now, I want that letter back."

"Fool!" Glazunoff said disdainfully. "Do you think I keep it in my pocket? It went long ago to other people, was translated, will be given to the press to-morrow night."

Lee, rotund and sparkling-eyed, seemed for a moment aghast.

"Impossible!" he exclaimed.

"Nothing is impossible," said Glazunoff, with a slightly bored air, "as you, yourself a man of science, should know. That letter will be of great interest to French readers."

Lee broke into a sudden laugh, soft and exultant.

"Ah, liar!" he retorted. "You don't know what was in the letter, then! You haven't had it translated! You aren't aware that it contained the contribution of Chinese laboratories to the ultra-sonic work of Solomon's chemist Pearson—which you, certainly, would never make public!"

Glazunoff turned livid at this mockery. Lee had pierced his bluff.

"Well?" he snapped. "End this foolery."

"I shall," said Lee. "The letter is lost. You read my papers. I can do nothing; but I can save my face—have you forgotten that we of the older world believe in saving face? I can kill you, and—"

The Mercedes, over the viaduct, was purring out along the Le Bourget road, fields on either side, the gray gleam of the hangars out on the left and ahead. The Sunbeam followed at a little distance. Abruptly, with a twist of his wrist, the chauffeur spun the steering wheel, then applied the brakes.

The big car went into the ditch, came to an abrupt halt there.

Lee was flung from the seat, and Glazunoff fell on top of him, striking. On the front seat, the Chinese there was hurled against the windshield; as he struck, the chauffeur gripped his pistol, tore it way, struck him across the head. He fell limply.

The Sunbeam came up alongside, and the Russian chauffeur covered its driver with the pistol. After an instant the left side door of the Mercedes opened; Glazunoff stepped out, cool and rather disdainful. The road was empty, the two cars were alone. The insistent hum of a machine came from overhead.

Glazunoff gave his chauffeur quiet, swift directions, while the driver of the Sunbeam, helpless, made no protest. The Russian knew that Dr. Lee was altogether too big a man to be sequestered without a large and serious outcry being raised; something which was by no means to be desired just at this moment. On the other hand, Glazunoff wanted, and knew that his master wanted, certain information.

The chauffeur dragged out Lee's unconscious body, bleeding from the mouth, and hurriedly loaded it into the Sunbeam. Then, at a command from Glazunoff, the Sunbeam's driver turned his car and departed.

The Chinese whom the chauffeur had knocked out was now put into the tonneau of the Mercedes and bound securely, his mouth wrapped with car-cleaning cloths. Boris Glazunoff glanced at his watch, and nodded with a satisfied air.

"Good work, very good work!" he told the chauffeur approvingly. "Go on to the airdrome and take your time—we're still ahead of the London plane."

THE UNFORTUNATE yellow man in the rear of the car was the same who had come with Dr. Lee to the Abode of Bad Spirits—beyond doubt, his chief aide. Glazunoff went through his pockets and located some papers and letters; and had excellent cause for feeling that he had accomplished a very good day's work. The death of Matsura was doubly compensated for, he reflected.

From the window of his room, which overlooked the garden, Jimmy Warden beheld the return of the Mercedes. Dominetti and Glazunoff alighted, then a smaller bound figure was carried out of the car and brought into the house.

The afternoon was not yet over, and Warden conjectured that Dominetti's first thought would be to interrogate him; indeed, five minutes later, one of the Russian servants brought a request that he come to the salon at once.

There he found Halsey, Glazunoff, and Dominetti himself, who occupied the seat at the desk, and the bound but no longer gagged figure of Lee's aide—a rather thin little man, imperturbable, whose sloe eyes looked out upon the room blankly enough. Beside the chair in which the yellow man sat, stood the two large Russian servants.

As Warden entered, Dominetti stood up and extended his hand, smilingly.

"Ah, Mr. Warden! Our last meeting was one thing—this is another. I am glad to see you here, and doubly glad because of your errand. Take a chair, make yourself comfortable and, I warn you, do not interfere. This man, who is an assassin, must be questioned—and let me remind you that I shall not tolerate any intervention."

Cold, inhuman, his glittering gray eyes alive with savage emotion, Dominetti's words and air belied his surface appearance of an impeccable gentleman. The man fairly radiated energy and dominating vigor.

Again, as in London, Warden felt that miserable sensation of futility, of helplessness, as he sank into a chair.

Too, he had the feeling that something terrible was about to happen, something from which at all costs he must hold himself aloof—and in this he was right.

Dominetti resumed his seat and fastened his gaze on the unfortunate saffron man.

"From the papers found in your pockets," he said, his voice metallic and sharp-edged, "you are Wu Hong Sze; is this correct?"

"Yes," the prisoner responded in English.

"I have heard of you," went on Dominetti. "You are a graduate of Chicago; when Dr. Lee went into politics, you refused a professorship of physics at the University of Tokyo in order to take up Lee's scientific work, in acoustics and geophysics. Your discoveries in the way of solutions have been followed by Glazunoff, here, for some time."

He glanced at the Russian, who nodded. "Yes. The flocculation of solutions—his apparatus is now in use by the American Department of Agriculture, I understand."

"You flatter me," said Wu, irony in his voice.

"Not at all," replied Dominetti, and took up a paper from the desk. "Here is a letter in Chinese which Dr. Lee was bringing to Mr. Solomon from certain of your associates in Nankin. Will you kindly translate it for us?"

"Certainly not," returned Wu Hong, calmly.

DOMINETTI LAID aside the letter. "Very well: it has already been translated, and deals with the destruction of protoplasm and blood corpuscles by means of ultrasonic waves," he said. "Now, I desire certain information from you. I wish to know where Dr. Lee is living in Paris, and when he is going on to the League conference at Geneva. These two things. No more. Then you shall go free."

"I have nothing to say," Wu Hong answered.

Dominetti leaned back, made a sign to the two Russians. They leaned over and seized the arms of the Chinaman, loosing them from the bonds.

Next instant, a scream broke from the unfortunate man as his arms were twisted around the high back of his chair. Warden half started up, then sank back, white-faced, as a pistol in Halsey's hand covered him.

Another scream burst from the tortured lips of Wu Hong— one of his arms fell, dangling horribly.

"These two things, no more," said Dominetti. He might have been carved of stone as he sat there, looking into the distended eyes of the yellow man.

"Nothing," gasped Wu Hong.

The word trailed away in a gasp and a low moan, as his other arm fell, broken. His saffron features darkened, his teeth were clenched on his upper lip, and the blood came from it. But his

staring eyes, fastened upon Dominetti, were resolute, unflinch-
ing.

"Your knives," said the Italian.

Warden closed his eyes as the Russians produced long blades.
He sat there quivering, at each instant dreading to hear another
of those terrible cries of man's agony—but he caught only a
stifled gasp, a groan. He dared not look to see what was happening.

"Bah! Take him away," came the voice of Dominetti.

Sick and faint, Warden looked up as a broken, crim-
son-smeared thing was borne out of the room. Halsey looked
rather white, and brought a bottle of whisky from the massive
cupboard, with glasses. Glazunoff poured drinks, and, smiling,
brought a glass to Warden.

"Here you are—look as though you needed it, old chap," he
observed.

Warden gulped down the whisky thankfully, and tried to pull
himself together. Dominetti was swinging around his chair, to
face Warden. Had the man really hoped to extort his information from Wu Hong—or was the scene of horror merely a
prelude, deliberately designed to break down the American?

"Come, come, you must not take these things so much to
heart," said Dominetti. "Now, Mr. Warden, let us put our cards
on the table! Here, take a cigarette and make yourself comfortable."

Warden accepted the cigarette and lighted it at the match
Dominetti held.

"You do not, by chance," asked the Italian smoothly, "know
anything about this Dr. Lee?"

"No," returned Warden. "I know nothing about him."

Dominetti nodded. "Probably not. Before proceeding to your
actual business—yesterday you mentioned a certain treaty. May
I inquire just how you learned of this treaty?"

WARDEN SAW Glazunoff watching him with a half-smile—so, then! They knew the treaty had disappeared, knew he must have taken it. Here the truth, the desperate truth, must serve him, and nothing else.

"I found it in a room of which you know," said Warden calmly. "It seemed to be the only thing worth taking—so I took it."

"Yes?" Dominetti smiled, and his voice was very soft. "And where is the document now?"

"At the American Embassy I presume," said Warden. "I sent it there by messenger."

There was an instant of startled silence. Halsey appeared to know nothing about the treaty; his manner was somewhat puzzled, curious.

Glazunoff, at Warden's words, caught his breath and sent a half startled glance at Dominetti, as though in fear. But the Italian's singular gray eyes did not swerve from Warden, and displayed no hint of emotion.

"You are a more dangerous antagonist than I had believed possible, Mr. Warden," he said. "Well, as to the treaty, let it pass. Now for your own status. Are you still an antagonist? Are you working for Solomon?"

"No," said Warden. "My only interest in this affair has been to get Miss Tully out of the hands of that dog Halsey. It was accomplished. Having been dragged into the business, however, I undertook to act as representative for Prince Sergei."

"And it interested you, eh?" Dominetti laughed lightly. "You are no doubt aware of the agreement between Sergei and Rome, eh? You know a great deal?"

"Certainly." Warden was cool enough now, perfectly master of himself, speaking without hesitation yet weighing every word before it left his lips. "I was informed of all the details of your own scheme to back Grand Duke Basil, and I'm aware of the meeting to-morrow."

"Proving that you are a man to be trusted," said Dominetti. "Good. If others trust you, I can trust you also—particularly as you are in my hands. You came to issue some ultimatum on the part of Sergei, no doubt, but things have changed. You are now aware that Prince Sergei no longer desires power and glory—all he desires is to save his own precious skin, eh?"

"Yes," said Warden bitterly.

He knew what this defection would mean to Solomon, whose dream had been a glorious one, and practical enough to boot— that swift march of fifty thousand men into the heart of old Russia!

"Yes, blast him!" the American went on. "The fool had only to use what was given him, carry out the plans made for him— and now his yellow streak has smashed everything! He deserves all he gets. I've no sympathy for him; however, I'll have to act for him."

Dominetti watched him, half-smiling, as he spoke. The sincerity of Warden was clear enough to all three other men.

"Sympathy, no," said the Italian slowly. "His weakness has astonished even me, I must confess. I broke down Solomon's organization in order that we might strike at Sergei—but we need not have uncovered him, perhaps, so carefully. He was not worth the effort, eh? Well, fear not. All his life the man will be haunted by the great chances he flung away, but I do not think he will live so very long."

Glazunoff and Halsey exchanged a glance, but Warden did not observe it. He was getting out the typed document that Glazunoff had prepared for him, and now he laid it before Dominetti.

"GLANCE OVER this," he said. "I don't know just what, precisely, Sergei wants in the way of terms—I presume in regard to finances and other things, since his own brother is paying you a thousand francs a month hush money."

"Eh? Eh?" At this calm thrust, Dominetti started, and his eyes widened on Warden. "You American devil—who told you that? Sergei himself did not know it!"

"I learned it," and Warden shrugged carelessly. "What matter?"

He could perceive at once that this trifle had raised him appreciably in the estimation of the enemy. Irony! If only Sergei Romanoff had not that fatal yellow streak, what might yet have been accomplished!

Dominetti returned the paper, beaming.

"Excellent," he stated in his cold manner. "I want that paper signed before witnesses to-night. Suppose you telephone Sergei now, read it to him, ask for his consent; then we can send it over at once to his hotel. The Hôtel de Choiseul, is it not? You can tell him that in return for his signature I will obtain a signed document indorsed by Grand Duke Basil, Prince Seminoff, and Baron Tondern, the chief leaders of Basil's party, agreeing to the following conditions:

"Sergei is to be retained in his titles and estates, upon the recovery of Russia. As Basil is childless, Sergei is to be nominated heir to the throne. Until Russia is recovered, Sergei is to be given a yearly grant of fifty thousand pounds for life, to be paid from the funds of the late dowager empress. Satisfactory?"

Satisfactory, indeed—it was madness! Even Glazunoff stared at his chief, startled by such terms. Warden met the cold eyes, which gave no hint of what was in the mind of Dominetti.

"You will give a guarantee that cannot be broken? But why?" asked Warden cautiously. "You offer a large price for a signature—"

"Which I need," said Dominetti. "Boris, get Sergei on the telephone."

That there was some trick to it, Warden was convinced; yet, if such a document were given Sergei and were made public—

"Wait a minute," said Warden calmly. "It is understood that Sergei will receive this abdication at once for his signature; but he will not return it signed until I telephone him that the other document is in my possession, some time to-morrow—"

Dominetti laughed. "You suspect me? Well, it shall be as you say. No, my friend—our cards are in sight."

Warden knew better. That Grand Duke Basil should recognize Sergei as his heir, was nothing short of absurd; the two men were bitter enemies. That Sergei should be given an annuity of fifty thousand pounds, was amazing. Dominetti must want that abdication very badly, or else had some trick up his sleeve.

"And perhaps he's doubtful of Sergei's good faith," thought Warden. "Well, we'll soon know about it now—if Sergei is playing some game, he'll refuse to sign that paper. If he's really abandoned Solomon and thrown up the whole thing, like a yellow cur, then he'll be glad enough of the terms!"

Two minutes later Warden took up the telephone and found Sergei on the wire.

CHAPTER XVI

CAPITULATION

J IMMY WARDEN was stunned, incredulous, bewildered.

Even now, the morning after his telephone conversation with Prince Sergei, he could scarcely believe he had heard aright. He had read over the abdication, he had repeated the terms offered by Dominetti—and Sergei Romanoff had jumped at them, had swallowed hook, line, and sinker, almost frantically. His very voice had betrayed, all too clearly, his eagerness to grab at the proffered bait.

There was some trick about it, of course; yet on the surface Dominetti had played fair and probably would continue to do so. Warden's one hope now lay in Solomon. He had a firm belief that somehow, at the last moment, the pudgy little cockney would show up with an ace of trumps. Sergei had been swung one way, and might conceivably be swung another way; or the deal with Dominetti might be halted.

Warden breakfasted with Glazunoff, and the two men stepped into the garden for a smoke and a stroll. Glancing at the open doors of the garage, Warden saw his own—or rather, Solomon's—Hispano standing there, and this recalled Ahmed ben Zain to his mind. He asked Glazunoff about the Arab.

"We're holding him. He got a rap over the head, but is all right now."

"And when does the party take place? To-day is the twenty-fifth, I think."

"Basil will be here for luncheon," said Glazunoff. "The others meet here at three o'clock. You can settle your business at luncheon with Basil."

"I fancy it's already settled, if Dominetti says so."

Glazunoff merely laughed dryly.

The morning dragged. It was well past noon when Jimmy Warden received the expected summons, and descended to the salon where Glazunoff was mixing cocktails. Halsey was not present, nor did Warden see anything of him all that day until evening.

"This is Mr. Warden, gentlemen," Dominetti said affably. "As I have told you, he represents Prince Sergei—very agreeably to us. Grand Duke Basil of Russia, and Baron von Federn."

The three men bowed, appraising one another. The German baron was a stiff, precise, silent man, speaking rarely. Basil, on the other hand, was a very handsome man of forty, cruelty lurking in his somber eyes, his mouth strong and passionate. Basil might be no angel, but he was certainly no weakling; Warden felt a keen regret that Sergei did not possess a bit more of his cousin's strong character.

They went in to luncheon, and Warden perceived that Dominetti had previously discussed him with Basil, for the grand duke showed no surprise over the capitulation of Sergei.

The meal passed with quiet talk, which revealed a most surprising knowledge on the part of Dominetti of nearly every important personage in Europe—an intimate personal knowledge, as of long acquaintance. When the meeting of the afternoon was mentioned, Dominetti nodded toward the American.

"I am going to ask Mr. Warden to be present at the meeting," he announced. "He knows already a large part of our plans, it appears, and it is just as well that he should know all. I hope to get in touch with Mr. Solomon to-night or in the morning, and settle matters with him—and it may be that Mr. Warden can be of mutual assistance. And now, if your highness is ready, we may touch upon the agreement with Sergei."

O N E O F the Russian servants came into the room and spoke with Glazunoff, whose eyes went to Warden.

"Mr. Warden is wanted on the telephone."

"By all means," said Dominetti, making a gesture.

Warden rose and accompanied Glazunoff into the salon, and took up the instrument from the desk, while the Russian lifted the separate receiver from the rack and held it expectantly to his ear.

"Warden—oh, it's you, North! How's everything?"

"Fine," said North. "I'm at Rue Montorgeuil."

"Solomon there?"

"No," responded North. "I paid your bill at the Hôtel d'Angleterre and all's jake. I'm instructed to ask whether Dominetti will see me some time this afternoon or early this evening. Solomon wants to get in touch with him through me."

Warden glanced at Glazunoff inquiringly. The Russian nodded, his eyes gleaming.

"Seven o'clock."

"All right, come here at seven to-night," said Warden.

"Right," North responded and hung up.

"All's jake!" This meant but one thing, of course. North had received the message about the Hôtel d'Angleterre, had interpreted it aright, and had taken care of June Tully. And beyond doubt he was now in touch with John Solomon, since he was at Solomon's house.

Dominetti, with more than a hint of triumph showing in his vibrant gray eyes, confirmed the appointment made by Glazunoff.

"Excellent!" he exclaimed. "At seven to-night, we shall receive a capitulation from this mysterious Solomon—eh, Mr. Warden? Oh, you do not think so? Well, you shall see. And now let us get to business, it is necessary to have the document written, signed, and sent to Prince Sergei, as I am anxious to receive his abdication during our meeting. Boris, suppose you write it out.

"Remember, Dominetti's listening!"
Warden warned Solomon.

His highness can sign now, can send it for the other signatures, and it can then go at once to Sergei."

Glazunoff wrote out the paper, in Russian, and followed the terms dictated by Dominetti. Warden perceived that Grand Duke Basil was none too happy about signing them, but dared not refuse. His signature was witnessed by Warden and by Baron von Federn; then Glazunoff, pocketing the document, departed to obtain the other signatures of the chiefs of Basil's party.

So, to the uneasy astonishment of Warden, the affair was concluded. He could discover no trick in the matter, yet was convinced there must be something shady in the transaction. It no longer bothered him greatly. June Tully was safe, well beyond the power of Dominetti, well beyond the reach of Halsey, and this counted for everything.

Then, North's message! Why was he coming here to-night, if not to present an ultimatum from Solomon. True, there had been no jubilation in his voice, yet it was now or never if action were to ensue; and Warden did not doubt for a moment that at seven that evening, John Solomon would deliver some blow to send all the enemy's finely planned schemes staggering into utter ruin.

So Mr. Warden was distinctly more cheerful as the day wore on.

THE MEETING took place in the stately dining-room, about the lengthened table, and if the presence of Warden caused any surprise to the others, none betrayed it. Warden was thrilled—he might have been all his life in the diplomatic service with never a chance to participate in so historic a conference as this promised to be. These men might not represent his cause, they might well be enemies—yet the thrill was here.

Dominetti headed the table, and opposite him sat Grand Duke Basil. Also present were several Russians, heads of the aristocratic party who acknowledged Basil as heir to the throne. Von Federn sat silent, intent, alert. Here on the left was Baron Yamanaka, correctly frock-coated, smiling, a man empowered to speak for the Empire of the East. And opposite him, Fakri Pasha—a virile, handsome Turk, proud in his consciousness that at his back was the new and rising Eurasian power.

Last of all, into the room came a man whom Warden recognized with intense amazement—the last man whom he would have expected to see lined up with the Russian aristocracy. It was Emile Marconnet; a great leader of the French Socialist party, the man who held the balance of power in the Chambre, the enemy of militarism and political expansion, the most execrated and yet most potent man in all France!

As Marconnet took his seat, Glazunoff came in and leaned over Warden's shoulder.

"I have the document. Will you come and telephone Sergei?"

Warden assented. In the salon, he presently had Prince Sergei on the wire, and told him that the terms were signed.

"Very well," said Sergei's petulant voice. "They must be in my hands before I surrender the abdication. I cannot take chances. I must verify the signatures."

Glazunoff nodded, and Warden informed the prince that

Glazunoff would come at once with the all-important document.

Hoping against hope, Warden returned to the conference, scarce listening to the pompous address being delivered by Grand Duke Basil. So Sergei would not take his word for it! Good. Perhaps it was all a ruse, perhaps Sergei would not yield the abdication, perhaps Dominetti would find himself balked at the last moment. There was still a chance!

The conference was unhurried. Wine was served, but tasted sparsely. One man after another spoke; Dominetti held his peace, patient, letting the others exhaust their oratory. Then, when his moment came, he was on his feet, speaking curtly, with dynamic force that fairly swept the table alert and into a wave of energy.

"Gentlemen, let us get down to facts," he said, and his voice shook them all with its trumpet-like vibrancy. Never had Warden more fully realized the essential power of quiet restraint. "We know for what purpose we have met here. Within six months the reign of chaos will be ended in Russia, and the rightful Czar will be crowned in Moscow. Gentlemen, I give you the health of Basil, Czar of All the Russias!"

There was a murmur of applause as those around the table, Warden excepted, lifted their glasses. Then Dominetti went on, having accomplished his dramatic gesture.

"We have certain proposals to lay before you, gentlemen; you have certain proposals to lay before us. The *pourparlers* are ended—we have come to the point of definite agreement. Will your highness kindly state in concrete fashion how you propose to act?"

GRAND DUKE Basil rose, and while every man there knew that he was but the mouthpiece of Dominetti, none the less his stately manner and words were impressive.

"I propose," he said simply, "to act. Behind me are my party, the exiled patriots of Russia. We have ample funds. At this moment we are gathering, in Germany and Poland, thousands of men—old soldiers of the Imperial armies. I propose to march directly upon Moscow, attacking Russia from the west."

"Without the consent of Germany," murmured Emile Marconnet in his sardonic fashion.

Baron von Federn rose and bowed.

"With the consent, approval, and aid of Germany," said the dry, precise Prussian voice. "With munitions and war supplies furnished by Germany. With two army corps of German veterans as the nucleus of the army, and with five thousand German ex-officers to assist the work. The German general staff has worked out complete plans of campaign."

Von Federn bowed and sat down; his concise words had electrified the assemblage. At this moment Glazunoff entered the room and took the one vacant chair at the table. The gaze of Dominetti rested upon him briefly, whereupon he responded with a slight gesture.

"Come!" Emile Marconnet, without rising, leaned forward and shook a finger at Basil. "You talk well; but, before we go farther, let us be practical. You have not the backing of the Imperial party—it is divided. There is that handsome dreamer, that proud weakling, Sergei, to consider. If you start your work with dissension behind you, then you must fail."

Glazunoff handed a folded paper to Grand Duke Basil, who glanced at it, flushed with triumph, and passed it to the nearest man.

"M. Marconnet, this document answered your objection. It is the unqualified abdication of Sergei Romanoff; he withdraws from any political pretensions, and urges his followers to join my faithful party."

There was a sharp intake of breath about the table. Yamanaka gave Dominetti a covert glance of admiration. The Japanese diplomat knew who had obtained this abdication.

For five minutes more the document was discussed, read over, handled. But Jimmy Warden sat in crushed futility. The worst was true. Sergei's yellow streak was no ruse, after all. Solomon's great dream had gone down in ruin, smashed by the very man he was raising to power!

Dominetti rose. "It is understood," he said suavely, "that even with German help, your highness might be unable to cope with the vast man-power of Russia, whose Red armies have attained enormous proportions. Therefore, since it is to the interest of all civilized peoples that the Russian Empire be restored to normal conditions, I desire to lay before you certain help which is offered our party. I believe that Baron Yamanaka has a proposition to set before us."

THE LITTLE Japanese rose and beamed around.

"I do not speak officially, *messieurs*," he said, "but I have reason to believe that Japan would be very glad to undertake action against the present Russian government, which has caused my country great trouble. With a notice of thirty days, we could move one hundred thousand men out of Manchuria against the Siberian provinces, striking directly inland. At the same time, our fleet would occupy Vladivostok. Within three weeks all of Siberia would be paralyzed or in our hands."

"Excellent!" Dominetti exclaimed, glancing at Fakri Pasha.

The Turk rose and swept the table with a half hostile, half proud look.

"Angora has not been idle since the Greeks were kicked out of Asia," he said in guttural tones. "We are ready, gentlemen. The French must be thrown out of Syria, the British out of Irak. However, we prefer to deal with our foes one at a time. I propose that instead of turning against the French the forces we have prepared, we move at an agreed date against the Crimea and the Baku oil fields. Thus, while Japan attacks on the east and Grand Duke Basil on the west, we shall deliver a vigorous blow from the south."

"And what if France withdraws from Syria, eh?" the Frenchman demanded. "What if she obtains the consent of the League to turn over her mandate to the English, eh? Bah! We have no business in that country. Good! France withdraws; I answer for it. But, about the Russian loans and bonds which have been repudiated by the Soviet Government—eh? Come, your highness! What about them?"

There was an instant of silence.

Warden could not but perceive the perfect manner in which Dominetti's scheme was fitting together. The repudiation of the Russian loans had caused suffering throughout France, the small bonds being held by uncounted thousands of Frenchmen. If Basil were to assume payment, then nothing could keep France from backing him. If Emile Marconnet were the agent of this assumption, then Marconnet would be the next prime minister of France.

"The first act of my government," Basil answered, "will be to assume repayment of these obligations."

"I am satisfied," said Marconnet simply, and emptied his wine-glass.

"But I am not," said Baron Yamanaka, rising to his feet. "Gentlemen, I understand that there is a movement counter to ours afoot, inspired by Italy, whose chief agent here is a man by the name of Solomon. Signor Dominetti, I should like to ask about this."

"So should I," put in Fakri Pasha, glowering across the table. "We know that man in Turkey. The devil himself were a better foe to have! What about him?"

Dominetti's inflexible eyes, his dominant, icy personality, held them all silent and intent. And suddenly Warden perceived more strongly than ever that it was Dominetti who was the motive power here, the force behind this whole vast scheme to change the face of the world. This Italian exile, by his genius, had welded together adverse forces, had planned out every move in his gigantic game of chess. Upon him the whole thing depended.

"TO-MORROW NOON, gentlemen," said Dominetti slowly, "we shall meet here to draw up the agreements and conclude our plans. I shall then present to you the signature of this man Solomon—his signature to an agreement placing five millions of dollars in our campaign fund, and binding him to leave France within twenty-four hours."

"How do you know?" demanded Fakri Pasha bluntly.

"I know," said Dominetti, "because at seven o'clock to-night he is sending his chief agent to me asking for terms—capitulating. Are you satisfied?"

Warden smiled ironically. Solomon capitulating, indeed! Dominetti would find himself neatly fooled there.

They were satisfied, however. And now began a discussion of terms, of a thousand involved details, taken up unhurriedly, coldly—a bargaining across the board which went on while the afternoon fled and the daylight died.

Of them all, Dominetti alone had nothing to ask; which meant that he had reached some private agreement with Basil for his own ends. Basil, indeed, was not holding out on terms with any one. Japan, Turkey, France—all had their will of him, and his promises were unhesitant. If he ever attained the Russian throne, thought Warden, Russia would be a smaller empire than it had been these two hundred years.

Sandwiches and coffee were served, and a huge samovar of tea. It was well after six when the company began to break up. Warden had sat silent, listening, appeasing his hunger while the others talked.

At six thirty only Grand Duke Basil and his Russian friends remained, talking loudly with Glazunoff, settling details. Then the others took their departure, and Basil, with Dominetti, Glazunoff and Warden, adjourned to the salon.

It was only now that Warden, with a start, realized that all this while Dominetti had made no mention to the others of the death ray—of that amazing and fearful apparatus whose secret was his alone, now that Pearson was dead.

Precisely at seven o'clock North was brought into the salon.

Warden felt his heart sink. North looked at him, nodded slightly; but the iron-hard features were set, desperate, pale.

"Well?" asked Dominetti, tense for all his control. "You have a message from Solomon?"

"Yes," said North, equally curt. "We are beaten. Solomon has sent me to ask what terms you will grant him."

CHAPTER XVII

TO THE VICTOR, THE SPOILS!

WARDEN SAT there, stunned. All his house of cards had fallen down around him; hopes, efforts, battling—everything had gone down in ruins!

This meeting of men, this game of plotting and wits into which he had almost imperceptibly been drawn, had ended in ghastly reality. He had entered upon it as an actor playing a rôle, and now he saw himself taking too real a part: the part of defeat. Sergei had sold out!

The brains and vision and ability of John Solomon, like those of so many human things, had been vastly overrated. The brains and ruthless efficiency and cruder methods of Dominetti had smashed their way to victory.

Watching North, Warden wondered how the man could take utter disaster so calmly. True, it was the calm of hopelessness, of despair; North was still the man of iron, yet he showed the bitterness of his situation in his features, as he eyed the victors impassively, with never a look for Jimmy Warden.

Those victors, all three of them, accepted victory in their own fashion. Glazunoff was nervous, smoking interminable cigarettes, eyes all ablaze in his pallid face, eagerness straining at the leash within him. Grand Duke Basil poured more liquor, his hand shaking a little. His cruel, handsome, virile countenance was alight, his somber eyes were glowing with strange fires; in this moment he beheld himself the focal point of half the world, the dominant figure of to-morrow's history, with the destiny of nations in the hollow of his long and slender hand.

Dominetti was different—and here he showed the real power in him, the real strength that underlay his nature. No sign of emotion was visible in his high-browed, tapering features. Those light and vivid gray eyes, so startling in contrast with the black hair and swart skin, rested upon North searchingly, almost meditatively—if their great vigor was not increased, neither was it diminished. The man I seemed impervious to exultation, even in this moment of triumph.

"So, the great Solomon demands terms!" said Dominetti slowly. "The mysterious is defeated; the incredible is become supplicant to the actual! And you, Mr. North, are the man who was to have destroyed me—and who, instead, begs for my terms! Very well. Where is this Solomon now?"

"At the Hotel Continental," said North.

Dominetti's brows lifted slightly.

"So! Does he know"—and Dominetti glanced at his wrist watch—"that ten minutes ago his house in Rue Montorgeuil was seized by my men, who are now in possession of it?"

North changed countenance slightly. This was, obviously, news to him—and most unwelcome news, too. His eyes went to Warden for an instant, in appeal, in helpless desperation. But Warden could give him no help here.

The telephone sounded. Dominetti picked up the instrument, and then looked over it at North with a thin smile, as he listened.

"Very good, Mr. Halsey," he said. "She is unhurt? That will be very pleasant, for you. Kindly place her in a room under guard, as I shall want to ask her a few questions before she is turned over to you. The place was unoccupied? Very well. I shall arrive in a few minutes to inspect it for myself. No, your six men should be plenty."

Dominetti laid down the instrument and lighted a cigarette.

"Suppose you telephone Solomon now, Mr. North," he said calmly. "My terms are very simple. He must meet me there at his house, alone, within twenty minutes, and we shall then settle terms personally."

NORTH, WHO was very pale, stepped to the desk, then paused.

"Let me—make one appeal," he said uncertainly. "Miss Tully cannot be given to Halsey like a chattel!"

Dominetti silenced him with words of chilled steel.

"You are not dictating what can and cannot be done, I am."

With an effort. North regained control of himself. Jimmy Warden found the eyes of Dominetti upon him, and sat up straighter.

"And you, Mr. Warden," said the voice of steel, "must accept defeat gracefully. Remember that you are acting for Sergei, not for yourself."

"Yes," said Warden.

He saw no hope, nothing to be done here. Afterward, perhaps; at least he could cope with that brute Halsey, if he could not cope with this man of steel!

North was calling the hotel. Then, abruptly, he had Solomon on the wire, and the others watched him, listening in fascination. Dominetti had taken up the extension receiver and was listening in on the conversation.

"He agrees," said North, after repeating the simple message. "He wishes to speak with Warden a moment."

Dominetti nodded, still with that thin, half-amused smile on his lips.

Warden took the instrument from the hand of North.

"Warden speaking," he said. "Solomon?"

"Yes, sir, and werry 'appy I am to 'ear as 'ow you ain't dead."

"Huh! You're happier than I am, maybe," commented Warden with bitterness. "This phone has an extension, remember."

As he spoke, he looked at Dominetti, and met a trace of pleased admiration in those gray eyes.

"That don't signify, sir. I ain't got nothing to say as can't be 'eard by anybody, as the old gent said when 'e was courting of 'is third. We're beat, that's all there is to it, just like that. This 'ere Dominetti is too much for me, and I ain't as young as I was, sir. I just wanted to ask if you'd be so good as to stand by me, sir, you and Mr. North both, when 'im and me meet. You won't 'old it against me, sir—being beat like this 'ere?"

"Nonsense! Of course we don't," Warden replied, a trifle impatiently. "If we've lost the fight, we've lost it."

"Yes, sir," said Solomon's wheezy accents. "And being sorry for yourself ain't a bit o' use, I says. Werry good, Mr. Warden. If you and Mr. North will stand by me, we'll see it through together. That's all, sir."

Warden set down the instrument, with a half-pitying smile as he looked at North.

"All broken up," he said curtly. "Wants to know if we'll stand by him to the finish. Poor chap! I expect he takes it hard."

Grand Duke Basil broke into hearty laughter. Glazunoff smiled, and even Dominetti indulged in a chuckle. He, too, had listened to Solomon's half-broken words. But Warden caught a swiftly repressed glow in the eyes of North—a flame that startled him beyond measure, inexplicably. North had received some message there. What was it?

DOMINETTI ROSE. "We'll let Mr. Warden and Mr. North stand by their chief in the moment of disaster, gentlemen! By all means, I'll have another bit of news for Solomon," he added slowly, "and also for Mr. Warden, which will cap our victory, I trust. Eh, your highness?"

He looked at Basil, and the Grand Duke laughed and nodded.

Something in that laugh, something in the acid voice of Dominetti, struck Warden cold. What did they mean? However, he had no opportunity to seek further. Dominetti turned to Glazunoff.

"By the way, Boris, good news for you. Halsey says that he found some sort of machine there, completely installed, with electrical connections; a notebook beside it with Pearson's name on the cover. Do you want to come along? It looks as though—"

Glazunoff bounded to his feet.

"Splendid!" he cried out exultantly, his pallid features all gleaming with joy. "The machine! Solomon installed one there. You recall—a huge box was taken from the laboratory to Rue Montorgeuil? Undoubtedly this was it. Eureka! We don't need to mourn Matsura, now! I can handle it, certainly!"

"Very well," said Dominetti, and waved his hand at the grand duke. "Congratulations, my dear Basil! You shall still have the machine of death to serve you! Shall you accompany us?"

The Grand Duke stood up. "I think not," he answered, and lifted his glass. "To the success of our plan, gentlemen!"

He drank his own toast, then bowed and shook hands with Dominetti, who ordered one of the guards at the door to have the grand duke's car ready. Then, when Basil had departed, Dominetti gestured to Glazunoff.

"The Mercedes. Mr. North and Mr. Warden can crowd in with the driver. You and I in back. There is no danger whatever; these gentlemen are too intelligent. Eh, Mr. North?"

"I'm afraid so," said North gloomily. "We're not fools."

"Precisely; as both of you have shown me." Dominetti suddenly gave them both a warm, flashing smile that was almost friendly. "You are beaten, gentlemen; but you have been terrible antagonists, and I salute you. If ever you decide to change flags, get in touch with me. And now, let us go. I shall join you at the car."

Glazunoff had departed. Dominetti walked briskly out of the room. The hats and coats of Warden and North were brought in, and the two men looked at each other silently for one long instant.

"Careful!" said North. "He meant something. Take it literally. Stand beside him."

Warden was scornful in spirit at these words. Solomon, indeed—to be taken literally! As though anything could be expected or hoped for now, when everything was lost, when utter disaster was openly admitted, when terms had been asked, when he himself had found his assumed mission a real one!

"Did June get to the embassy with the treaty?" he asked.

North gave him one look and shook his head. That look spoke volumes.

As the two men were escorted outside and ushered into the waiting car, Warden remembered Dominetti's baleful hint about "another bit of news." What could that be? Meant not only for Solomon, but for him as well? Some sort of fresh triumph, no doubt, some new disaster; perhaps in regard to the treaty, perhaps not. Well, no matter! The game was lost.

Only one thing remained: June Tully. Dominetti was bound, obviously enough, to turn her over to Halsey.

"And for her sake I must get out of this with a whole skin, somehow," thought Jimmy Warden. "Now it's only a question of preserving my neck. Once away, I'll go after Halsey on my own—and I'll settle the scoundrel this time!"

THE PROSPECT was satisfying; but, as the big Mercedes hummed through the drizzle of rain, Mr. Warden could not see any immediate assurance of its fulfillment.

On the other hand, he could see where Dominetti would make a huge clean-up inside of three days—the publication of that treaty would cause a tremendous crash in French stocks, which Dominetti would have sold short. To Warden, this was the keenest blow of all. The instant that document was made public, the United States would become a target for the scorn and fury of half Europe. Had he only kept it himself—well, what use to mourn? The game was lost. Sergei had given up; Solomon had capitulated.

If North had, as Warden suspected, any lingering hopes as to Solomon's activity, they were destined to be very speedily set at rest.

When the Mercedes drew up before the bronze gates of the house in Rue Montorgeuil, they stood open, and Halsey appeared at once, beckoning the car into the courtyard. As it passed inside, the gates clanged shut again. Halsey held open the car door. He was quite himself now—the glare of floodlights illuminating the courtyard showed the unconcealed triumph in his face.

"I'm expecting Solomon to come here at any minute," said Dominetti sharply, on alighting. "He hasn't arrived?"

"I only wish be would!" Halsey snarled.

"Good! Have him brought to me immediately when he comes. Two men on guard at the gates, the others scattered about the house. You yourself keep an eye on North and Warden, here; the chauffeur can do that, too. Any new developments?"

"Yes," said Halsey with a smile. "Come inside."

They entered the reception salon, the chauffeur removing cap and coat and following them, pistol in hand. Dominetti threw one swift glance about the magnificently furnished room, then turned and stared incredulously at an object Halsey was handing him. Warden gave North a took, and received a helpless shrug in return.

It was the morocco-bound copy of the treaty!

"Eh?" The face of Dominetti drew into taut lines, his eyes fairly blazed at Halsey. "Where did this come from?"

"Your friend Miss Tully had it," and Halsey laughed complacently.

"So!" Dominetti turned, whirled on Warden, regarded him with cruel exultation. "I see! Your messenger did not take this to the embassy after all, eh? My poor friend, you have lost out—how do you say?—all along the line. And you have nothing to say about it?"

"Why say anything?" returned Warden stolidly. "It's immaterial now. The war's ended."

"Right!" Dominetti pocketed the document, laughing slightly.

Glazunoff intervened with ill-suppressed eagerness.

"Well, do your talking if you like, but let's have a look at that apparatus, Halsey."

"Follow on." Halsey waved his hand. "Yonder is Solomon's private office—plenty of records and interesting documents on file, it seems. They'll give you a pleasant hour or two, Signor Dominetti!"

HALSEY LED them through the corridor into another portion of the house which was new to Warden. As they followed, Warden touched North's arm; for the moment they could speak without being heard, as Dominetti was in advance with Halsey.

"Too bad! She should have delivered that treaty!"

"Not a chance," murmured North. "Saw John yesterday morning. He looked it over, said it was of no interest, and told me to take her here and await word from him. I found the gates and everything wide open."

"My heavens!" muttered Warden. "The man's gone stark, staring mad, North!"

Probably North was of the same opinion, for he merely shrugged and made no response. Beyond a doubt, thought Warden, John Solomon was out of his head. The destruction of his organization, of all his plans, must have floored him completely.

Now, with no little pride and triumph, Halsey swung open a door and they passed into a strange room, lighted by a huge crystal chandelier. Not a stick of furniture was in the room, and the floor was bare. Against one blank wall, near the door, hung a gorgeous old Chinese rug of rich gold and blue, a rug at least ten by twelve feet in size. Opposite this wall were windows, uncurtained.

To the right was a long empty wall; in the center of this wall had been a doorway, which was now bricked up; the bricks and mortar were fresh and unplastered as though the job had been done recently and left unfinished.

Opposite this bricked-up doorway, against the fourth wall of the room, was a complicated array of machinery—or rather, a series of machines—connected with the wall by an electric cord which passed to a switch and plug.

Glazunoff advanced upon it eagerly. Dominetti turned to North and Warden—behind whom, at the door, waited the chauffeur, pistol in hand.

"Do you know what this machine is?" asked Dominetti.

North shook his head.

"Never saw it before," said Warden curiously, and so evidently was he telling the truth that Dominetti turned to watch Glazunoff, whom Halsey had joined. Immediately afterward Warden recalled that immense packing-case which he had seen unloaded in the courtyard, and surmised that the machine had arrived in it.

"Looks like a combination of X-rays and ultra-violet light," said Halsey lightly.

Boris Glazunoff, examining the mechanism, sniffed silently for a moment. Then he turned to Dominetti.

"I can't quite make it out," he said, his eyes glowing. "But we've got it, no doubt about that!" He touched the large apparatus at one end, which was connected with two other instruments, not unlike cameras in appearance, by a long tube of crystal or fused quartz. "This must be Pearson's experimental apparatus—here's the aperture for the passage of the ultra-sonic wave, and here's a test tube still containing some sort of blood—you see the microscope mounted here at the side to observe what passes in the test tube? Yes, this must be Pearson's perfected machine!"

"We'll find out," said Dominetti, looking at the apparatus curiously.

"Right," Glazunoff replied. "It'll take ten minutes or so to get the tubes heated up—perhaps longer. I'll give you a demonstration of something you never saw before!"

GLAZUNOFF WENT to the switch, connected it, stood back. Instantly there was a faint, insistent humming sound, which quieted down to an imperceptible drone; through the long quartz tube, began to play a faint greenish light.

Dominetti looked at Halsey.

"Where is that American girl?"

"Locked in her room, upstairs," said Halsey, and his eyes went to Warden sardonically. "She's safe enough."

"I'll question her later, then." Dominetti checked his words, and across his face flitted an expression of astonishment.

Warden turned. Stepping past the guard at the doorway, coming placidly into the room, was John Solomon. The startled chauffeur had lifted his pistol, but Dominetti's gesture caused him to lower it.

There was no menace in that pudgy little figure. It was grotesque enough, and to Warden was rather pathetic. Solomon wore his Basque *beret,* and his two hands were busily carving tobacco from his black plug into the old clay pipe. His round features were quite blank, devoid of expression; his mild blue eyes ignored every one else, to rest upon Dominetti with a species of pleading, apologetic in their humility.

Warden suddenly felt ashamed of his presence at such a scene.

"Good evening, Mr. Dominetti, sir," said Solomon. He came to a halt just in front of the Chinese rug hanging on the wall. "Werry 'appy I am to see you 'ere, sir, you and your friends both. You and me, sir, 'as 'ad a lot o' conflict, and we've done each other a mortal lot o' damage—but now it's ended, and a werry good thing, too, says I. There ain't nothing like ending of a thing shipshape and proper, as the old gent said when 'e fired the 'ousemaid. And I 'opes you says the same, sir."

Warden had a comical feeling, for an instant, that these words were ambiguous—that it was Solomon, not Dominetti, who was here to dictate terms. Then the feeling vanished at once.

"How the devil did you get here?" snapped Dominetti.

"Why, sir," and the blue eyes met his gaze blankly, "I just stepped in, so to speak."

"Hm!" Dominetti surveyed him with interest and a trace of contempt. "You run true to form, eh? Just like all the English—

as soon as you kick them hard, they kneel down and lick your boots! Well, you're prepared to receive my terms, are you?"

"Yes, sir," said Solomon mildly. He pocketed his knife and plug, and tamped down his pipe. "If so be as you 'ave a match to spare, Mr. Warden, we'll 'ear what's to be done in a bit o' comfort. It's wonderful what 'elp a taste o' baccy can be, sir!"

Warden recollected his instructions. He moved over to Solomon's side, handed him a box of matches, and North joined him. The three of them stood facing Dominetti, who was closest to them. The chauffeur-guard stood at the entrance. Halsey stood near Glazunoff, who, after a brief inspection of Solomon, had turned again to the apparatus.

"So you know your house of cards has collapsed, eh?" Dominetti flung at him, half sneeringly. "You and Mussolini— bah! Warden, here, is negotiating on behalf of Sergei; you know that Sergei has given up his fine dreams, do you?"

"Yes, sir, I expect 'e 'as," said Solomon, with a wheezy sigh.

"There's something else you don't know, then," and the singular gray eyes of Dominetti were fairly alive with energy. He gestured. A man who had appeared at the door came forward and handed him a bit of paper, then departed. Dominetti, smiling, opened the paper, read a line of writing there, and crumpled it up. His gaze, with a trace of exultation, went again to Solomon.

"Ten minutes ago," he said calmly, "Prince Sergei was found dead in his hotel room."

CHAPTER XVIII

THE FINAL CRASH

THERE WAS no doubting the words; that air of quiet assurance told its own story. Dominetti's agents had struck their final blow, and their deadliest one. At the words, Solomon blinked, then a trace of agitation showed in his face.

"Dang it! You've went an' done it," he said tremulously. "Murdered 'im!"

Dominetti shrugged lightly, and got out a cigarette case.

"What do you expect?" he retorted. "Well, so much for your fine little plot, Solomon. It's finished. You're smashed. And you're in my hands now, to boot; you and the two chief agents left to you—for don't think you've fooled me. I know very well that Warden's your man, and you planted him to represent Sergei. And the terms are mine to dictate."

Warden felt a singular sense of futility, of helplessness. So Dominetti knew or guessed the truth; had again been playing him along for a sucker!

This also explained the trick in the Sergei negotiations. Dominetti had been willing to promise anything, had made Basil and the others promise anything, in order to get Sergei's abdication—knowing that their promises would never become public, while Sergei's abdication was already given to the press—or would be given in the morning.

Solomon was obviously hard hit by this news. He struck a match and held it to his pipe with trembling fingers.

"Yes, sir," he said apologetically. "No doubt about it, sir—'ere

I be, just like that, and no 'elp for it, neither, as the old gent said when 'e buried 'is third. And what might be your terms, sir?"

Dominetti eyed him with those inflexible gray eyes.

"Before you leave this house, Solomon," the words came with careful deliberation, "you are to place one million pounds to the credit of Grand Duke Basil at the National City Bank, or Barclays. I understand you've leased this house: I want the lease assigned to me. I want an agreement from you to leave France within two days. That is all."

"All, sir?" echoed Solomon blankly. His surprise was not assumed.

"Yes, all. Think I care about killing you? Bah! I kill those who are dangerous—those who serve you, but not you—poor little old Englishman! Live out your life, broken and smashed—fool that you were, to set yourself up against me! Well, what about my terms? Do they suit you?"

Solomon puffed placidly at his pipe for an instant.

"Yes, sir, they're werry good, and not so 'ard, neither," he admitted. "What about Mr. North and Mr. Warden 'ere? You ain't a goin' to 'urt them, nor Miss Tully?"

"I've already offered them jobs," said Dominetti. "As for Miss Tully, she does not enter into the matter. We'll not discuss her."

"No, sir," said Solomon, to the disgusted astonishment of Warden. The pudgy little man fumbled in his pocket, with a worried air, and produced a small red-covered notebook. "If so be as you'll look over this 'ere statement of accounts, Mr. Dominetti," he said humbly, "I'd be werry glad. I try to keep me accounts in order, sir; I 'aven't 'ad time to enter up poor Prince Sergei, but you'll find everything else shipshape."

He handed the red notebook to Dominetti.

DOMINETTI TOOK the notebook with an amused air. Before he could open it, a sharp exclamation broke from Halsey.

"What's wrong, Boris? Good God, man! Look at him, Dominetti!"

Glazunoff, standing watching the apparatus, turned to meet their gaze. The quartz tube, its quicksilver spluttering in white fire, was sending off a strange and unearthly light, but it was not the light which made Glazunoff look so singular. His eyes were distended, and his face was dark with suffused blood.

"Nothing's wrong," he said irritably. "This thing is superb, magnificent! I'll show you something in a few minutes, Dominetti—I'm just getting the hang of it now. Marvelous! Is this Pearson's machine, Solomon?"

"Yes, sir," returned Solomon, looking a trifle agitated. "I ain't werry certain about it me own self, sir—Mr. Pearson, 'e never 'ad no chance to work it."

"I'll do that for him," and Glazunoff laughed.

The laugh had a strange shrill note which drew Warden's eyes for a moment. Excitement, perhaps, had caused the change in the man—then, looking at Halsey, Warden started slightly.

Halsey, too, had that odd expression—distended eyes, suffused features—and was lighting a cigarette with strange, jerky motions, as though all the blood in his body were in violent movement. The thing was indescribable, yet distinctly horrible to see—and might have been only imagination.

Dominetti apparently saw nothing wrong, for now he stepped back beneath the great crystal chandelier, close to Halsey, for better light by which to examine the little notebook.

Afterward, Jimmy Warden wondered whether that entire scene had been plotted out in the brain of Solomon—whether that very backward step of Dominetti's had been in the mind of the little cockney.

The Italian held up the notebook, opened it, scanned one page and then another. His air of amused contempt quickened into undisguised interest; then it passed into slowly gathering anger.

A low oath broke from his lips.

He turned another page, glanced at it—and then, exploding in sudden passionate fury, he dashed down the little book to the floor and flung a frightful, inarticulate cry at Solomon, the cry of a wild beast who finds himself trapped beyond escape.

Then, abruptly, he calmed himself; but the gray eyes were lurid with baleful fires.

"You fool!" he said slowly.

Solomon sighed wheezily.

"Yes, sir, just like that. It's a werry good play, Mr. Dominetti, to let the other chap do the 'itting—to let 'im 'it 'ard, so to speak."

Dominetti looked incredulous, amazed. "But—you're a fool!" he cried out. "You can't mean that—it's impossible!"

"Lots o' men are fools, sir," said Solomon, the blue eyes quite blank. "And it ain't a 'alf bad notion, neither."

AN EXCLAMATION from Glazunoff broke in upon them.

"Dominetti!" he cried. "Look here! Come here, look! You can see the protoplasm disintegrating before your eyes—"

Glazunoff, gesturing to the microscope beside the apparatus, looked like a madman. His face was a queer purplish black—perhaps due to the spluttering glare of the quartz tube at his elbow.

"Yes, sir, just like that," said Solomon in a low but piercing voice that held them all spellbound. "And if there was another machine like this 'ere, pointed at a man, you'd see 'is blood corpuscles boilin' and disintegratin' too. If there was a false brick in that 'ere doorway across the room, and a machine was sending of a sound-beam—"

Warden was the only one who thought to glance at the bricked-up doorway, and he barely repressed a startled cry. One of the bricks had vanished, in the center of the new work.

"Shut up, Boris!" exclaimed Dominetti, as Glazunoff tried to urge him toward the apparatus. "Solomon, what do you mean by this nonsense?"

"I means, sir," said Solomon placidly, "as 'ow you're beat—just like that. All around the clock, so to speak. That 'ere treaty you forged, for one thing. It's a werry smart bit o'work, but it won't never come to light, sir.'Cause why, your whole blessed game has gone to smash, just like that. An hour ago Inspector Leblanc was arrested and coughed up all 'e knew. At this werry minute, the police are occupyin' of your 'ouse in Boulogne. To-night Baron Yamanaka is being ordered 'ome by 'is government. So is Fakri."

"You're mad!" screamed Dominetti, and turned furiously toward the man at the doorway. The Italian's features, like those of Glazunoff and the watching, frowning Halsey, were a queer dark color. "Here, you—shoot this fool!"

The chauffeur lifted his pistol. At this instant, from other parts of the house, came the reverberant sound of heavy shots. As the pistol swung up, an unseen weapon smashed out its report. The chauffeur swung around, fell heavily. In the doorway where he had stood, came an Arab, white-clad, smoking, automatic in hand.

"Good Heavens!" A sudden wild and horrible scream broke from Halsey. "You heard what he said—what's wrong with us? Let me out of here—quick, quick—"

Halsey took a step forward.

Too late!

He reeled, clutched at Glazunoff, who was supporting himself against the apparatus, staring at Solomon from horrified, distended eyes. The arms of Glazunoff gave way; he and Halsey both fell limply against the machine, and their bodies slithered to the floor.

Then Warden saw a fearful and incredible thing. Glazunoff had fallen with one arm far outstretched. As Warden looked at it, the fingers of his hand vanished. The hand itself began to vanish. The hand, wrist, arm—

For an instant Warden lost his head. Horror seized upon him, wild blind panic. All these things had taken place in the fraction of a moment. Warden did not realize what he was doing until he found himself in the doorway, struggling to get out of this room, away, anywhere! Then, as the Arab caught his arm, he glanced back.

He had a glimpse of Dominetti standing there, motionless, speechless. In the man's face was a look beyond words, a look of such utter terror, of such horrible fear and agony, that it remained planted in the brain of Warden till his dying day. Then he turned and broke—fled out of the room, came to a halt in the corridor beyond, weak and trembling.

"Werry good, Dr. Lee," said Solomon, puffing unmoved at his pipe. "Cut 'er off, just like that, Mr. North. I expect as 'ow—"

BUT NORTH had fainted—iron man that he was, he could not look upon what was passing in the hall where Dominetti had just crashed to the floor—disintegrating in the midst of his shattered schemes for world conquest!

Solomon motioned to the Arab, who caught hold of North and dragged him out. Then Solomon himself turned and left the room, and walked over to where Warden stood in the corridor.

"Well, sir?" he said, with a wheezy chuckle.

Warden turned away.

"Never mind talking now, John," he said. "I—I'm sick."

An Arab appeared, and saluted.

"Solomon Effendi! We have them all. Four are dead. The others live."

"Very good," said Solomon in French. "Kill the others, place them all in this room. Bring in the acids and bombs from the secret passage. In ten minutes, you will be the last man here; in fifteen minutes, fire the bombs and get away."

Dr. Lee, who had come in time to hear these instructions, caught at the arm of Solomon.

"Stop, stop!" he cried, his saffron features convulsed. "Are you mad? Would you destroy this house—these things here—this apparatus which is a marvel of scientific—"

Solomon knocked out his clay pipe and pocketed it, quite unmoved.

"Dr. Lee," he said calmly, "you 'ave the secret of this 'ere ultra-sonic wave. Others 'ave it likewise. If so be as you want to go ahead with it, go on. But what's in this 'ere 'ouse belongs to me, sir, as the old gent said when 'e caught the butler a kissing of the 'ousemaid. I'll 'ave no truck wi' this 'ere devilish contrivance, you 'ear me?"

Sudden passion shook the voice of Solomon, and for once his face was swept by something very like horror and repulsion, and his placid blue eyes blazed out.

"I'm done with it!" he cried. "I'm done with all this 'ere scientific deviltry, that's what! I'm a goin' back to simple things, just like that—I'm a goin' to Egypt, and I'm a goin' to stay there the rest o' me days! You get out, Dr. Lee—just like that. Get out, and get out quick! Mr. Warden, you 'op upstairs and get Miss Tully, and you get out, too. Fetch 'er down to the 'Otel Continental, sir—I 'ave a suite there."

And, stamping away down the corridor, Solomon was lost to sight, muttering something very like oaths to himself.

Just what happened next, Jimmy Warden never knew exactly. He had a dazed memory of two Arabs guiding him, helping him break down a locked door, of June Tully rushing into his arms. He did not come clearly to himself until he found the two of them standing on a street corner, waving to a cruising taxicab.

A medley of throngs around, of confused cries, wakened him. People were running toward a spouting blaze somewhere back in Rue Montorgeuil. A company of firemen, their brass helmets glittering in the street lights, went clattering and roaring past. Then he was pushing June Tully into the cab and following her.

"Hotel Continental," he directed.

"Oh, Jimmy!" June's voice came at his ear as he put an arm around her in support, and a slender hand clasped his own firmly, confidingly, "What has happened, Jimmy? Where are we?"

"We're going away from here, damn it!" Warden said savagely. Then, realizing the situation, he drew the girl closer and gazed appealingly into her deep brown eyes. "June, dearest, will you go away with me? Away—the two of us?"

A moment later he rapped on the window.

"Don't bother about the Continental," he ordered the chauffeur. "See if you can catch the boat train at the Gare du Nord."

He never saw nor heard of John Solomon again.

EDITOR'S NOTE: Readers of the John Solomon stories have found brought to completion his amazing world duel with Dominetti. But one particular—the mystery of the little red notebooks—the author may not explain without the express consent of John Solomon himself. What did these notebooks contain—what secret, what astounding proclamation? We cannot say, as yet.

Solomon himself, strangely horrified and repelled by the results of his delving into science, kept his word and went back, with his secrets, to the Eastern lands where he first attained fame and fortune. It is very probable that the startling rumors that have recently come out of the Libyan desert are due to his activities there; and if so, we trust Mr. Bedford-Jones will get in touch with John Solomon and report these matters to our readers.

ABOUT THE AUTHOR

H. BEDFORD-JONES is a Canadian by birth, but not by profession, having removed to the United States at the age of one year. For over twenty years he has been more or less profitably engaged in writing and traveling. As he has seldom resided in one place longer than a year or so and is a person of retiring habits, he is somewhat a man of mystery; more than once he has suffered from unscrupulous gentlemen who impersonated him—one of whom murdered a wife and was subsequently shot by the police, luckily after losing his alias.

The real Bedford-Jones is an elderly man, whose gray hair and precise attire give him rather the appearance of a retired foreign diplomat. His hobby is stamp collecting, and his collection of Japan is said to be one of the finest in existence. At present writing he is en route to Morocco, and when this appears in print he will probably be somewhere on the Mojave Desert in company with Erle Stanley Gardner.

Questioned as to the main facts in his life, he declared there was only one main fact, but it was not for publication; that his life had been uneventful except for numerous financial losses, and that his only adventures lay in evading adventurers. In his younger years he was something of an athlete, but the encroachments of age preclude any active pursuits except that of motoring. He is usually to be found poring over his stamps, working at his typewriter, or laboring in his California rose garden, which is one of the sights of Cathedral Cañon, near Palm Springs.

www.ingramcontent.com/pod-product-compliance
Lightning Source LLC
Chambersburg PA
CBHW030533030726
47495CB00004B/979